1971

the
billikin
courier

the
billikin
courier

T. C. LEWELLEN

RANDOM HOUSE/New York

the
billikin
courier

ONE

LONELY GUNFIGHTER. FOUR FEATURE FILMS ONLY 50 CENTS. BEST DEAL IN SAN FRANCISCO. CINEMASCOPE. BUGS BUNNY CARTOON. NEWS OF THE DAY. THE PICTURE YOU'LL TALK ABOUT FOR YEARS.

Right. I couldn't even remember the plot of one of the four films I had just seen.

Vaguely I recalled there was something I was supposed to be thinking about. It wasn't very often there was anything I was supposed to think about—except the next meal or the next bottle. The idea that it might be important was mildly fascinating.

Then I remembered the man in the alpine hat. I turned and looked back at the doors. The ticket taker, a teen-age kid with acne and wearing a 1930 tuxedo that was two sizes too large, briefly caught my eyes and dropped his gaze to the ticket box in embarrassment. The alcove was cut in half by the shadow of the marquee. From the inside light I could barely discern the blurred silhouette of a man standing motionless against the frosted glass of the doors. Seven hours of ten-year-old lousy movies. By God, I was making the bastard work for his pay.

I turned again and walked south along the sidewalk toward Market Street. The pavement was almost deserted beneath the last remnants of sunlight, and I felt as though I were walking inside a surrealistic painting where light and shadow had been exaggerated and carefully arranged into a patterned loneliness. After less than a half a block I stopped and feigned examining a display window. My eyes moved back toward the theater. Alpine Hat was bent over with his hands on his knees, reading a film poster.

I glanced back at the window. The store was deserted, and beyond my reflection there was only bare floor and a few counters and tables draped with white dust-covers. Down the street came the singsong voice of a newsboy crying the latest on some scientist's suicide. Inadvertently my focus drew back to the reflection in the window. There was no longer any shock or shame. That had all been expended a long time ago. What I saw was a thirty-two-year-old bum, the eyes squinted and bagged with too many whiskey nights, the dark hair uncombed, uncut, unwashed, the chin stubbled with four days' whiskers. What was left of Robert Chessick. It hadn't really been a bad face once. You could still see it in the straight nose and the narrow lips that a long time ago had been proud and taut. Now I had to admit to a certain weakness about the mouth. At least my six-two height hadn't diminished any, but I was about thirty pounds underweight. The clothes didn't fit. The flannel shirt was too small, the black work pants too large. You couldn't be particular when you were grabbing off a washline.

Footsteps. I swung my gaze back toward the theater again, giving up any pretense at examining the window. Alpine Hat was approaching at a leisurely pace. He was a real dandy. The hat was fashioned of closely woven straw and dyed a light green. A small red feather jutted from the band. Plaid sports jacket. Tan pants, maybe silk. Patent-leather shoes with buckles. His face was shadowed beneath the brim of the hat, but I remembered the effeminately handsome, intricately lined features and the mustache shaved to perfection. If it came to a fight, he would be no problem. Even in the shape I was in, I still remembered enough of my Army karate to kick a kneecap out of joint.

I stepped out into the middle of the sidewalk. He slowed his pace and raised his head from the pavement to look briefly at some point on my chest.

"Excuse me, please," he said softly.

I moved again as he attempted to pass. This time he stopped. His eyes held on my mouth.

"You got a nail?" I said.

"I beg your pardon." There was a slight accent that I couldn't place. Maybe British.

"A weed. A cigarette."

"I'm sorry. I don't have any. I don't smoke."

"You should try it."

"Yes, certainly. Now if you don't mind."

"I do mind," I said.

He dropped his gaze back to the sidewalk like a reprimanded child. "What do you want then?"

"A dollar for a flop. A bed."

He stood for a moment without replying, then slowly removed a wallet from inside his jacket.

"Better make it two," I said. "Inflation, you know."

He dipped into the wallet again.

"Cost of living just went up. Better make that three."

"Do you want me to yell for the police?"

"Cost of living just went down again. I'll settle for two."

Still not looking at me, he lifted the two bills. That's when I froze. Maybe it was nothing more than the incongruity that sent the shock wave down the yellow streak on my back. But there it was, just below the uplifted bills, the bright shiny tip of a sleeve knife. I had seen only one before. While the unit was still at Fort Benning, a Spec Four in my platoon had used one to cut up a Pfc. It was an ugly, nasty little thing that came out fast on nothing more than the flick of the wrist. But you had to be damned good to use one. Flick, catch and cut in one motion. Fighting down the momentary fear, I took the two bills and stuffed them in my shirt pocket.

"Is that all?" he asked.

I swallowed hard and stepped back so if he decided to use that knife, I would have enough room to turn and run like hell. "No, just one more thing. You've been following me. I'd kind of like to know why."

For the first time he raised his head and looked me full in the eyes. His mouth widened to a grin. "Don't be absurd," he said. "Why would anybody want to follow *you?*"

He moved past me and up the sidewalk. I watched him until he reached the corner and disappeared around the side of a building onto Market Street.

It was a good question, I thought. There were probably a couple million people in Frisco with skeletons in their closets—a clandestine love affair, a business secret, a reefer in the pocket, an illegal ticket on a horse race, or just enough money to be worthy of the attentions of a con man or a blackmailer. Why the hell would anyone bother with a burned-out ex-second lieutenant-schoolteacher who had been on the bottle for eight months? Even in the Army, I had never had access to any information more secret or more important than the time my platoon was moving out. Besides, a couple drinks and everybody's-buddy Chessick would tell anyone anything he wanted to know. It was part of the atonement. My life was an open book. Pretty cruddy—but open.

And Lorrie? No, the divorce was final six months ago. She was married to greasy Harry the math prof now, I'd heard. And she wasn't exactly the private-detective type.

When I reached the corner at Market, I stood for a moment looking up the sidewalk. Alpine Hat was gone. Maybe it had all been my imagination. It wasn't inconceivable that I could crack again. Perhaps the damage was more permanent than I thought. What did they call it in college? Paranoia. Delusions of persecution. The next step was to rationalize that if someone was going to the trouble to persecute me, I damned well must be important. The incarnation of Jesus Christ or Napoleon. To see how it would feel, I shoved my hand into my shirt and assumed a classic Napoleonic stance.

A young couple passed arm in arm. The girl glanced back once and giggled to her boy friend, "Did you see him?"

"Yeah," he said, loudly enough to be heard for half a block, "this town's got a monopoly on nuts."

Obviously Napoleon wasn't working. I tried Jesus Christ. "The meek shall inherit the earth," I called after them in my most Christlike voice.

"You like it—it's yours," Boy Friend answered over his shoulder. The girl cuddled, giggling, against his protective biceps.

I couldn't think of a fitting reply, so I settled for "Thanks," and stood watching the couple move on up the street. I felt strangely elated. I had just witnessed true love in bloom and I had two bucks in my shirt pocket—the biggest single panhandle of my career. It would be a problem deciding how to spend it. Two bucks would buy a half gallon of lousy wine or a pint of lousy whiskey or a couple shots in a lousy bar. Two bucks. If Alpine Hat was that easy a mark, maybe I should be following him.

I walked east on Market toward the waterfront. It was dinnertime for the people who lived by schedules, and the streets were as deserted as they ever got until after two A.M. on a weeknight. The sky was in the last phase of dusk and the shadows of the immobile bus-waiting forms were spread on the pavement like elongated people run over by a road grader. The stores were closed and deserted. In sporadic hot-dog cafés, vaguely human forms slumped on tired elbows at the counters. A newsboy passed, yelling mechanically and without enthusiasm, "Treason suggested in scientist's suicide." They had been shouting about him for two days now and I wished they would hurry up and bury the bastard. Bury the whole rotten city with him.

There had been a time when I had actually liked San Francisco. A young Pfc. then on leave from Fort Ord. You could always tell a city by its skyline, and of course there wasn't another more imposing. San Francisco seemed to exude an atmosphere, a personality all its own, like a neurotic girl, at the same time both vivacious and somber.

But that was San Francisco. San Francisco belonged to the rich and the happy. The businessmen and the beatniks and the young lovers. This was another city. Frisco. Just plain Frisco and to hell with all your patriotic natives. Frisco of the pornographic bookstalls and the dive movie theaters and the back-alley cement canyons with the empty tragic wine jugs of one more hopeless, forgotten night. Frisco of the fairy bars and the Salvation Army and Brother Bob's Rescue Mission. Before we serve the soup, let's all join our voices in a hymn of praise. Put a nickel on the drum/Save another drunken bum/Salvation Army, Salvation Army/Put a nickel on the drum and you'll be saved. Frisco, the loneliest city in the world.

After several blocks I turned into a familiar side street. The brief elation I had experienced had eclipsed as quickly as the sun behind the skyscrapers, and the mood had mellowed to an indiscriminate gray. Sometimes when I thought about it—and it couldn't be avoided when every hour seemed suspended outside of time—I really believed that when the atonement or expiation or whatever it was I was after had been accomplished, I might find a decent job and take up life in the other—normal—world. Maybe even get married again. I was like a jailed man who had to put in so much time before the crime was sufficiently punished. Except that for me there was no specific date when I might say,

All right, it's finished. Through. Done for. There was no moment when I might wake up and find the records stamped *Paid in Full.*

Sometimes I thought there should be something more. A sudden flash of lightning, a burst of pain, which in a single instant would obliterate Chessick the dreamer, Chessick the coward, Chessick the failure in everything he touched. But there was no lightning. There was only the hopeless, endless, aimless, quiet walking through dawn and afternoon and evening, a quality of mere timeless movement. And maybe I was a failure at that, too. I couldn't even sink low enough to make the punishment unbearable. Eight months and I hadn't even succeeded in the simple goal of becoming a full-fledged lush. I was one of those rare men who for some combination of metabolism and mentality could never build up an honest need for alcohol. Even now, as I stood on the sidewalk contemplating the sunken door of a familiar bar, I knew that getting drunk would be nothing more than impotent gesture.

For a moment before entering I examined each end of the street. An aged couple, a pregnant woman, three teen-age kids, an old woman walking a dog. No sign of an alpine hat. I smiled, repeating his words over in my mind, Why would anyone follow *you?*

TWO

She was a naturally beautiful girl. There
was nothing especially unusual about that except she knew
how to wear it. That was rare in California, where it seemed
there was a special class in junior high school that taught
them how to paint their faces like Tijuana whores and pad
their skimpy chests with weather balloons. This one was
different. She wore no make-up at all, not even fingernail
polish, and I was willing to bet she was a natural blonde.
Her breasts would be all her own, too. You see strange
things in Frisco bars. She was small all over—up, down and
around—but you knew that if you got your hands on any of
it, it would every inch be firm and honest. She wasn't the
type you noticed fast, or at least on her own side of the
world she wouldn't have been. You had to look at her for a
while. And then after your mind had stripped her naked

three or four times, like you did any broad, you would find yourself watching her face and that long, straight blond hair, and you wouldn't be raping her in some back alley, but drifting in a rowboat up a melancholy river with drooping sunset trees lining the banks and she would just be there, curled up under your arm, warm and small, yet big enough to fill the massive void of your loneliness, and if you didn't catch your dream fast, you'd be asking her to marry you and really believing in happily-ever-afters.

"So the ol' lady says—she says, 'Mack,' she says, 'Mack, ya gotta cut out the boozin' or I'm gonna'—now get this—she says, 'I'm gonna go home ta muddah.' How ya like that, uh? After all I done. Ya know whad I says? Uh? Uh? Ya wanna know whad I says? I says, 'Baby'—I says—'Baby, go!' " Mack burst into a sustained rasping laugh and reached across the table and tugged at my shirt sleeve. "How's that? Uh? Did I tell her? Did I, uh?"

"Yeah, you told her," I agreed without enthusiasm. I would have preferred to do my drinking alone, but two bucks doesn't go far even in a dive. There was always a lush with a problem who would buy himself a sympathetic ear with a few drinks, and you couldn't always choose your benefactor. Mack was as good as any other.

"So whad does she do, uh? I'll tell ya. I'll tell ya whad she does. She starts bawlin', that's whad. An' then the kids start bawlin'. So whad I do ta make 'em do that? I says to myself. I says, Whad I do? Well, ya know whad I tell 'em. Ya wanna know, uh? Ya wanna? I says—I says, 'Shaddap!' Did I tell 'em or did I tell 'em? Uh? Uh?"

This time I ignored the persistent tugging at my arm. I was looking again across the whiskey-stained table and past Mack's contorted pug-ugly face and the other tables and tragicomic immobile faces to the girl at the counter with her mop-haired boy friend. Yeah, she didn't need paint and balloons. She could afford to wait until you noticed her. Money. Class. A different school. Maybe the whores in her district didn't have to appeal to the acne-faced kid who would run home and masturbate at the sight of a bare neck. No, this baby was manufactured with solid-gold machinery for the cultured taste—for the eye which would automatically break down a Rembrandt self-portrait into its compositional elements and know all about the "artistic qualities" but nothing of the depth of sadness in that face. No, she was no Rembrandt. A Mondrian maybe. Pure, perfect composition.

She was the type I found easy to hate. At the back of my mind I still held some notion that beauty was the greatest thing on earth and money a close second. She had perverted them both. I had seen her before. You got to know the slummers after a while—the rich bitches and bastards who made the rounds of the back-alley bars now and then so the rabble would know they were being well looked after. Every once in a while her picture popped up on the society page of a park-bench newspaper. Beautiful Carla Markham, daughter of financier Carl Markham, frugs with film star George Letrec on the lawn of . . . Carla Markham models a gown for high society fashion show . . . The local news hawks seemed to get a kick out of photographing her. But her pictures should have been on the sports page. Rumor had it she was trying to set a new record for the ninety-yard dash between bedrooms. A couple of my grubbier wino friends claimed they had been in those bedrooms. After you hear it a few times from different sources, you begin to believe it might not be all brag.

Come off it, Chessick. Your gutter is too low for prudery.

Mack was leaning forward on the table with his face in his arms, mumbling incoherently. He began to cry. For a moment I sat patting him on the head and thinking about all the Macks in the whole vast bloody ugly world who would be crying on their barroom tables tonight. Such sentimentality was too luxurious to be sustained for long—especially when my glass was empty. I picked through the change in my pocket and decided I had enough for a beer at least. I wasn't drunk—at least not nearly as much as I would like to

be—and I made it to the bar through the maze of tables
without seriously offending anyone larger than myself.

"Beer," I said. "Thirty-five cents' worth."

" 'Nother dime," the bartender said.

I contemplated the quarter and two nickels on the counter. "So what'll it get me?"

"A sweet good night," the bartender said.

"Put it on my bill," a voice said.

It was Miss Markham's companion, a young man of maybe
twenty-five who looked like a refugee from a Beatle movie
—hair down over his ears, some kind of sports jacket without
a collar, pants tight enough that they might have been sexy
on a girl. Carla's eyes remained on her drink.

"Make it Scotch," I said. "Best you've got. Double shot."

The young man looked me over with a smug expression,
then commenced nodding his head up and down with a
slightly jerky motion in time to the rock 'n' roll music on
the juke box. "So how's it hanging?" he said.

I almost laughed. Rule #1 in the Slumming Guidebook:
Play it cool. Make friends with the natives. Guaranteed to
impress your girl.

"I'll survive," I said.

"Glad to hear it, man." Boy Friend began to play the
counter with his fingertips as though it was a bongo drum.
"So where's the action?"

I had to think about that for a minute. "Have you tried
Carla Markham's whorehouse?" I said.

I was watching both their faces. Boy Friend's reaction was
what I might have predicted. Pure shock. He froze momentarily, then his lips broke into a nervously defensive grin,
and he turned to Carla to see if she had gotten the joke. She
hadn't. In fact, there was no visible reaction at all. She
didn't even look up. Her hand held steady on the glass a few
inches off the counter, her eyes gazing into the liquor. Boy
Friend turned back to me, laughing softly as though it was a
good joke, even if possibly a bit risqué. I knew he was praying to Mammon that Carla hadn't heard. With a painfully

deliberate nonchalance he set a five-dollar bill on the counter and got up.

"Well, I'm glad to have met you," he said, smiling to me, then turned to the girl. "Hey, Carla, whaddaya say we make the jazz scene at North Beach. This place is a drag."

She didn't move. Not even her eyes. Very slowly she said, "Hit him."

"Ah, come on, Carla. He didn't mean anything."

"Hit him."

For several seconds he stood watching her, his body as taut as a strained rubber band, his eyes frantic, his mouth working for words. Suddenly he turned on me with his fists balled at his sides. "You better apologize, mister."

I just sipped my Scotch and contemplated him. There's a certain feeling of freedom and power you get when you fall so low you don't give a damn what people think. "You know," I said, "I'm all for you young people rebelling against your parents and conventions and the atom bomb and this world-you-never-made and all that—but is it absolutely necessary to run around looking like a fag?"

Boy Friend's body went limp. His eyes glazed, staring through me into nothing. Abruptly he whirled and walked quickly to the door. "Are you coming with me, Carla?"

"No."

"I'll tell your father."

Her only reply was to raise her glass to her lips and sip slowly. His body shaking with frustration and anger, Boy Friend disappeared through the door.

"He was really a nice guy," Carla said without looking at me. "He just wanted to show off, that's all."

"Can't say he's very good at it."

"And I'm sure you are. You must be very tough, Mr. . . ."

"Chessick. And in the shape I'm in, a girl scout could whip me with one hand."

For the first time she turned and gazed at me. Her eyes covered every inch of my body. She might have been examining a dissected frog in biology class. "Yes," she said, "I believe you."

"Thanks, my masculine self-image needed your confidence."

"Oh? Do you get emasculated often?"

"Daily. It's my favorite sport."

"And your second favorite sport, I suppose, is castrating harmless young men in front of their girl friends."

"Third. My second favorite is insulting beautiful blond rich bitches who drag their boy friends to two-bit dives to watch the animals."

"My psychiatrist would love you," Carla said. "You'd prove all his pet theories about the male castration complex."

"Yeah. I don't doubt your psychiatrist would love me—if I gave him half the chance. But there are people in this room with honest reasons to drink themselves into a stupor. Like Mack over there. Four kids, a shrew for a wife and arthritis in both hands so he can't get a job at the only thing he knows—lifting a shovel. He's a good man. He's got courage and honest emotions—maybe even the last remnant of an obsolete thing called human dignity. I think he's earned a right to cry in his beer without being local color for the snob-hill gang."

"You're getting serious," Carla said.

"Sorry. I never could be clever for more than a minute at a stretch."

Carla sipped absently at her drink. She had a magnificent mastery of the art of voiding the face of any expression at all. For all the warmth of her flesh, for all the promise of her body, she might as well have been a plastic mannequin in a store window. It was a skill not everyone could acquire. You had to be burned out inside. I was an authority. I was pretty good at it myself.

"He wasn't lying," she said after a while. "He will tell my father. Dad will send someone. Have you ever been beaten up by two private detectives?"

"Not recently. Sounds intriguing."

"It gets to be a bore. Let's get out of here."

The bright red Corvette was parked at the corner in a taxi zone—one of the minor luxuries of the rich, I thought. I didn't bother to open the door for her, but she didn't seem to expect it.

"Didn't your boy friend's poppa buy him a car this week?" I asked.

"I like to do the driving," Carla said.

"Yeah, I noticed that."

She knew the car and the controls well enough that she didn't have to prove it with sudden bursts of speed. I had always been a Volkswagen man in my more affluent days. A car was transportation, plain and simple, and driving one of those shark-finned French juke boxes would have been comparable to walking into the public library with my fly open. But this Corvette, for all its whorehouse glamor, was all man underneath the transvestite clothes. It moved with power and precision and for real—without swagger. We crossed Market, running south on some nameless but familiar street where the buildings wore blank, anonymous faces. It was past midnight and the winos would be curled up in the alleys, covering themselves with cardboard and garbage-can rags against the cold. We picked up the freeway off Mission Street, and Carla maneuvered easily up the labyrinthine ramp and then opened it up to ninety with a lot to spare, heading north toward the Bay Bridge.

"There's a hotel near the Berkeley campus that's used to odd pairing," she said. "They'll think you're a student."

"I didn't know it mattered."

"My father's goons are pretty good at the hotel beat. They won't find us there."

"I bet you were voted Girl of the Year by the detectives local."

"You don't approve?"

"Sorry, baby. I'm an old Indiana boy."

"That's all right," Carla said. "Most men are really puritans. They don't think anything of putting down two dollars on the janitor's daughter for a quick disease, but they look at me and start building pedestals. I'm not the pedestal type. Don't worry, Mr. Chessick, I won't hurt your pretty little conscience for long. In a few days you will hate me quite sufficiently."

"Do I really have to wait that long?"

Carla glanced at me. Obviously I wasn't being properly grateful. "I can see this is going to be an exciting night," she said.

The hotel was a converted Victorian mansion that seemed a strange repudiation of the concepts that had built it. It was a family place. A portly mother in toe-length dress. Father cultivating a mustache and singing on the barbershop quartet at Rotary picnics. Twenty-seven kids and a dog. It was different now. Arty fag movies in Room 12. A lezzy orgy third floor to the left upstairs. Pick up your cat-o'-nine-tails, rubber suits and twelve-inch-heel lace boots at the desk.

The room was small, hardly bigger than a large closet, and this one didn't cater to any esoteric tastes. You could find a hundred identical rooms in the uptown slums. A single steel-frame bed. Chest of drawers. Bathroom down the hall. The only concession to the more artistically inclined was the hook in the ceiling, from which, I surmised, you could string up your playmate with the help of a rope if that's where your interests lay. Nothing but romance.

Yeah, romance. I guess I had been fool enough to let some idealistic notions in that direction creep into my mind. Maybe I was even ready to build a pedestal if she would give me half the chance. But as she said, she wasn't the type. As I had suspected, Carla had a remarkable body. But there was something unreal about it, something as cold and distant and impersonal and unachievable as the center fold-out in a *Playboy* magazine. Even when she was in my arms, I might as well have been collecting a dime thrown to the street-corner clown. We made love. Great euphemism that. Manu-

factured love. Assembly-line production. We dragged the
bits and pieces out of nothing more than memory and fitted
them together into an efficiently functioning machine—a pop
artist's machine that destroys itself by draining all its own
energy, leaving nothing more than a pile of useless junk.

And afterword she cried. That hurt. I was a sucker for
tears and hers were real. She lay on her side with the covers
pulled demurely up to her chin and her face against the wall
and cried for almost an hour. I made no attempt to comfort
her. One consoling word can be more devastatingly intimate
than twelve hours of impassionate intercourse. I was screwed
up enough without getting hung up on some neurotic
broad.

After a while I got up and fumbled a cigarette from the
pack we had bought on the way. I stood there leaning
against the dresser and thinking about the good times in bed
with Lorrie. For all her outward modesty, my wife had been
a real hellion in the sack. Ex-wife, I reminded myself. Ex-
wife, ex-son, ex-everything. Ronnie was five years old last
week. He would have had the usual party. Maybe some of
the kids would ask about Dad. What would Ronnie tell
them? Back fighting in Viet Nam probably. The kid had
been real proud of that second-louie bar. Did you kill lottsa
Cong, Dad? Mommy says you got wounded real bad. Can I
see the medal? Can I show it around?

Sorry, son, they don't give medals for where I was
wounded.

Carla was asleep. Her breathing was soft and steady, and
every so often she would begin to say something and it
would break in a muted sob and then she would be sleeping
again. There was something very warm, very gentle about a
sleeping girl. She seemed . . .

Forget it, Chessick. All the tears in the world wouldn't
change the situation a jot. She was a cheap rich slut looking
for kicks wherever she could find them. I couldn't afford to
start getting sentimental now.

I crossed to the window and pulled the curtain with my

forearm. The moon was a diluted yellow glow through the thick, moving haze of clouds. The air smelled like rain. Below the window was an alley and across it an old wooden warehouse running the length of the block. A man sat in one of the doorways, huddled into his coat and discernible only by the orange glow of his cigarette. So Berkeley had its bums, too. The moon sought a hole in the clouds, and I watched absently as the pastel light swept the darkness from the alley back toward the warehouse. Then in the moment before the clouds again covered the alley in blackness, I saw quite distinctly the alpine hat and the red glint of a feather.

Panic surged up from my entrails and burst in my head. Then it was gone and there were only the questions clicking off with mechanical precision in my brain. Was he one of Old Man Markham's private eyes? No, this was the second day I had been tailed by Alpine Hat, and it would have been impossible for anyone to foresee the accident of my picking up Carla in a bar. Blackmail? No. A setup? But too much was chance. How could anyone have known I would chase Carla's mop-haired boy friend away? No, not a setup either. Then what? At least one thing was sure. Alpine Hat wasn't just part of my imagination.

A direct confrontation. The bastard wouldn't find it so easy to lie his way out this time. I was already dressed and halfway to the door when I remembered his sleeve knife. I needed a weapon. Something small and inconspicuous. My eyes scanned the darkened room. There was nothing. Carla's purse lay on the floor beside the jumble of clothes. Quickly I picked it up and felt through the contents. Keys, lipstick, a small cellophane package probably containing a sanitary napkin, wallet, scattered coins, handkerchief, a pack of cigarettes, a lighter. Then I found it. A four-inch hat pin with a round plastic ball on one end. It wasn't ideal. I would have to go for the eyes or the flesh of the stomach. Against that knife it would be all but useless, but I hoped to hell it wouldn't come to that.

I shoved the pin in my pocket and went into the hall. The

hotel was silent. A balding night clerk slept with racking snores in a chair behind the counter. Outside the air was cool and a wet breeze was blowing in from the bay and rustling the treetops along the sidewalk. The ground was bathed in a sickly green pallor from the filtered moon. I cut across the front of the house on the lawn and around the side. When I reached the other corner I hesitated in the shadow of the wall, watching the vague figure in the doorway across the alley. He lit another cigarette, and in the brief flickering glow I could see it was the same man I had met earlier.

I fingered the hat pin, at the same time trying to remember the basics of my Army karate. Front kick the best bet. Bring knee waist-high and shoot in with focus on the toe. In and out fast. It's the shock that counts. But what was there to be afraid of? A fop who probably couldn't punch a hole in wet toilet paper? Everything else about him was show. Why not the knife?

Abruptly I shoved away from the building and crossed the back yard to the alley. When I reached the pavement I stopped. I could feel Alpine Hat watching me through the darkness. His cigarette arced away off a flicked finger and splashed brief sparks along the pavement. Slowly he rose to his feet. I moved forward.

And then everything was bright and scintillating. I began to fall. I fell down into the dark earth, and far above me I could hear the soft patter of rain.

I lay for a long time, even after I was awake, listening to the rain on my back and shoulders. My left hand was sticky and burning. The back of my neck throbbed in rhythm to my heart. The pavement was hard and wet and cold against my cheek. Painfully I pulled myself up into my jacket. There was no strength in me to move. No reason to move.

Suddenly I heard the splash of running feet very near. A kid's voice called and echoed. The voice grew more distant, and then other voices—far away, too—picked it up, calling

back and forth. I opened my eyes. It was early in the morning and dark with clouds and the rain made quick little
darting splashes on the concrete. The air smelled salty and
there was the acrid odor of dead fish. Gulls cackled overhead.
Down the pavement in front of me a small group of people
were gathering.

I struggled to my knees. When I lifted my hand from the
pavement a pink splotch beneath spread outward and flowed
away in narrow streams. There was a new purple scab ex-
tending all the way across my left palm. I looked around. I
was on a wharf, a windowless concrete building on one side
and a railing and a drop to the sea on the other. Behind the
crowd that was forming on the street was the imposing skyline of Frisco. I knew the place. This was a favorite pier for
kids to go fishing.

I pushed myself to my feet and stood for a moment waver-
ing back and forth, then took an unsteady step toward the
crowd. As one the entire group backed away several steps. A
woman screamed something and pointed at me. A police
siren cut the air, growing closer. It seemed like a hell of a lot
of trouble over a drunk. But all I needed now was a bunch
of cops. Maybe there was a way out behind me. I could dive
into the water and hide under the pier in the pilings if necessary.

I whirled and started to run. But my feet weren't moving.
I was frozen in place, staring down, my entire body numb.
Alpine Hat lay on his back. His face was white and staring.
Staring with three eyeballs. At the very corner of the left
eye, so that it touched the flesh of the nose, was what looked
like a red pearl. But it wasn't a pearl. It was the plastic end
of a four-inch hat pin.

THREE

The cop was a big guy, shoulders half a mile apart and a pug face in between that would have made Bela Lugosi look handsome. His nose had been broken so many times it could no longer remember which way to hang, so it just struggled out in all directions from the middle of his face. Whoever had worked over his eyes had done a good job. All the flesh had been pushed back into the sockets, so now all you could discern was the soft glint of two steel-black pupils gazing out through what resembled layer upon layer of wrinkled wads of chewing gum. He stared at me across the desk, with his mouth twisted in an expression of such total disgust that I figured he was deciding whether to spit in my face or mop up the floor with me.

"Chessick? Robert Chessick—dat right?" he asked.

"Yeah," I answered, rubbing the back of my neck. It

didn't hurt that much any more but I needed his sympathy.

"You a Polack?" he asked unsympathetically.

"I don't know," I said, "I never thought about it. I suppose I have some."

"I'm a Wop," he said. "I hate Polacks."

We weren't getting off to a good start. I sat there watching his squat, knobby fingers on the desk and wishing to hell I was back in some peaceful gutter, wishing I'd never laid eyes on Carla Markham or Alpine Hat or . . .

"Maggie," he bellowed so suddenly and with such force that I almost bolted from my chair. I swung toward the door, expecting to be besieged by a full platoon of the Gestapo torture brigade, brandishing rubber hoses, lead pipes, two-inch-wide leather belts with rusty, bloodstained buckles . . . Instead, in walks—*clickety-click*—six feet of scarecrow, uniformed policewoman. She had a face as white and drawn as a corpse, and wow! what a figure—21-21-21. All she needed was a mustache and . . .

"You called," she said sharply.

"Yeah," Pug-Face the Cop said. "I gotta have a witness. Da Supreme Court says I gotta have a witness." He swung his attention back to me. "Your rights is ya don't gotta say nuttin' an' anything ya do say we're gonna throw atcha in court, so it's better off ya don't say nuttin'. Okay? You heard dat, Maggie? I told 'im, din't I?"

"Yes, sir."

"Ya wanna confess?" Pug-Face said to me. "Inna old days I wouldn't even 'a ast ya. Jus' take ya in da back room an' slap da crap . . ."

"Sir, that could be construed as a threat," Maggie cut in.

"What! I din't threaten nobody. That weren't no threat. You, Chessick, did I threaten ya, uh?"

"No. I don't think so."

"Dere, Maggie. He said I din't threaten 'im. You heard 'im. An' din't promise ya nuttin' nor make no deals neither, did I, uh? Did I?"

"No," I admitted.

"You heard 'im, Maggie. He said I din't make no deals."

"Yes, sir" Maggie said. "But you have to tell him about the lawyer."

"Oh yeah. I forgot. Da Supreme Court says I gotta tell ya ya don't gotta say nuttin' wit'out a lawyer should be present. Yer a bum, so da court gotta appoint a mout'piece fer ya, so ya don't gotta say nuttin' till da trial. But don't get no ideas 'bout gettin' off innocent. Ain't no court-appointer shyster gonna go to much trouble freein' no bum. Hell no! Dis state's gonna hang your ass, Chessick."

"Sir, that's prejudgment. The Supreme Court says every man is innocent until proven . . ."

"Screw da Supreme Court," Pug-Face bellowed. "Get 'im outa here. Goddamn Supreme Court. Buncha Polacks. Lousy buncha Polacks. Get 'im outa here."

I didn't wait for another invitation. I was out the door fast, dragging all forty pounds of Maggie clinging to my arm like a spindle-fingered leech. A cop who was on guard at the opposite door poised his hand above his pistol butt when he saw me run out. I stopped, grinned and wiped my palm across my forehead. My armpits and the back of my shirt were drenched in sweat. I was vowing to myself that if I ever met old Chief Justice Polack Warren, I'd give him a big hearty kiss on the cheek. But the Supreme Court had only saved me from a beating. That wasn't going to help me when the cyanide capsules started breaking on the chamber floor. And that's right where I was headed—the San Quentin gas chamber. Old Pug-Face might not win the Nobel Prize for smarts this year, but he damned well knew what he was talking about. No lawyer appointed by the court was going to spend much of his hundred-dollar-an-hour time trying to clear a burned-out tramp on an open-and-shut murder charge. I could already hear what the bastard would say: Hat pin in the eyeball. Pretty gruesome. Might be able to swing the temporary insanity bit, especially if we emphasize your previous experience working the booby-hatch beat. If we're lucky we'll get you off with ninety-nine years.

There was one other alternative. I didn't like it much. I wasn't the type to go begging handouts from old college buddies, but there's a first time for everything. Besides, I was quickly developing a real zest for life.

"All right," Maggie said. "Back to your cell."

"Wait a minute," I said. "I want to phone a lawyer."

For a long time Bob Merril just gazed at me through the wire screen, nodding his head back and forth with exaggerated sadness. The years had been good to Merril. They had put a maturity and toughness into his craggy face, yet the charm was still there. His innocence and trust in humanity couldn't be contained in anything as small as his heart, and they had worked their way up into his eyes and mouth. I felt guilty sitting in front of him, accepting all that good, decent, honest sympathy that no bum deserved.

"Ah, Chess," he said. "Why didn't you call me before? God, it kills me to see you like this. Eight months without a decent meal. What's a friend for, anyway? Didn't you know I was in San Francisco?"

"Yeah, I knew. I saw your picture in the papers during the Lovejoy trial."

"But for chrissake, that was months ago. Why didn't you . . ." He stopped abruptly. His eye caught mine for just an instant, then fell back to the counter. "That Viet Nam thing?" he asked.

"Yeah." I felt a sharp pang of shame that he knew about it. It had been nearly nine years since we had parted ways —me drafted into the Army with a master's degree, Merril continuing on for his degree in law. When I got out of the Army that first time he had already left Indiana for the West Coast. Merril had never been one of my best friends—that would have been as stifling as having Jesus Christ in tow—so I lost track of him. It had never occurred to me that Merril might still be corresponding with someone in Indiana, that the story of Lieutenant Robert Chessick—war hero—might traverse nine years and thousands of miles.

"Ah, Chess," Merril said. "Shell shock is common in war. You don't have to let it mess up your whole life."

"Yeah, well, there's not going to be much life left to mess up if something doesn't pop fast. They're already fitting me for a casket at San Quentin."

"It doesn't look good, Chess."

"If it's hopeless, just let me know. As I said on the phone, I don't have any money. I can't pay you and . . ."

"Damn it, Chess, your credit's good with me. So let's kill that subject right away. Now tell me honestly—did you do it?"

He was looking me directly in the eye when he asked, and there was something about the sincerity, the trust, in his face that would have made it damned hard to lie. If I had any doubts about Merril's ability as a lawyer, that dispelled them. It takes a certain amount of deep-down guts to ask an old friend if he's a murderer.

"No," I said. "I told you on the phone . . ."

"You can't see a man's face over the phone. I believe you, Chess, but I won't kid you. That makes it all the more difficult. If you killed him, your . . . uh . . . previous mental instability would be good grounds for an insanity plea. But since you're innocent, we're going to have to go for broke. Either scot-free or the gas chamber. Is that all right with you?"

"If that's the way it is."

"Okay. Here's how it sizes up. I did some checking before I came down. The dead man's name was Louis Owen. He was a shoe salesman—emigrated from Wales two years ago and has been living in San Francisco ever since. He's a bachelor, lived alone in an apartment in Oakland. No criminal record. The police have already searched his room and quizzed his neighbors. The neighbors claim he was a friendly, easygoing man with no bad habits, aside from keeping rather odd hours. His room turned up nothing out of the ordinary, with the possible exception of a wardrobe that was costly far beyond the means of a door-to-door shoe salesman.

It appears probable that Mr. Owen either had some sort of independent income, which would be strange, since a man who was working just for the pleasure of it would hardly choose selling shoes. Either that, or he had another job, though nothing's turned up yet."

"What about the sleeve knife?"

Merril scratched his head and shrugged. "Dead end. There was no sheath for such a knife on the body, nor was any weapon found on the pier."

"Then what the hell did this?" I said, holding up my bandaged left hand. "Maybe I imagined everything else, but it's damned hard to just think up fourteen stitches."

"Whoa," Merril cautioned. "No one suggested you imagined anything."

"Well, why not? I'm a mental case, aren't I? And this is a nightmare. They go together. Nightmares and nuts. None of it makes any damned sense. How do I know I'm not cracking again? Maybe I did kill him. Maybe I thought I was being persecuted or something. How do we know I wasn't seeing alpine hats all over the place and killed the first one I came in contact with? Maybe my mind just made up the story about Carla and the hotel in Berkeley because I couldn't face being a murderer. So then I slash my hand and throw the knife away and pass out from loss of blood. That makes more sense, doesn't it?"

"No," Merril said. "For two reasons. First, if your mind were trying to repress the knowledge of a murder, wouldn't you at least conjure up a story that was somewhat logical? What you told me on the phone was too illogical for even the mind of a madman—and I don't believe you're mad, Chess."

"And the second reason?"

"Your hand. It rained all night and you were lying face down with your cut palm on wet pavement. The blood would have been constantly washed with water, and in a cut that large, no scab would have formed. I talked to the doctor who treated your hand. He is convinced that by all the laws of medicine you should have bled to death. Yet, not only didn't you die, you didn't even lose a significant amount of blood."

"What are you getting at?"

"That protective scab which formed across the cut on your palm could only have occurred in a warm, dry place—such as a car traveling from Berkeley to the San Francisco waterfront. And since you didn't lose much blood in the process, I would assume that someone put a tourniquet on your arm."

I leaned back in my chair and sighed. For a second I had almost convinced myself that I was insane. That would be the easy way out. But Merril wasn't going to settle for any easy ways.

"But nothing that would hold up in court," I said.

"Afraid not. There's no way to determine precisely what time your hand was cut. But for the moment it's about all we have to go on."

"What about Carla Markham or the Berkeley hotel."

"I haven't checked them out, but I wouldn't rest any hopes there. The hotel—if it's the type you describe—would hardly be too enthusiastic about testifying in court. And I sincerely doubt that a girl of Carla Markham's social position would find the prospect of a starring role in a murder trial especially thrilling."

"That leaves her boy friend out, too. How about the bar where I picked her up?"

"There would be a slight chance that the bartender would remember you. But it would be dangerous testimony. That would place you in downtown San Francisco only hours before the murder—and within easy walking distance of the scene of the crime. He would be of no help in placing you twenty-five miles away in Berkeley."

"In other words, we've got nothing."

"Oh, I wouldn't say that. If this had to happen, it's as good a time as any. The prosecution won't get much help from the police for a while. The entire force is tied in knots over this Kreigger deal."

"What Kreigger deal?"

"Oh, this scientist who committed suicide the other day. Kreigger defected from a top-secret laser project. The F.B.I. believes that before he killed himself he hid some important microfilm. The whole police force is out searching for it—so they're not going to have much time to investigate you. Which is one shot in our favor, since my experience has been that the police are working for the district attorney— and he's the one who'll be prosecuting the case."

"If that's the only thing in our favor . . ."

"Don't get pessimistic. Remember, I haven't even started really investigating yet. Something will turn up."

Merril rose and headed for the door, but before I could even yell my thanks across the room, he turned and came back. For a moment he stood hunched over the back of the chair, then, not looking at me, he said, "By the way, Chess, I wasn't planning to tell you this—but I suppose you've got a right to know everything. Before Owen was killed, he was kicked twice—once in the knee and once in the groin—very hard. A dislocation and a complete rupture. Traces of the microscopic material of Owen's pants were matched to the same material on the toe of your right shoe."

FOUR

I was hardly a stranger to the Frisco jail. In my eight months on Booze Alley there had been three or four brief stints in the drunk tank. A collection of lushes is as amiable a group as you'll find. They understand the problems of their kind, and to a man they are ready to respond with honest tears to a tale of woe, with loving aid and assistance to a case of the DT's. The drunk tank is like a convention hall where you return periodically to renew old acquaintances. Nobody stays there very long, so you just enjoy the warmth of a real bed and hot potato soup for as long as it lasts, and you don't even notice the steel bars.

To outward appearances the felony tank is just like the drunk tank—a rectangular room with three four-bunk cells along each side. That's where the similarity ends. Some men have been in there for months awaiting trial, never setting foot outside the barred doors. All of them have nothing to look forward to except ten or twenty or thirty years at the Big Q—San Quentin. Some will go to the gas chamber. There is no honest humor in a felony tank. There is only the quiet surge of long hours of hopeless waiting, of desperation, of fear. They play poker in whispers, betting grains of tobacco and roll-your-own papers. They steal the metal cups and boil flax over stoves fashioned of rolled toilet paper and drink the foul concoction for the mild kick.

There is no separation of the queers and perverts. At night you can hear the dark, ugly sounds of animal passion from the next cell. Then when it is over and you can think again, you lie there and listen to the metallic ring of your breathing echoing from the steel walls. You lie awake and remember things you haven't thought about for years—the sun on the pavement when you were a kid, the first high school dance. You even remember all the things you were once going to do, as if someday you might still have done them.

In the morning I woke early and lay with my eyes closed until I heard the metallic crunch as the cell door was electronically unlatched by a button outside the tank. We assembled briefly in the larger cellroom to receive our cold dehydrated scrambled eggs and to dip lukewarm coffee from a kettle. In fifteen minutes the white uniformed cook's crew returned with the guard to gather and count the eating utensils. I went back to my bunk and read a few pages of a bad Zane Grey western that I had picked at random from the paperbacks strewn about the floor. Then I closed my eyes and waited, suspended and hovering in a world without time.

That afternoon I was taken again to the visiting room. Merril looked at me sadly through the wire screen.

"Nothing?" I asked.

He shook his head. "The hotel in Berkeley wouldn't talk. Carla Markham refused to see me. I can subpoena them into court, of course, but I wouldn't chance it unless I could speak with them first."

"So we're right where we started—nowhere."

"That's about the shape of it. I checked again with the doctor who treated your hand, asked him about any injury to your neck. No bruises or marks. Whoever hit you did a professional job. Nothing new has turned up about Owen."

"Then it's cut and dried," I said.

"There's another angle we can try. When did you first notice Owen following you?"

"Monday morning."

"Had you done anything Monday? Try to remember anything that happened Monday. Did you meet anybody—do anything? Try to remember. We've got to find a motive."

"I have tried to remember. I woke up in an alley Monday morning. Then I just wandered around the city until about noon. I picked up a free meal at some Baptist rescue mission. Then I panhandled fifty cents and sat in a movie for six hours. I slept in the bushes in a park on Telegraph Hill."

"Could he have been following you before without your knowing it?"

"No. Not him. He was too much a dandy, too obvious for the places I go. Maybe somebody else."

Merril sighed. "God, Chess, I don't know what to tell you. I don't know where to turn next. Until we find out why Owen was following you, I don't even know where to start looking. But don't give up hope. I'll delay the trial as long as possible. Something's got to break."

"Yeah," I said. "Sure." I gazed at my hands on the counter. "Merril . . ."

"Yeah, Chess."

"If I pleaded guilty—could you establish temporary insanity?"

I could feel Merril's eyes boring into me. I didn't look at him. "We're not beaten yet," he said.

The barred door clicked shut behind me. I stood for a moment examining the anonymous faces circled about a dice game. A few pairs of eyes lifted toward me, then looked away. For all I was to these men—or to the world—I could already be dead. Slowly I walked to my bunk and sat down with my face in my hands. After a while I could hear myself laughing in a dry, empty monotone.

"Chessick," the guard said.

I pushed myself off my back and crossed to the tank door. The guard slid the door open and closed it behind me.

"It's about time," I said. It was Saturday afternoon and I hadn't seen Merril since Thursday.

"You got no complaints," the guard said.

I walked ahead of him silently down the steel, murmuring corridor, past the row of dismal tanks and trapped men to the big steel door. The guard pushed a buzzer beside the door and a narrow slit opened. A pair of eyes looked first at me, then at the guard. The door swung open. We crossed the corridor to the elevator. I noticed the guard didn't lock me behind the wire cage that divided the elevator in half. When the door opened we stepped into a wood-paneled hallway with offices.

"You came too far," I said. "The visitor's room is one up."

The guard glanced at me distainfully and nodded along the hallway. I followed it past the open doors. We were on the ground floor and I recognized the offices as interrogation rooms. The hallway opened abruptly into a large room with a long desk. Several cops and a few civilians were standing about. Merril was sitting on a bench beside the door and he rose and waved when he saw me come in. The guard motioned me to the desk. I had to wait until the desk cop finished booking a young hood in a leather jacket; then he came down behind the desk to me.

"Chessick," the guard said.

Without speaking, the desk cop crossed to an open safe and returned with a box of manila envelopes. He searched through it briefly, then drew one out.

"Chessick, Robert W.?" he said.

"Yeah," I said.

He handed the manila envelope across the counter to me. There was a white business form stapled to it. "Check the contents and sign the receipt," he said mechanically.

I opened the envelope. Inside I found my old plastic wallet, a dirty handkerchief, a quarter and two nickels.

"It's mine," I said.

"Sign the receipt."

"I'm not signing anything until I know what's going on."

The desk cop looked at me quizzically, then turned to the guard.

"He hasn't been told," the guard said.

The desk cop expelled a long-suffering sigh and turned back to me. "A witness was on the pier," he said. "Saw the whole thing. Saw you kill Owen."

I just gazed at him with my mouth open.

"Self-defense," the cop said. "You're free."

FIVE

Merril had brought me an inexpensive suit of clothes to celebrate my release—pants, sports jacket, shirt, tie, underclothes, socks. I changed in the police station men's room and walked out on the street with an unfamiliar feeling of respectability.

It was a good day to be let out of jail. A real travel-poster day. The sun was descending into the Pacific Ocean somewhere in the vicinity of Fleishhacker Zoo and it cut the sky across—half blue, half gold—and had left some gold trim on the tops of the buildings. It was a day when the young lovers came up from Palo Alto and Sunnyvale and San Jose to browse the stores and to walk the parks hand in hand and to gaze at each other over a cozy candlelit dinner at Fisherman's Wharf and to dream of the night's love-making, and maybe church in the morning when they would feel warm and holy. A good Saturday when the shopping mothers rushed home on buses with kids in tow to bake TV-dinners for late-golfing fathers.

Merril was parked almost half a mile away, and we took our time getting there, stopping to look in windows and to admire the girls—and for me—to feel free and alive again and to pretend that nightmares ended abruptly and could be forgotten. We stopped and got a hamburger at one of those long, narrow-counter places with the stainless-steel atmosphere and the stainless-steel waitresses.

"Like to invite you home for the night," Merril said. "But what with the kid now, we've got a full house."

The statement was rather jarring. I had been so wrapped up in myself for the last few days it hadn't occurred to me that Merril might be married, let alone a father. "Christ," I said, "'I hope I'm not keeping you from dinner."

"Oh no. This is Marriane's night to teetotal with the local Ladies Social Climbers Club. I have nothing more important pending than a couple hours in front of the idiot box."

"How long have you been married?"

"Five years November 17. Damn, Chess, didn't you know? I thought I'd told the whole world. Well hell, you knew her. Marriane Harper. She was a junior at Indiana when you graduated."

That was even more jarring. Marriane was the most expensive bitch I ever got into bed. Not expensive in the way Carla Markham was, no, Marriane was from the lower-middle, but she had expensive tastes. I always suspected she had diamonds painted on each contact lens so she wouldn't have any trouble keeping her eye on her goal. She was the one who made me trade in my practical old college Chevy on a nearly new Cadillac. We were real close for all of the forty-three days it took for the finance company to repossess. So people change. Give her the benefit of the doubt, Chessick. Besides, whatever else she had been, she was a fine— damn fine—lot of woman.

"No," I said, "I didn't know. Congratulations. I remember she was a lovely girl."

"Lovely! She's beautiful, Chess. She gets more beautiful every day. No kidding. Our daughter's a real doll, too. She's five now. Let me show you a picture . . ."

He must have had a dozen pictures of the kid in his wallet, and as he said, she was a real doll. The face might have been Marriane's when she was a child—the smooth skin, the dark, glistening hair. Only one thing bothered me. It was too much Marriane—Marriane and someone else. Not Merril. It fitted together real neat. Five-year-old daughter, five years married. It had entered my mind—before I could censor it—that Marriane had been after more than Merril could offer, unless she needed a husband so urgently she couldn't let dreams any longer stand in the way of practicality. I had seen that happen a few times before, and some fine marriages had come out of it. The way Merril was in love with both Marriane and the kid, this was probably a good one. At least I liked to think so.

"Beautiful," I said. "You must be a proud father."

"Yeah. Thanks, Chess. Hey, you'll have to come out to dinner one of these nights. Marriane would love to see you again."

I seriously doubted that, and the prospect wasn't too appealing to me either. "Well, let me get this other thing settled and I might start socializing again."

"Are you still worrying about that? It's over. Forget it. Self-defense. You're a free man."

"All right. Maybe it's over and maybe it isn't. But I still have the feeling . . ."

"What? So the witness's testimony wasn't logical. It saved you from the gas chamber, didn't it? Look, Chess, I'm a lawyer, right. Well, if I've learned just one thing in this profession it's this: If the verdict's innocent, for God's sake, don't question it."

"Maybe. But something tells me that the verdict—the real

verdict—isn't in yet. And the real judge and jury in this case aren't sitting in any courtroom. They're hiding someplace out there—waiting."

"What the hell kind of talk is that?"

"Listen to me, Bob. I had a lot of time to think sitting there in jail. Sure it's illogical—sheer madness. But somewhere, behind what we can see, I sense something perfectly logical. Somewhere there's a pattern. A motive. Someone went to a helluva lot of trouble to frame me. Somebody smart. Particles of Owen's pants on my shoe. That was pure finesse. Then this witness—what did you say his name was?—Aaron? —He stuck his neck way out to get me free again. What if there had been a flaw in his story? What if he made just one little slip? That would have implicated him in the murder —and through him maybe a lot more people. No, it was too big a chance to take just out of magnanimity. Somebody went to a hell of a lot of trouble to put me in jail—and a lot more to get me out. Why?"

"All right," Merril said, "I give up. Why?"

"You," I said.

Merril looked at me curiously. "Will you talk some sense, Chess?"

"Okay, look at it this way. Somebody wants me dead. For some reason they find themselves with a corpse on their hands, so the easiest way is to frame me for murder. I'm a bum. No money, court-appointed lawyer, quick trial, gas chamber. They don't figure on you—a high-class professional criminal lawyer who cares, who really cares. You phone Carla Markham, check the hotel in Berkeley—show every sign of beginning an intensive investigation to determine my innocence. You may find out something and they can't take the chance, so they set me free for no other reason than to get you off the case."

"Come on, Chess, you're grabbing in the dark."

"What the hell else can I do? Or there's another possibility. What if they were afraid you'd get me off with a prison stretch. I'd still be alive—but I would be quite safely protected behind bars. If they really wanted me dead bad enough, they would have to set me free so they could get to me themselves. Doesn't that make some sense?"

"No," Merril said, "it doesn't make any sense at all. Look, I know this has been a trying week, but don't start imagining things. Face a few facts. You don't have any money, you've never seen any top-secret event, you don't know anybody, you don't do anything. You're a tramp, Chess, a bum, plain and simple. You're of absolutely no importance to anybody. Just what the hell remotely conceivable reason is there for anyone to want you dead?"

"That's it! Because I'm a bum. Look, Bob, if you were going to choose out of all of San Francisco just one man to kill—and if the name didn't matter—who would you choose? The mayor? The president of a bank? Somebody with lots of friends? No! You'd choose somebody who was expendable, someone who could simply disappear off the face of the earth without anybody paying the slightest attention. A bum. Me."

"It doesn't work, Chess. It just doesn't work. You're conjuring up a madman who wants to kill somebody—anybody —for no reason at all. It just doesn't jibe with your theory that there's some kind of organization behind it."

I had no answer. I sipped silently at my coffee.

Merril sighed heavily and leaned forward on the counter. "Okay. So what are you going to do about it?"

"Talk to the witness—Aaron—personally."

"That could be a mistake. You haven't been tried, so there's no question of double jeopardy. If you convince Aaron to revoke his story to the police, you could still go to the gas chamber."

"Well, what the hell else can I do? You want to come with me?"

Very slowly Merril's lips curled in a smile. He sat looking at me with exasperation for several seconds, then reached in his pocket and withdrew a slip of paper.

"What's that?" I asked.

"Aaron's address," Merril said. "I rather thought you might be bullheaded about this thing."

It was one of those dingy, multicolored testaments to modern mobility—a rental trailer park in San Mateo with hundreds of what the salesmen call "mobile homes" stacked side by side like so much cordwood, sort of a slum for the man on the move. I've seen such places that were clean and well laid out with walks and shrubbery, but this wasn't one of them. It was the fast-buck type of project that California entrepreneurs love to bulldoze out of an orchard on Wednesday and start renting Thursday. The ground was cluttered with overturned garbage cans, tricycles, filthy kids and yapping dogs.

Number 38 was a long, rusting green affair, wheel-less and balanced on stacked concrete blocks. A small, unpainted plyboard and tarpaper shack had been added around the door as a sort of foyer. A blue Ford was parked in the indented tire strips in the dirt that served as a driveway. I tried knocking once lightly, and when there was no response, I knocked harder. There was a burst of coughing, a lot of padding around, then finally the door opened.

I don't know what I expected, but he wasn't it. He was a short, squat man with a beer paunch that hung slightly over his beltless trousers. His face, still bloated with sleep, was innocuous enough—the sort of bland, jowly, everyman sort of face that you pass a thousand times a day on the street and never bother to notice.

"You Kenneth Aaron?" I asked.

"Yeah . . . uh . . . you'll have to pardon me . . . uh . . . I don't remember."

"My name's Chessick. This is Bob Merril."

Aaron raised a hefty arm and rubbed his eyes, then stood gazing at me blankly for a while. Then suddenly he burst into an embarrassed grin. "Ah, yes. Mr. Chessick. Of course. Of course. I am sorry. Please come in. Please. You'll pardon the house. I just moved in a few days ago and it's still quite a mess."

That was an understatement. Drawers were open and dripping with underclothes and socks. Shirts and pants had been left at random on everything that would hold them. Ashtrays, crowded with shaggy, stumped cigars, dirty dishes, silverware and beer bottles were strewn about the table and sink. Aaron grappled a load of clothes from the couch, motioned to us to sit down and tossed the clothing through the bedroom door. "I really should get a wife," he mumbled. "We bachelors have such a hard time at housekeeping. And I'm afraid I'm terribly lazy. But please sit down. Would you like some coffee?"

"No," I said. "Just answers."

If he detected any antagonism in my voice, he didn't show it. "Yes, of course. I really am very sorry about that, you know. I can't tell you how sorry."

"Sorry about what?"

"Why, I mean not going to the police sooner. It must have been horrible for you . . . I mean knowing you were innocent. But it was my job, you see. I'm a real estate salesman. I just got the job, you see. A really good job. The very finest homes for people on the way up. We don't take general listings. I work for the builder, you see. Very status homes." All the time he was talking he was moving aimlessly, picking up junk from one part of the room and setting it down at random in another.

"God damn it," I said, "will you sit down?"

Immediately he scurried over to a chair, sat down on an ashtray, stood up, set the ashtray on the floor, then sat down again with his hands between his knees and his eyes on the floor like a chastised child.

"Now," I said, "what was this about your job?"

"Why, that's why I didn't go to the police sooner. I'm really terribly ashamed, but my job . . . I mean it's very bad publicity. They might even have put my picture in the paper. And we do sell status homes, you see . . . and my boss said—when I first came to work, he said—'Our salesmen must keep out of trouble.' Those were his very words. Then I read in a magazine how in New York the people just stood by and watched a lady get murdered because they didn't want to get involved. It sounded so horrible. And then I thought to myself, But here you are letting that poor man stay in jail when you could help him, and I thought, Well, Kenneth Aaron, I guess you're no better than those other people. So I stayed awake all night and I thought to myself, Well, darn it anyway, I don't care if I do get fired. I'm going to help that poor man."

"A truly commendable sacrifice," I said with as much sarcasm as I could shove through my teeth.

Merril nudged me with his elbow as a signal to shut up. "Tell us exactly what you saw," he said.

"Why, the whole thing. Just like I told the police. But I do want you to understand, Mr. Chessick, that I am terribly sorry that I didn't tell them sooner. It was horrid . . . truly horrid of me."

"Damn it, will you just answer the question. What did you tell the police?" I said.

"Why, just what I saw. I was driving by the pier . . ."

"You're sure it was the pier? Not a hotel in Berkeley?"

"Berkeley? No. No, I don't ever go there. It was the pier in San Francisco. You know, down by the waterfront. Well, like I said, I was driving by— It was quite late—I had just seen a movie, you see—and had a beer . . . It's very lonely when you're not married, so I go to the movies a lot. And, well, I was driving by and I saw these two fellows standing there . . . I mean you and the other guy . . . and I'm new here, so I didn't know how to get back on the freeway to San Mateo, and no one else was around, so I thought I would ask you. So I parked the car at the sidewalk and started to walk over . . . You were way back from the street . . . and I stopped because I could hear you and this other fella . . .

the one with the funny hat . . . you were arguing about something. I guess you didn't see me."

"How did you happen to see them?" Merril asked. "It must have been pretty dark."

"There was a light on the wall, a sort of spotlight. In fact, there were three of them. I guess they were to keep burglars out or something."

"That checks," Merril said to me. "I looked over the area. The lights are high up on the wall and quite dim, but bright enough to make out faces at night."

"Yes, that's right," Aaron said. "But they were talking real fast and I couldn't tell what they . . . I mean, you . . . and the other fellow . . . were arguing about . . . except it might have been about money. Anyway, the guy with the funny hat got real mad and then all of a sudden he went like he was going to hit you . . . and I saw real fast . . . almost like magic there was a knife in his hand. He swung the knife at you, but you grabbed it in your hand and kicked him and then it looked like you just hit him in the face with two fingers. He fell down and then you stood there for a long time looking at your hand where you had caught the knife . . . It was bleeding real bad . . . and then you fell down."

"Didn't it occur to you that that was rather fast for a man to faint from loss of blood?" Merril asked.

"I don't know anything about that. Really."

"The knife," I said. "What happened to the knife?"

"I was coming to that. I mean, I was real scared . . . 'cause neither of you were moving. So I ran over to see if I could help. First thing I did was pick up the knife and throw it up the pavement a few feet. I guess maybe I thought that one of you would wake up and cut me with it or something. I could see that you were breathing, but it didn't look like the other guy was, so I tried to feel his pulse . . . and I found this little leather thing around his wrist."

"The knife sheath?" I asked.

"I don't know what it was. Anyway, I was real scared when I saw this guy was dead, and . . . well, I guess I panicked, you might say, and I ran away. And before I got to the car I remembered I had touched the knife and the police might take finger prints and think I did it. So I came back and got the knife, and then I remembered I had touched the leather thing on the guy's wrist, too, so I came back and got it."

"And where are they?" I asked.

"I gave them to the police when I told them about everything."

"You're a damned liar," I said.

Aaron hunched down in his chair as though I were going to hit him. Merril nudged me again to shut up, but I wasn't about to be quiet. I wanted to back this fat worm against the wall. I wanted to get him so mad he would be talking without thinking.

"Now you listen to me and you listen close," I said. "I was hit on the head and taken to that pier by the same man who killed Owen, and for all I know that was you. Well, I damned well don't like being tailed all over the countryside and I don't like being framed for murder. I don't know what this is all about, but let me tell you one thing certain. I'm not going to let it drop until you and your rotten mob have done as much sweating as I did. You understand that?"

Aaron stared at me with mouth and eyes wide. "What . . . what . . . what . . ."

"Oh, for God's sake. Didn't you hear me? I'm calling you a repulsive little fat pig of a liar."

"What . . . what . . . what . . ." Aaron said.

Merril grabbed my arm and pulled me through the door, trying to calm me. Outside, the last of sunset was gone and the sky was heavy blue with black patches of cloud. Behind me, Aaron's dull voice droned on through the open doors in that same flat monotone, like a stuck record. "What . . . what . . . what . . ."

Merril loaned me twenty bucks and drove me to a shabby
$2.50-a-night hotel on a Frisco back street. He wanted to
lend me more, to set me up in a comfortable motel, but I
wouldn't hear of it. We sat in the car in front of the place
for a long time without speaking.

After a while I said, "What do you think? About Aaron, I
mean."

"I don't know," Merril said. "I thought I had been in this
business long enough to spot a liar—even a practiced liar—
half a mile away. I'd swear he was telling the truth. Every
reaction was right. If he was lying he should have gotten defensive when you pushed him, but he didn't. Just confused.
That's the way people act when they're telling the truth."

"All right. I got the same impression. But damn it, I'm
not going to throw in the towel and admit I'm crazy yet.
You've defended enough criminal types. What kind of man
would be able to lie so convincingly?"

Merril thought it over. "Well, there's your compulsive
liar. He's convincing because he half believes his own lies—
sort of makes up his reality as he goes along. But he's always
on the defensive. When he's backed into a corner he'll start
padding and expanding. Aaron's story was too consistent for
that type."

"What else?"

"There's only one other type that could possibly get away
with it. The technical term is 'sociopath.' They're the ones
who sell people the Brooklyn Bridge—the ones who beat the
lie-detector tests. It's a fairly rare form in its pure state. Ego-
tism carried to an absolute degree. Completely amoral. Go-
ering and a couple of other Nazi bigwigs were the type.
Maybe Stalin. It's not insanity or even neuroticism. It's just
as though an ordinary person were stripped of conscience.
Since they believe that other people are merely things to be
used, they can put on any face necessary to reach their goal.
They aren't all criminals. Some make it in big business or
government or the military. But they're all totally ruthless,
and totally convincing in any role they decide to play."

"Then they're capable of killing?"

"Yes. They wouldn't kill for fun or even temporary profit. Their minds are too logical for that—like a calculator. But if something stood in the way of a long-range goal, they could kill their own mothers with no more emotion than if they were swatting a fly."

"And if Aaron's the type, I take it that it wasn't a good idea for me to call him nasty names."

"Wouldn't make much difference," Merril said. "Such men have invisible walls around them. Insults don't even get through. But I hope you weren't serious about investigating further. These people may have no more need of you. If so, they may just leave you alone. But if Aaron really is a socio-path and you got in his way, he wouldn't hesitate to kill you."

"I was just trying to scare him . . . see how he would react. If it's all over, I'm willing to leave it that way. I'm no hero. I proved that a long time ago."

I got out and closed the door. "Chess," Merril called through the open window, "give me a call in the next couple of days. I'll see about getting you a job."

"Right," I said. "Thanks. Thanks for everything."

I got a small room on the third floor, with a neon sign blinking blue and red through the cheesecloth curtains. Quickly I folded my new clothes over a chair and fell into bed. My body was more tired than I had thought, but my brain was working overtime. The whole rotten situation was like a disease eating away inside my skull. I was like the blind man trying to describe an elephant by feeling its knee. There was too much that was out of my reach. I couldn't even formulate questions, let alone answers. So maybe Aaron was telling the truth. Someone who looked like me or was dressed up like me fought Alpine Hat. Or Alpine Hat was already dead and . . . It kept coming back to one thing. Old funny-farm boy Robert Chessick was slipping off his nut again.

After a while I slid into a thin veneer of sleep and dream.

I dreamed about Carla. She was dancing in a meadow in the sunlight and her white hair flowed in the wind. I went up to her and she smiled at me and opened her arms for me. Her body was soft and warm. It grew dark and began to rain. Carla fell down on the pavement. I kneeled beside her and took her head in my arms. She looked up at me. At the corner of her left eye was the round ball of a hat pin.

I pulled myself up from the nightmare and opened my eyes. The ceiling blinked red and blue from the neon sign beyond the window. I was very tired. I closed my eyes again.

"Mr. Chessick," someone said.

SIX

I was sitting bolt upright in the bed. Automatically my hand searched the nightstand for the lamp. I heard the click of the switch, but nothing happened. The room remained dark, with only the rhythmic pattern of blue and red flashing a dull neon glow through the gauze curtains. In the sporadic light my sleep-dazed eyes could barely make out the vague silhouette of a man seated in a chair at the foot of the bed.

"I hope you will forgive the intrusion, Mr. Chessick," a voice said. It was a husky voice that came through the throat, almost without benefit of lips or tongue, and the words rolled with a slight garble over trapped mucus. The stranger seemed to be deliberately disguising his voice so I would not recognize it again. Perhaps I had heard it before, at another pitch. There was something strangely familiar

about the deliberate concentration on each separate word. "I
felt it necessary to pull the plug on your lamp. I have reason
to believe that you are being watched by the . . . uh . . .
opposition, and I would rather they did not know I was talking with you."

My initial panic settled into a lethargic curiosity. If this
man was going to the trouble to disguise his voice, he probably didn't intend to kill me. At least at the moment.
"Okay," I said. My voice sounded flat, as though played on a
cheap tape recorder. "Maybe you can do some explaining."

"I rather thought that any explaining should come from
you. However, to allay your fears, let me assure you that I'm
on your side."

"And which side is that?"

"The side of the United States Government, I should
hope. Though you will forgive me if I retain certain suspicions until we complete our conversation."

"You're a cop?" I asked hopefully.

"In a manner of speaking. Yes, you might say I'm a federal cop. My name is Ladd—a code name, of course—and I
am an agent with the Special Department of Interior Counterespionage. It's a small and unheralded department of the
Federal Bureau of Investigation. The F.B.I. is simply the
term for the overall organization, which like any other government bureaucracy is broken down into separate compartments, each with a specific function. Our specialty is counterespionage within the United States—mainly, of course,
against the Communist underground. We do much the same
work as the C.I.A. does outside the United States. In fact,
sometimes I'm not quite certain whether we belong more to
the C.I.A. or the F.B.I. One must suffer such confusions in a
bureaucracy, I suppose. But I shouldn't bother you with our
petty interdepartmental jealousies."

"It's damned well about time you people decided to show
an interest."

"I assure you, Mr. Chessick, we've been interested for
some time. I believe you were briefly acquainted with one of

our agents. Quite a dandy. Always wore an alpine hat with a ridiculous feather in the band. Hardly the proper uniform in a profession which prides itself on anonymity."

"Alpine Hat was an F.B.I. agent?" I said incredulously.

"Yes, unfortunately. Every once in a while a nut slips through. My office is in Washington. I assure you if I had any knowledge that such a man was in the field, he wouldn't have lasted with the department for five minutes. He thought he was a spy, or some nonsense. Even carried a knife up his sleeve. Good God, the things I must put up with! Even the idiots running the department on the West Coast here had enough sense not to use him on an important assignment. But then we didn't really think you were very significant. The element of murder somewhat changes the situation."

"Well, what in the hell is the situation?"

"Frankly, I haven't the slightest idea. I was hoping you could tell us. You see, we happened on you very much by accident. Our department constantly has a number of Communist agents under surveillance. Many of them we could arrest at any time and be sure of a conviction, but we have found it more profitable to follow them in the hopes that they will lead us to someone higher up. It's quite a chain. One man leads us to another, and he to another, and so on. Well, by this complex process we discovered that two very professional agents were following you. These were not the sort of men who make many mistakes, so naturally we figured you must be of some importance to them. We did a swift, but thorough, check on Robert Chessick—college, teaching job, Army records, and so forth. Of course, it was evident why you are, say, on the bum. I mean Viet Nam, the mental hospitals. There is no evidence that your present life is in any way a sham. In fact, I should say it seems quite logical."

"All right. You get an A for research," I said with more anger than I intended.

"Let's make that a C," Ladd continued. "It seems we

missed the most important element—the reason the Commies continue to keep their best men on your tail, and yet haven't bothered to pick you up for questioning."

"Questioning about what?"

"Oh, come now, Mr. Chessick—I won't tell you how we learned but I assure you that we knew all about your activities last Monday night."

"Monday? What are you talking about?"

Ladd ignored the question. "We would have questioned you ourselves, of course, except we're rather curious about just what the Reds have in mind, and we didn't want to tip our hand quite yet."

"Wait a minute. Back up. What's this about my activities last Monday?"

I could almost feel Ladd's distainful smile through the darkness. "Excuse the oversight," he said. "I had forgotten that you have a tendency to consume inordinate amounts of alcohol. Let me refresh your memory. You are acquainted, of course, with the incident of Dr. Otto Kreigger."

"Never heard of him."

"Oh, come now. He killed himself in a San Francisco hotel room about a week ago."

"Yeah. All right. 'Scientist commits suicide. Possible treason.' I remember the headlines. I didn't read the story."

"Then let me fill you in. Dr. Kreigger was a brilliant young physicist—a true prototype—in Germany when Hitler came to power. Unlike many of his peers, Kreigger held some very definite political convictions. He didn't know exactly what he was for, but he was very much against fascism. Though he wasn't a Jew and really had nothing to fear, he saw the writing on the wall—it was more obvious than even we like to admit—and escaped to Britain in 1936. His career is not exciting, but it is quite remarkable. He had a doctorate in theoretical physics—not nuclear, certainly—something to do with radio and light waves. As a German, he was ineligible to assist us in the war, though it is now evident that Britain might well have perfected her radar much sooner had they accepted his talents. But one must understand the attitudes of war. Anyway, he was sent to an internment camp in Canada, where he may or may not have become acquainted with Klaus Fuchs.

"Of course, the postwar prejudices of the United States were relatively short-lived—much to our benefit, I believe. We had never been bombed, never seen our civilians systematically massacred, so we forgot a lot sooner than Britain did. Which is one reason why the United States was able to steal Kreigger from the English without much argument. Oh, we made a thorough security check. I've done that sort of work and not much misses our eye. Kreigger had an amazingly clean record. He had left Germany of his own will. From confiscated German files, we learned that as a student he had been ardently pro-American, had never belonged to the Communist Party or any other revolutionary organization. No crime record or any hint of homosexuality which might mark him for blackmail. Actually, a better security risk could hardly be found. The United States immediately put him to work on radar. It appeared a wise decision. Kreigger was in every way an ideal scientist. He rose rapidly. In the fifties he was given an enviable post at the BMEWS site at Clear, Alaska."

"BMEWS?" I put in. "Ballistic Missile Early Warning System?"

"Correct," Ladd replied. "Along with the DEW Line and the White Alice Project, BMEWS is one of the cornerstones of our retaliatory defense system. The Clear Site consists of three huge radar screens—each one the size of a big apartment building. Its function is to spot any Russian missiles coming over the pole or across the Bering Strait. You can see that his position was a most important one."

"Yeah," I said. It seemed that with each word my heart would cease to beat. The perspiration rolled down out of my hair and along my forehead and cheek. Whatever Ladd was leading up to, it was already evident that the stakes in this game were of mammoth proportions.

the billikin courier 53

"Clear is hardly the ideal spot for comfort. It's located between Anchorage and Fairbanks and the only access is by railroad. But Kreigger seemed to enjoy it well enough. He had always been a solitary man and he had nurtured a number of hobbies. Anyway, he remained several years at his own request. There is no evidence that he had any contact with the Communists at this time. Later his brain was again needed for research. Lasers this time. You might have guessed, if you know anything of the subject, that the United States has been involved for a number of years in attempting to adapt the laser as a weapon. An extremely powerful laser that could shoot a beam of tightly condensed light several miles into the atmosphere would be the most important development in weaponry since the atomic bomb."

"If any of this is classified, I damned well don't want to hear it," I snapped.

Ladd laughed softly into the darkness. "You mean you're afraid you might give it away? I assure you, I myself know only half of what the Commies do. But where was I? Oh yes, a laser such as I have described would be the perfect defense against missile attack. Now we depend entirely on bullet-like projectiles—anti-missiles. But a laser, aimed by radar, could scan the sky. With a number of these placed strategically along our borders, we could destroy any missiles aimed at the United States. The implications are staggering. We could destroy Russia or Red China without fear of retaliation. On the other hand, if Russia had such a weapon, they could destroy us."

"And Kreigger . . ." Before I could finish the sentence the words constricted in my throat and I burst into a fit of coughing.

Ladd waited until it was over, then his voice continued in the same halting, deliberate monotone. "Yes, Kreigger. We have reason to believe that Kreigger made a significant breakthrough. Oh, we certainly don't think that he actually perfected such a weapon—even on paper and in mathematical terms. We live in an era of team research. Kreigger was responsible for only one aspect of the laser. However, a single important breakthrough could make a difference of several crucial years in attaining the final goal. We're not sure what Kreigger's discovery was—but we do know it was of tremendous importance to the project. It appears that he tried to give that discovery to the Russians."

I felt no fear now. There was only a dull, lethargic whir in my brain and my body was numb, as though some mad dentist had novocained every inch of my flesh. I could only sit and stare into the neon-flickering darkness with a dazed awe at the sheer magnitude of it all.

"And me?" I said.

"You? Well, it would appear that in some way we cannot yet understand, you, Mr. Chessick—and you alone, out of all the three billion people on this earth—are the key to the hiding place of those plans."

SEVEN

       I was sitting up full now, my back curled over the low steel frame and resting against the wall, my knees pulled up under the covers. Ladd had chosen his position well. The red-blue-black neon through the curtains cast its alternating color on the wall directly behind him, so he remained but a sporadic silhouette. The interims of darkness were too brief for my eyes to adjust, and Ladd remained merely that black shadow, indistinguishable even to size since there was nothing visible to relate it to. For several minutes the room was dead silent, with only the exaggerated rasp and suck of breathing. I knew Ladd was waiting for my reaction. But there was no reaction. None. Only a dull sense of floating outside myself, of hovering in a void.

       "Why me?" I said finally. How many times in the last fifteen minutes or half hour or week or year had I spoken those same two words. And yet it was the only question that made sense. I could hear it pounding a slow tattoo in my brain, and it had picked up the rhythm of the neon lights, alternating the color of its voice. *Why me? Why me?*

"There are several possible reasons," Ladd said. "I suppose the main one was that you just happened to be available. Then, too, you are—shall we say—expendable. But we mustn't be too prone to conjecture. Theory too often obscures fact, and I personally would be very careful about attempting to fathom the mind of a scientific traitor. In the old days it was simpler. Money, blackmail, the excitement of espionage. You can afford to be simple when not much is at stake. But all that changed with the atom bomb, of course. Your classical nuclear scientist who gives the enemy secrets is a very different man from your simple mercenary traitor of the past. Now there is a whole world at stake. One can almost understand the torment of suddenly waking up one morning and discovering that you have in your brain secrets which can drastically change the course of history. It would be a cold-blooded man who would not ask himself, 'Am I really utilizing my knowledge to the best advantage of man? Isn't there a slight possibility that the wave of the future—the destiny of man—may lie not in American democracy, but in Russian Communism?'

"Kreigger was a very lonely man. During his years in Alaska especially, he must have had more time to contemplate such treasonable questions than even he wished. He was hardly the first to answer in favor of Communism. The list is lengthy—Nunn May, Klaus Fuchs, Ponticorvo, the Rosenbergs. It wasn't money that made these scientists turn against the countries that fed and nourished them; it wasn't blackmail that drove them to betray their way of life. There is something vastly more powerful than all the money in the world. Idealism, Mr. Chessick, the conviction—arrived at after years of torture and doubt—that their scientific knowledge must be used according to their beliefs. I find it rather ironic that the very same conscience and sense of personal responsibility that we so highly value are precisely what convince men like Kreigger that they alone have the right to decide for all of humanity how their knowledge will be used. I'm afraid I'm boring you."

"No. Go on."

"Well, Kreigger's beliefs appear to have fermented for many years, then exploded all at once. Unlike his precursors, he decided *totally* in favor of the Russians. There is a distinct possibility that he was somewhat mad. You understand the pain he must have borne alone for those many years of doubt. He was not furtively contacted by the Reds until recently. They gave him a phone number to call if he ever decided to defect—and the fact that he failed to turn that number over to the security police shows that his decision was pretty well made before he was ever contacted. Last Monday afternoon he used that phone number to make an appointment to meet a Russian agent here in San Francisco. He then returned to his laboratory and destroyed all the plans on the laser project with the exception of some microfilm he took with him. This he did quietly and inconspicuously. As head of his section, he could come and go as he pleased. He was, however, not the only man acquainted with the new discovery. There was one other—his chief assistant—Dr. David Bowles. Kreigger picked Bowles up at his home that evening—rather unexpectedly—and the two of them went for a drive. Bowles was found later that night in a patch of trees off the main highway—with six small-caliber bullets in his chest.

"It was all very hasty. I suppose when Kreigger phoned the Communist agent, he was constantly afraid that he would change his mind. There was an element of panic in it—as a man who suddenly decides once and for all to commit suicide must run directly into the bathroom and pull the trigger before he allows himself to think about it too much. The Russians must have recognized Kreigger's panic and figured they would have to take advantage of it now or not at all, much as they would have preferred several weeks to make the elaborate preparations necessary for spiriting a celebrity out of the United States. Everything was thrown together quite hastily. It is hardly any wonder that the man assigned to make the contact should discover at the last minute that we were tailing him and be forced to break the appointment.

"Kreigger was running scared. He had timed his flight to California to leave only minutes after he had killed Bowles. In fact everything—his arrival at the San Francisco airport, the cab ride to the place of contact—everything was timed down to the second. It would only be hours before Bowles' wife phoned the police to report her husband had not returned. Kreigger's superiors would be notified, the laboratories checked, the pile of burned records and the open safe would be found, the F.B.I. would be notified, the airport checked. So you can see that Kreigger was working against a tight deadline, with the police just hours, then minutes behind him. You can imagine his panic when his contact did not show up. No message. Nothing. His entire life, everything he had convinced himself he believed in, all those years of torture and doubt and decision, everything gambled on the single turn of a card . . . and lost. And the worst of it was that it was lost not because of a mistake in his planning or judgment or timing, but because some man he had never seen was late. At any moment he would be arrested. All of his grandiose dreams of a new world would be destroyed. And yet for all the frustration, the blinding fear—Kreigger's mind would still be working with that habitual mathematical precision. Outside the fear, separate from the panic, a part of his mind was yet rational, highly ingenious. That part would be theorizing, developing alternatives, weighing, selecting . . . He could not allow himself to be arrested, for then the information would revert to the government which he had ineradicably chosen as the enemy of mankind. He could not commit suicide, for then all the years of work would be for nothing. He had destroyed all the plans except for the microfilms he carried with him, and if he destroyed those . . . What would you do, Mr. Chessick?"

I thought about it for a moment. "Get drunk," I said.

Ladd laughed low in his throat. "Yes, I suppose most of us would. But that was too simple. Kriegger was a genius, remember. He possessed an amazingly complex mind. He would have solved the problem somehow. For example, he might have hid the documents in a place where they would not be discovered for years. But that would have been insufficient. It would be too possible that the plans would never be found. He knew, of course, that his steps would be thoroughly retraced, that every inch would be searched by both the Russians and the Americans. But the United States —able to work in the open—would have a decided advantage in such a search. No, he couldn't permit that. He would have to leave a clue—something to give the Commies the edge. We have reason to believe he did just that. And once it had been accomplished, he locked himself in his hotel room, stuck the same pistol in his ear with which he had killed Bowles—and pulled the trigger."

I leaned forward on my knees, studying the darkness. It was doubtful that Ladd was giving me the whole story. No, that couldn't be expected. There would be just enough that I needed to know in order to answer questions. But fantastic as it all seemed, there was an indisputable logic to it. I had known loneliness and doubt and fear, the desperation of staking a lifetime on a single irrevocable act. I felt I knew, even more than Ladd, that Kreigger would have acted, thought, in just the manner described. "And the clue?" I said.

"We thought you could tell us," Ladd said slowly. "After all, you were the last man to see Kreigger alive."

He might just as well have hit me in the face. I stared into the darkness, stunned. "Good God!" I said. "Are you mad! I've never met the man in my life. I never even heard his name until now."

Ladd merely snorted with irritation. "Kreigger was hardly in a position to introduce himself formally. I doubt very much that he would have felt called upon to show you his credentials. He was a thin man, five feet nine. His hair was spotted with gray, as was his mustache. A rather bushy mustache. I suppose you might say he was rather avuncular in appearance. Sound familiar?"

"No!"

Ladd expelled a breath of air in a long-suffering sigh, as though to suggest that such well-established facts should not require reiteration. "As I said before, whiskey can be very damaging to the memory. Let me refresh you. On Monday, the seventeenth—last Monday—you met this man in a small uptown bar. He bought you a drink and then suggested he buy a bottle and the two of you drink it in his room. You followed him to his room at a nearby hotel, where you remained for about two hours. Then you came out alone and . . ."

Suddenly I threw my head back and laughed. It was the first really good laugh I had had in a long time, and the sound of it seemed to wash me clean. The whole insane nightmare dissipated in the echo between the walls, leaving a vast ocean of relief. When it was over, I gasped, "So you see, it is a mistake. Someone who looked like me. I never met Kreigger. Never. On Monday I was at a movie all afternoon."

For a long time Ladd didn't speak. My laugh had become a girlish giggle, and I tried to smother it in my hand. Ladd's voice emerged very slow—very deliberate. "You're lying, Mr. Chessick. If you think you can get away from it that easily . . ."

"So throw me in jail. Give me a lie-detector test. I tell you, last Monday I was asleep in a lousy movie. I remember the day clearly, because that morning I noticed Alpine Hat following me. I thought he was a cop and memorized what I had done the night before just in case I was to be pulled in on a dope charge or something and needed the alibi. I even remember the movies."

"How long were you there?"

"About six hours. I fell asleep. The usher woke me up and threw me out because I was snoring. You see, I'm clear. It was a mistake."

"You're damned certain of this?" Ladd said levelly.

"Damned certain."

The pause was long this time—several minutes. I didn't dare break the silence. I could feel Ladd's intensity transmitted on the air like electricity. It's over, you bastard, I thought. Over. Give it up. Find another sucker. This baby's got an alibi.

Finally Ladd's voice again broke the stillness. "Well, I suppose that changes everything."

"You're damned right it does. It was all a mistake. I've got a normal face. A couple days' beard. Any face with a beard looks the same. So somebody saw a man come into a hotel with a beard. He describes a guy who looks like me, dresses like me. There are thousands of them in Frisco. It could have been anyone. Anyone except me. I was somewhere else."

The dark figure rose slowly against the colored wall and disappeared against the blackness of the door. "All right, Mr. Chessick. I will accept that for the moment." The voice was halting, confused, and yet there was something else, a sort of inchoate elation, as though Ladd had suddenly figured something out but was afraid to believe it quite yet.

"Wait a minute," I said. "What about those Commie goons who are following me around? It makes me nervous. Couldn't you just drop them a slight hint that they're wasting their time on the wrong man?"

"I'm afraid that will probably continue until it is absolutely certain you are the wrong man. You will be in no danger. Our men will also be watching you."

"And what do I do in the meantime? Twiddle my thumbs?"

"I would suggest you go out and get drunk. Just continue your normal life. As I have previously mentioned, the men who are watching you are highly trained professionals in the game of espionage. You would be making a serious mistake if you attempted to take an active part in such a deadly game—especially when you appear to be on neither side. Don't fight the problem. Just go about your business and pretend it doesn't exist. Don't try to contact me. When we have more to tell you or need your assistance, we will let you know. And by the way, don't leave town."

The door opened, but Ladd had taken the precaution of turning off the hall lights. For a moment I listened to the retreating pad of feet along the hall, then I was out of bed and running to the door. I wrenched it open and gazed into the hall just in time to see the dark form disappear around the lighted corner of the stairwell. "It's over!" I screamed. "It was a mistake. It's over—you bastard!"

Doors opened along the hall. Angry faces peered at me from unlit doorways. But I hardly noticed them. I was laughing too hard.

EIGHT

Like Merril had said, Marriane was more beautiful than ever. Or at least she was if your tastes ran to those narrow zombies who, according to *Vogue* magazine, spend their ageless lives cavorting on sunset beaches in original Dior gunny-sacks. I doubted if Marriane had ever done any professional modeling—too much like work—but maybe the gods had caught her staring longingly at those Dior pictures and taken pity. Zap. She was suddenly metamorphosed into a Paris original, irrelevantly stuffed with a woman's version of what a woman should look like. Me, I preferred them short, blond and firm—all right, like Carla Markham—and the long-lanky look ("Slender," *Vogue* would call it) left me cold. Which was an understatement in this case, because Marriane damned near frosted my eyeballs. If she spit, she would have put an icicle right through my forehead.

"Good morning, Chess," she said. Translation: You bastard, first you take advantage of my stupid husband's gener-
osity, steal time from his legitimate, paying clients for no
more reason than to save your worthless hide from the gas
chamber, you soil our name and the social position I've
worked so hard for, and then you have the gall to appear at
the door of our eighty-thousand-dollar split-level home in a
very—*very*—exclusive residential district. And I suppose you
even want to come in.

"Good morning, Marriane," I said. Translation: Let's go
find us a nice muddy gutter, baby, and we can pick up
where we left off when my Cadillac was repossessed.

She stood holding the door open and staring at me—
through me—as if I were a disguised Beelzebub trying to crash
the Pearly Gates.

"Uh, how are you?" I asked.

"I'm very well. And you?" she answered, holding the
door.

"I'm all right. Uh, look, I had an appointment to see Bob.
Can I come in?"

"Yes, we were expecting you," she said without moving.
"My husband doesn't usually take clients on Sunday."

I contemplated whether it would be more painful if I
punched her in the nose, kicked her in the knee, or just put
a run in her nylon socks with my fingernail. Luckily Merril
appeared behind her before I could come to a decision.

"Chess, come in. Come in," he said. "'I see you've met
Marriane. She was just thrilled when I told her you were in
San Francisco. Weren't you, dear?"

"Just thrilled," she said.

I walked in like a halfback, ready to straight-arm her if
she didn't get out of the way. It was a pad worthy of Marriane. Imported Swedish furniture. A rug you could get lost in
if you fell down. Original abstract expressionist paintings.
The interior decorator must have specialized in theater lob-
bies. But then most people have trouble just keeping up

with the Joneses. Merril—or his wife—was taking on the Vanderbilts.

"Nice place," I said. Translation: How do you get to the balcony?

"Thank you, thank you," Merril said. "We're quite proud of it."

"We're buying a summer cottage in Carmel next year," Marriane said.

Picking up Crosby's old place, though all we really want is the golf course. I shuddered at the thought of what all this was costing. If Merril ever decided to send me a bill, I would seriously consider going back and trying for the gas chamber.

"Well, it's not really settled," Merril said. "We may not be able to afford . . ."

"But really, we will have to have *someplace* after the elections. Did you know Bob was going to run for the senate? He'll win it, too. Won't you, dear?"

It sounded less like a question than an ultimatum. "That's nice," I said. "By the way, I'm sure you're quite busy. Maybe I should get right to the point."

"Don't worry about my time," Merril said. "But you did sound worried when you called this morning. Sit down. The coffee will be ready in a minute. But go ahead. Tell me everything."

"Yes. Anything for an old college friend," Marriane said.

"Well, it's sort of confidential. In fact, for all I know, it may be top secret."

"Oh, come on, Chess. Marriane knows all my clients' secrets."

Yeah, I thought, and she's probably using half of them for blackmail. "Well," I said, "last night I had a visitor." It took a while to tell it all. Merril listened intently, tape-recording it on his mind. Marriane just sat there in her best *Vogue* sit as though expecting a photographer to jump through the window at any second and snap her picture. I wondered if she ever went to the bathroom. Maybe that was too uncouth. Once she did rise and leave the room, but while I was listening for the humanizing flush of the toilet, she returned with coffee in a sterling-silver pot, poured it into cups made of anemic eggshells and resumed her pose. It was all very distracting, but I got the story out.

When I was finished, Merril rubbed his chin thoughtfully. "So Owen was with the F.B.I. What about Aaron?"

"Ladd didn't say. I guess I could have asked him, but my mind wasn't too logical."

"Yes, that's understandable. This Ladd—did he show you any credentials, anything to prove he was who he said?"

"No, it was too dark. I couldn't even see his face."

Merril rose abruptly, crossed to the phone and dialed quickly. It rang for a long time on the other end, then I heard the faint click. "Hello . . . Mike? Mike, you old clown, when are you going to drop out and see us? . . . What? . . . Oh, this is Bob Merril . . . Yeah, well, how're the kids? . . . Debbie's fine, just fine . . . What I called about, I need some information for a client. He claims he's been contacted by a man named Ladd with the F.B.I. . . . Right . . . Just a code name, uh? What's his real name? . . . Well, who would know? . . . Hmm, must be pretty high up . . . Special Department of what? . . . Interior Counterespionage . . . Right. I got it. Hey, you know anything about this Kreigger suicide? . . . Nothing. No leads, uh? . . . What? No, no, my client's not involved in any way in that. Just curiosity, that's all. Well, thanks a lot for the information . . . And give me a call at the office. Maybe we can get together for lunch . . . Right, Mike. We'll see you."

Merril returned to his chair and sat down. "Well, that checks. Mike's a private detective. Used to work for the F.B.I. I got his son off a statutory rape charge a couple years ago and he's been one of my best sources of information ever since."

"All right. So the F.B.I. really is on it. Where does that

leave me? Isn't there anything I can do to get them off my
back? There must be a law against just following people
around."

"I'm afraid not, Chess. You'd have to prove someone was
actually bothering you, and even then, as a man who was
just released from jail on a murder charge, you would have
quite a time getting anyone to believe you."

"So I just sit back and chew my fingernails until their feet
get sore?"

"I'm afraid that's about all you can do. Look, Chess, I
know this may be painful, but you are caught smack-dab in
the middle of a silent, all-out war between the two most
powerful governments on earth. These men are working
outside the law, and there's just nothing I can do, nothing
anyone can do."

"Well, couldn't I talk to the F.B.I. myself?"

"They wouldn't even admit they'd ever heard of you. And
it would be impossible to contact Ladd. He had a very good
reason for keeping his face hidden from you. As department
chief of the counterespionage apparatus in the United States,
he would be a perfect target for a Russian assassin. There
are probably only three or four top officials who even know
his real name. There's nothing you can do but wait."

"Wait, hell! It's a simple case of mistaken identity."

"That's what I can't figure out. Is it a mistake? Do professionals make such stupid mistakes? It's hard to believe.
Whatever gave anyone the idea you had seen Kreigger anyway?"

"I don't know. Ladd didn't say."

"What if it isn't a mistake?" Marriane said casually.

I turned to her, stunned, not so much by the question as
the new tone of her voice. It was almost seductive.

"But it was. Somebody else looks like me, that's all."

"But if it isn't," she persisted. "If you really do hold the
clue to the hiding place of some important microfilm—well,
if someone else—you—or Bob—found them first, and sold
them back to the United States Government—well, wouldn't

that be worth quite a bit of money—perhaps millions of dollars?"

"Marriane!" Merril exclaimed with honest shock.

I was fascinated. What an absolutely lovely voice Marriane had when she was talking about money.

"Baby," I said, "please believe me. It's a mistake. Besides, one man has already been murdered, and I have no desire to try for number two."

Marriane was gazing at an invisible hand on the ceiling that was counting out thousand-dollar bills. "Well, I do think it is a distinct possibility and should be taken into consideration," she said.

Number one: It wasn't a distinct possibility at all. The whole thing was mistaken identity, plain and simple. Number two: About the only thing a million dollars would buy for the discoverer of Kreigger's microfilm would be an elaborate mausoleum. I had a slight hunch that anyone who was even suspected of ever having laid eyes on those laser plans would meet a very swift demise. Number three: I had other things to consider.

I tried to consider all of them on the bus back to the city. I could just sit it out, pretend nothing at all was going on, as both Ladd and Merril had suggested, but that was most unappealing. The life of a bum is mainly one of complete boredom, of simply trying to fill up the endless twenty-four hours in an endless day. That I couldn't endure any more. I had to keep moving—do something—act—or I would go nuts again. It would have been simple enough to run, but running wasn't enough. They would just follow me. It took money to hide, and I only had about sixteen dollars left from the twenty borrowed from Merril. And who did I know with the thousands of dollars it would take to run in style? Carla Markham. Yeah, she would just love to hand me a blank check for that wonderful night in Berkeley. Unless . . .

Forget it, Chessick. Blackmail is a dirty, nasty business.

But then I was a dirty, nasty sort of people, and blackmail did have its more appealing aspects. The only problem was that my mind had already erased the image of Carla the bitch, Carla the rich whore, Carla the neurotic. Now I only remembered Carla the girl, Carla with the tears in her eyes choking back a sob in her sleep. She had said I would hate her in a couple days, and yet here I was thinking that just maybe she was the only beautiful thing that had happened to me in many a year. Memory is rotten in that way.

There was one other alternative. It seemed rather pointless, but at least it would keep me moving, keep my mind occupied. If I could only prove that it was a mistake, I might be able to convince whoever was following me to go find himself another boy. But I was no detective. Where the hell do you start?

I started at the public library. There is a very Sunday-ish quality about a library—any big-city library—an atmosphere of mute lost time and staid sobriety, as though everyone in the place is a Quaker scholar writing a concordance to the Bible. You look at the endless bookstacks and see an old monk with white beard shadowed against the stone walls of an ancient monastery. You stand lost and alone and vaguely afraid inside the labyrinth of esoteric knowledge, feel dead hands reach out from dead pages and smell the musty odor of generations moldering in unmarked graves.

For a long time I gazed in despair at the bookstacks—sensing that somehow I had stepped out of life, out of earth and into a monstrous gray dungeon—wondering what I was looking for. Finally my eyes picked out the reference section, and after considerable searching I found the latest *Who's Who in America*.

Kreigger was listed on page 1,188. Anyone who doesn't think Americans live in a computerized culture should thoroughly peruse the *Who's Who*. Typically, the section on Otto Kreigger possessed all the warmth and humanity of a scientific description of a species of clam. It was very revealing. Modern man—abbreviated, condensed, truncated, emasculated, synopsized, epitomized, abstracted, contracted, abridged, digested for quick consumption and summarized for easy reference. Someday, after 99.9 percent of the earth has been blown to hell or laser-ated by our most advanced scientific achievement, some lonely survivor will erect a monument to dead mankind and scratch upon it the fitting epitaph: HERE LIES MODERN MAN. DO NOT BEND, FOLD, SPINDLE OR MUTILATE. Kreigger's epitaph had already been written in the *Who's Who*—which is, I suppose, another one of the curses of fame.

"Kreigger, Otto R.," it began, already pregnant with meaning, "physicist; b. Berlin, Ger. Sept. 3, 1911; B.A. Univ. of Hamburg 1932; M.A.-PhD Frederick-Wilhelms Univ. of Berlin 1936; prof. Univ. of Cologne 1936; came to Britain 1936; came to Canada 1939; came to U.S. 1945; U.S. govt research 1945–48; prof. Univ. of Chicago 1948–1950 . . ." There followed a series of professorial and visiting lecture jobs at various universities throughout the United States, with a two-year gap between '57 and '59, during which, I conjectured, he had been involved on radar research, because in '59 he became an official at the Clear Radar Site in Alaska. The list of jobs ended there, when, according to Ladd, he was again given a top-secret assignment at the laser labs in Illinois.

The list of Kreigger's published works was impressive, but no more revealing than the sterile outline of his life. As early as 1935 he had, while still a student, rather presumptuously published *A New Theory of Light*. After that came an almost incoherent series of titles: *Physical Optics, The Atomic Theory of Light, New Studies in Aether and Electricity, Studies in Refraction*, a magazine article, "A New Look at the Contribution of James Braid," *Light and Radar, Polarization and Electromagnetic Theories of Light, The Multicavity Magnetron, Theory of Servomechanisms* . . . There was a long list, but at "multicavity magnetrons" my mind went sailing out through the walls and windows and began to seduce a sweet-young-thing on the Riviera. Just what in the hell was I looking for anyway?—a book entitled *How to Put the Screws to Robert Chessick?* Perhaps what I wanted was a portrait of Otto Kreigger, the modern Hamlet, tortured for years by indecision and finally risking everything in a sudden, frantic, irrevocable burst of passion. But I always was the type who wanted my history humanized. I could care less about the date George Washington was born. What interested me was his wooden teeth.

Kreigger was obviously not about to burst cherry-cheeked to life from the pages of the *Who's Who.* I tried the local newspapers. There the picture was a little more human, but hardly more accurate. Pandering to popular tastes, Kreigger was portrayed as an unredeemed Nazi devil who made Hitler look like a saint, a dirty, rotten, nasty, evil Judas who was selling out the world for forty pieces of Russian-mined silver. Ladd's version of the quietly fanatical idealist was easier to swallow. I've never met a man who was deliberately evil. It's too much work, and from the list of Kreigger's books, it appeared he had better things to do.

The factual texts of the news stories followed pretty closely what Ladd had told me, but were somewhat more detailed, especially about Kreigger's suicide. He had been found in the Llowell Hotel, a place I vaguely recalled from my meanderings along Frisco's back streets. Like many another "hotel" in the lower-class districts, the Llowell was a broken-down relic of the pre-earthquake days that bore a neon sign simply announcing "Rooms—$2.oo and Up," and pandered mainly to a very transient clientele—two or three hours at the most. The name of the hotel was only of passing interest. Ladd had spoken of a nearby bar where I was supposed to have met Kreigger. It was possible that he had gotten a description of me from a bartender or one of the waitresses. Anyway, it was worth a try—an excuse to be moving again. The atmosphere of the library was already beginning to seep into my veins like formaldehyde.

After almost an hour in that oversized crypt, it took a while to adjust my eyes to the sunlight. I was surprised to discover that it wasn't even noon yet, which left an excruciatingly long day to fill up before I could find a flop somewhere. I knew vaguely the direction of the Llowell Hotel, and with the help of passers-by, I made it on foot in under half an hour. If anybody was following me this time, they were doing a good job. Every few feet I would stop and look back. Nothing but the usual kids and Sunday lovers.

I passed the Llowell Hotel and walked on up to the corner where a red neon sign announced simply BAR. That about summed it up. It looked like any other low-class bar in any city in the United States. Coming in out of the sunlight, you got the impression that they forgot to pay their electrical bill—except the only decorations were a series of multi-colored electric beer signs, everything from rippling sky-blue waters to shooting stars bouncing around. The signs were everywhere, on the walls, on the counter, crammed in among the booze bottles. I suppose the whole world will look like that come Judgment Day. The heavens open and . . . Behold! A Schlitz Beer sign arcing from horizon to horizon.

The place was almost deserted. Two B-girls, a fat bartender with a towel stuck in his belt like an apron, one sad rummy staring mournfully into an empty shot glass. It was all too somber especially coming on top of a library, so before I sat down I dropped a quarter in the juke box, closed my eyes and punched six buttons. Before I even made it to the counter, the Rolling Stones hit me in the back of the neck with nine hundred amplified guitars, six banshees and an echo chamber.

Out of deference to the décor, I ordered beer. Somehow the bartender got the message. I watched his face for some sign of recognition when he took my money, but if he had seen me before, he wasn't very friendly about it. Competing with the Rolling Stones in their chosen field was beyond even thinking, so I let them have their three minutes before I made any attempt to talk. The second song was a little calmer—seems this hillbilly was about to be shipped to Viet

Nam and every time he turned around some college punk was asking him to give blood to the Viet Cong or something. And I thought I had problems.

"Hey," I said.

The bartender ambled over. "Uh?" he said.

"You mind if I ask you a couple of questions?"

He thought that over for a while. "Uh-uh," he said.

"You ever seen me before?"

He looked at me closely. "Uh-uh."

"Last Monday," I said. "I had a beard then. Different clothes."

He had to think on that for a long time. "Uh-uh," he said.

I had the feeling ace detective Robert Chessick—the Sherlock Holmes of Wino Row—wasn't doing so well. This idiot probably couldn't remember his own face between shaves. "Well, thanks anyway," I said and went back to nursing my beer. So I was out in the dark again. All I knew now that I didn't know this morning was that this particular bartender hadn't fingered me to the F.B.I. That left only a couple million more people to question. I settled back and listened to my final juke-box selection. Some pimply-faced kid was getting the shaft from his girl friend's daddy because she was rich and the singer lived down in the boondocks.

"You a fuzz?" a voice said.

She was a skinny girl with wire for hair, a pockmarked face and a chest that had been ordered from Sears Roebuck in a plain package. She sat down on the stool beside me and looked me over carefully.

"No, I'm no cop. Why, have there been cops in here?"

"One 'r two. They was askin' about Monday like you was. That's how come I figured you for one. You gonna buy me a drink?"

"Okay. What'll it be?"

"Bourbon on the rocks."

The bartender brought the liquor. I grabbed it and tasted it before she could get her hands on the glass. I gave it back to the bartender. "This baby's a little old for the Pepsi Generation," I said. "How about trying again with bourbon?"

The bartender mumbled something under his breath and exchanged the drinks.

"That wasn't very nice," the girl said. "I ain't so old. Besides, I can't drink no bourbon. It makes me sick."

"Okay. I'll trade you," I said, giving her my half-finished beer. "And if you tell me all about Monday night, maybe I'll even buy you a Pepsi."

"You gotta pay me money. I seen that in the movies. When cops want to know something they gotta give the girl twenty dollars. I seen that lotsa times."

Goddamn movies were starting inflation in the stool-pigeon market. "Yeah," I said. "But if they ain't cops, they kidnap the girl and tie her in a chair and burn her feet with cigarettes."

"Yeah, I saw that movie, too," she said enthusiastically. "Gee, would you really do that?"

"Matter of fact, I don't think I would. But then I don't have any money either. So why don't you be a good girl and tell me all about Monday and I'll buy you a Pepsi, okay?"

"Okay. But I want a Seven-Up."

"Anything your tender little heart desires." I gave the bartender a dollar for the soft drink and told him to keep the change, which made everybody happy. "Okay, now what happened Monday?"

"Well, that guy who killed hisself—you know, the one that had his picture in the newspapers—well, he was in here. Gee, if I'd known he was gonna be famous and all, I'd a ask him for his autograph. But—would you believe it?—you hardly even noticed the guy. I mean, he didn't look famous nor like he was gonna shoot hisself or nothing."

"How did you happen to notice him?"

"Gosh, I notice all the guys. Besides, he weren't very nice. I ask him to buy me a drink and he was downright rude.

Can you imagine that. I mean, he seemed so lonely and all. He must have been sitting there for two or three hours, not talking to nobody or nothing."

"Was he alone?"

"Yeah, when I saw him he was. But about ten o'clock I had to go upstairs for a while. I was—uh—feeling poorly. Say, you sure you ain't no cop now?"

"If I was a cop, I would have given you twenty dollars."

"Yeah, that's right. I forgot about that. Well, anyway, I was gone till nearly midnight and when I came back he was gone. Whaddaya think of that?"

"Not a helluva lot. In other words, it's possible that he could have been joined by someone else while you were gone?"

"Yeah. The cops asked Willie about that—he's the bartender—but he don't notice things much, so he couldn't remember."

"When did the cops show up?"

"Oh, they didn't come till the next afternoon. Lots of 'em. Gee, it was just like the movies—I mean, real exciting."

"And nobody else, just cops."

"Oh, no. That same night there was a fella and a lady come in—gee, musta been about three or four in the morning. An' he asked all sortsa questions about whatsisname."

"Kreigger."

"Yeah, that's it. I saw it in the newspaper under the picture. Yeah, Kreigger. Well, this other fella asked when Mr. Kreigger left and if I knew where he went and all sortsa things."

"This man. What was he like?"

"Oh, I dunno. He was kinda short and heavy and with a beer belly—but not so's you'd call fat though. And he seemed, you know, nervous and kinda shy, like as if he was scared of girls or something."

"Short, stocky, not much hair . . ." I suggested.

"Yeah, that's him. Hey, you know who he is?"

"His name is Kenneth Aaron and he sells real estate."

"Gee, you oughta tell the cops about that. They asked me all kinds of questions about who he was."

"Yeah, I'll be sure to tell them. What about the girl?"

"Oh, her. She was kinda pretty, I guess—if you like that kind. She had red hair—looked dyed to me—and she wore shades. A real phony type, ya know. And, oh yeah, there was a coupla scars on her wrists like she tried to kill herself or something and loused it up. I mean, jeeze, what a phony. You know her, too?"

"Not yet. But I have a feeling I might meet her sooner or later. What did they do when you told them Kreigger had already gone?"

"Well, she just sat there at the bar and had a drink. The fella, he went to the bathroom."

"The bathroom!"

"Uh-huh," she giggled. "Gee, I don't usually notice things like that, but, gosh, he sure did stay in there an awful long time. I was almost gonna send Willie in to see if he had fainted or something."

Things were slowly beginning to add up. By prearrangement, if Kreigger didn't make contact he would leave a message in the men's room, maybe scrawled on a paper towel and thrown in the wastebasket. But that would be too dangerous, because they could never be certain the contact man would get there before the trash was dumped. Besides, I had no assurance that Aaron was the contact man. If the F.B.I. had captured the actual contact, Aaron might have been sent in his place.

"Where is the men's room?" I said.

"Over there. Gosh, that was sure sudden."

"It's the power of suggestion, honey. Sit tight, I'll be right back."

The men's room was a small one-toilet, one-washbowl, no-mirror affair with enough prophylactic machines on the wall to give the place the appearance of a penny arcade. Instead of paper towels, there was one of those boxes that feeds out a circular dirty linen rag, and there was no wastebasket, which shot down that theory. The walls were scrawled with the usual vulgarities—outhouse poetry, sketches of gigantic misshapen organs, the names and telephone numbers of last week's girl friend, invitations from the local queer. The wall had been neither washed nor painted in years, so anyone who had to sit there for long could catch up on the latest in authentic Americana.

Something caught my eye. A single spot on the door—no larger than my hand—had been recently washed. The area had a whitish, bleached appearance against the filthy brown surrounding it, and I could barely discern the remaining outline. Then it clicked. So that's what Aaron was doing in here all that time—washing the back of the door with his handkerchief.

The light was bad and I had to move up close and hope no one opened the door and broke my nose. Whatever had been written in that space had been done with a black marking pen, and the washing hadn't been completely successful. The first thing I was able to make out was what resembled the vague outline of a Buddha with small pointed horns jutting from each side of the head. It was just an outline—nothing more—and the only details which had been added were two slit eyes and a single-line grinning mouth.

A grinning Buddha with horns. Well, that told me a hell of a lot.

Then I noticed that there had been two words written across the belly. Aaron had been especially meticulous in washing away these words, because they were even less clear than the outline. It was possible some drunk had drawn the Buddha, and Kreigger had merely chosen the belly as one of the few clear places on the wall to write his message.

I couldn't read it in the dim light, so I lit a matchbook on fire and held it close against the door. I could make out an R . . . then an O . . . then a B . . .

Then my mind found the pattern of the letters and they suddenly spread themselves across the door in blinking neon.

The blood rushed up from my feet and exploded in my head. I staggered backward a few paces and stared at the bleached spot on the door.

Written clearly, undeniably, inside the outline of the Buddha with horns were two succinct, very familiar words: ROBERT CHESSICK.

NINE

If anything, the Markham mansion was
smaller than I had anticipated. But then, on my first trip to
New York I had been surprised at the smallness of Manhat-
tan. I suppose the human imagination will always be capable
of building bigger than the human hand. So it took me a
while to get used to the fact that the Markham place didn't
exactly blot out the sky, nor was it of the Victorian design
fashioned by my expectation. Instead it was ultra-modern, of
the Frank Lloyd Wright–Edward Durrell Stone genre, a
three-story tiered pattern of diminishing rectangles in blaz-
ing white. It was a masterful study in pure composition and
artistic balance—the white of the walls subtly emphasized by
long blue windows. In sharp contrast to Merril's home, the
place was luxurious without ostentation. Inside you
wouldn't find any *nouveau riche* replica of a theater lobby.

This baby had been built by people born to so much money they didn't have to brag about it. The place reminded me of Carla herself, beautiful without the adornments of lipstick and green eyeshadow and golden earrings.

It stood in the center of a couple of acres of lawn and patterned shrubbery, the whole area surrounded by a high arbor which probably concealed a steel fence. The wrought-iron gate was wide open and I stood for some time apprehensively gazing from the sidewalk up the spotless drive, where ten or fifteen cars—mainly foreign sports models— were parked before the house. It was Hemingway, I think, who said that cowardice was merely the inability to suspend the imagination. He might have added the obvious moral: Don't anticipate. I tried to shove the memorized speech out of my head, for fear I would try to quote it verbatim and louse it up.

I started walking hesitantly up the drive. The day was passing well on into afternoon. It had taken over two hours to get to the Markham place. Not that it was hard to find— the phone book was quite specific—but the buses didn't run all the way into this neighborhood and I had to walk almost two miles. The decision itself had taken no more than a split second. There comes a time in every man's life when he had better run like hell, and one look at my name scrawled in the latrine of a bar I had never been in before was a pretty good reminder that my time had come. Sure, it could still be a mistake—there must be half a dozen Robert Chessicks in Frisco—but I wasn't about to stick around and find out. A thousand dollars in traveling money would take me a long way, but I needed it fast. That meant Carla Markham, and if the name of the game was blackmail, well, that was tough. After all, I reminded myself, I was a dirty, rotten, nasty-type character, and besides, if Carla Markham's tragic neurosis was the result of having too much money, I would be doing her a favor by relieving her of a grand or so.

I've never been especially clothes-conscious, but when you're standing in front of a pad like the Markhams', you automatically begin wondering if you're dressed for the occasion. The cheap outfit Merril had bought me wasn't exactly the latest in the *Playboy* fashion guide, and Merril had hideous taste in ties. My drip-dry, never-press white shirt must have looked as if I had actually followed the manufacturer's slightly optimistic instructions. At least I had stopped at the bus station for a quick shave.

A real-live French maid in a black uniform and wearing a doily for an apron answered the door. She looked me up and down with mildly disguised disapproval, announced, "The party is in the rear, sir," and closed the door.

"Thanks, baby," I said to the door.

I didn't like the idea of walking in on a party, but the possibility of a good stiff drink wasn't exactly unappealing. Besides, my mind had conjured a number of difficulties in even getting to see Carla, so it might turn out easier than I anticipated. As I circled the house I could hear the rising sound of voices. The back yard resembled a Warner Brothers version of a Parisian sidewalk café—a number of sporadic umbrellaed wrought-iron tables in various shades of white and blue. The color scheme was consistent right down to the white concrete of the swimming pool and the deep blue of the water. I was quick to notice that rich girls had softer skin and smaller bikinis than poor girls, which, I suppose, is a generalization deserving of profound philosophical speculation. Happily there wasn't a tuxedo in the place. In fact, half the group appeared to be ardent disciples of Allen Ginsberg. The girls bore long, well-ironed, usually blond hair above sweatshirts and leotards. Several of the young men wore blue jeans and khaki shirts and sported well-combed and perfumed beards. Three couples were involved in a slow, trancelike dance to a Brubeck record.

Carla, dressed in white blouse and black capris, both form-fitted for the specific purpose of tormenting hopeless males, was standing at the bar, passing out flippant inanities to the guests. Well, the bar was as good a place as any to make my move.

I edged in beside her and ordered Scotch-on-the-rocks from the butler who was pouring. Chevas Regal yet. I had arrived. Carla turned and looked at me with that special expression of hers that was no expression at all. I thought the least I deserved was mild surprise.

"Good afternoon," she said.

"Hi," I said.

"And when did they let you out of jail?"

"Yesterday."

"And now you've decided to go away for a while. I think that's a fine idea. Have you ever considered Tibet?"

This girl was positively amazing. "Tibet sounds all right," I said. "But there's a little matter of money."

"Yes, of course,'" Carla said. She turned suddenly, as though someone had just caught her eye. I followed her gaze through the dancing, mulling kids to the patio door. I don't know why I hadn't noticed him before, unless he had been inside the house. Maybe I had noticed but it was so traumatic I repressed it. I've seen practiced wierdos in my day, but this character was working overtime. He might have been a beatnik, except he was too old—over forty, I figured. Maybe a warmed-up leftover from the Lost Generation. Bushy beard half covering his face, hair sticking out all over the top of his head, faded *Mad* sweatshirt with a picture of the *What, me worry?* kid on the front. He looked as if he had refrained from bathing as a protest against the Depression. With his hands shoved deep into his pockets, he slouched over, grinned, and extended his hand.

"I'd like you to meet Deke," Carla said.

"Hi, Deke," I said.

"Deke handles all my blackmail," Carla said and walked away.

"Hey, wait a minute," I yelled. I tried to follow her but Deke was smilingly shaking my hand in a vise grip. Carla disappeared into the crowd.

"A truly magnificent creation, is she not?" Deke said. "One who might well have struck darts of envy to the very heart of Helen of yore."

"A real doll," I agreed. "Now will you leggo. You're breaking my gawddamn hand."

"I sincerely beseech your pardon, sir," he said, releasing me. "Ah, but before you depart, you must partake of another draught of the nectar of the gods. Jeeves, a parting drink for our dear companion here."

"My name ain't Jeeves," the butler said.

"Look, buddy," I said, "I'm not going anywhere until I talk to Carla."

"Oh? But I received the distinct impression that she had very little desire to speak with you. But perhaps you and I could engage in some friendly discourse. Have you read much Schopenhauer?"

"Who?"

"Schopenhauer. But then he is a bit passé, isn't he. Everything is existentialism or zen today. Terribly negativistic. Personally I incline to the philosophy of Nietzsche."

"What the hell has Nietzsche got to do with . . . Well, who are you, her bodyguard or something?"

"Ah, no. Merely a companion, sad to say—a miserable old man who has outlived his serviceability to the subtle concupiscence of maidenhood, one who must wander the dark realm of chastity with undiminished yearning. But I suppose one must choose the stoic view when there is no other. Ah, but she is a lovely girl, is she not? A bit mercurial perhaps. Manic-depressive, I believe the psychiatrists call it. But there is so little beauty on this dreary planet, even the gods must forgive such minor flaws."

"Look, buddy, why don't you go stand on your head in a corner?"

"How terribly crude," Deke murmured with a hurt look. "And I am so trying to be a gentleman. And blackmail is such an ugly business."

"That's between me and Carla."

"On the contrary. A swain of noble disposition must champion the cause of even lost loves. Besides, you might find blackmail difficult in the extreme. It would simply be the word of a common tramp against that of beauty and wealth. Certainly that hotel in Berkeley will not aid your insidious enterprise."

"You seem to know a helluva lot for an obsolete lecher."

"Carla tells me everything. She cried just terribly—was depressed for days—when she heard you were in jail for murder. Do you know she actually considered testifying for you? I dissuaded her, of course."

"Thanks, friend," I said. "Now I'll make you a deal. You go rape the first little girl you find and I'll go talk to Carla."

I started to move away, but he stepped in front of me. "Really, you are hard to get along with, Chess."

"Mr. Chessick to you, buddy. Now you want to get out of my way or you want a punch in the mouth?"

"A person would have to be quite a buffoon to *want* a punch in the mouth. However, I seriously advise against any such act of violence."

The Chessick temper flared into action. I reached up and caught him with both hands at his neck. There's a nerve center just under the chin, and I was going for that with an upward jerk of my thumb. But he was faster. His right arm came up alongside his head and his open hand clamped into a fist. His entire body tensed against my grip and then his elbow shot out across my outstretched arms and he came down hard on my wrists. My hands broke away from his neck. For a moment I thought my wrists were broken, but there wasn't much time to contemplate the idea. Simultaneously his knee rose into my groin and his elbow jerked back into my face. Then I was doubled up on the grass, clutching my stomach and trying to puke, but nothing would come up. "Oh my God," I mumbled.

"Are you hurt?" Deke's voice mumbled above me. "Really I'm sorry, but you shouldn't have resorted to violence, you know."

It was several minutes before I could move. I could hear the voices of the others forming a circle around me, but no one tried to give me a hand. Deke's voice rambled on apologetically above me. Very slowly I looked up, wiping the tears from my eyes with my sleeve. I was still on my knees and all I could see were Deke's hands hanging loosely at his sides. And what hands! Why the hell didn't I notice it before! Each center knuckle bore a circular black callus. I had seen that only a couple of times before in the Army. There was only one way to get calluses like that—years of striking a bamboo mat or a brick wall. Fists like that could shatter a fifty-pound block of ice. And there was only one sport which required such power. Karate. And this bastard wasn't any amateur either. The break he had used on my choke was a shoden karate move I, myself, had learned many years ago and all but forgotten. Deke must have held off on that knee to my groin or he would have shoved my balls clear up to my chest.

"Did I hurt you very badly?" Deke persisted. He reached to help me. I shook him off and struggled to my feet, still bent forward and clutching my stomach.

"Go to hell," I mumbled.

The crowd opened as I staggered through it. I fell twice and lay on the grass for a few minutes each time before I finally made it to the gate. When I reached the sidewalk, I dropped back to my knees and puked up every meal I had eaten for the last seven years.

TEN

So here I was, Chessick the Great, hero of a million daydreams, Robert Chessick of Scotland Yard, master detective, Chessick, the savage arbiter of law and justice. Right, baby. Here I was, Chessick the bum again, running again. Running blind, broke and scared from the shadows of men I had never seen.

At a gas station I picked up a ride with a reluctant truck driver south on 101, down through the dry brown, fish-smelling countryside and into the grim industrial kaleidoscope of South San Francisco. The driver chewed gum and talked about his wife's bowling score and the electronics correspondence course he was taking and the radio repair shop he was going to open someday. He turned off at San Mateo, and I got out and stood for three quarters of an hour jabbing my thumb at the passing cars, until a cop pulled up and told me to get the hell off the freeway. I walked back into the bushes until he left, then came back and started hitchhiking again. A kid about eighteen or so picked me up in a new Chevy. He had grown some peach-fuzz around his upper lip and colored it to a mustache with his mother's mascara. His high school teacher had told him he was a good writer, and as soon as he graduated he was going to get a job with a Frisco newspaper and go to Viet Nam as a war correspondent, " 'cause over there it's like *real*, man," and everything was phony in California. He had a fat Persian cat in the back seat, and I held it on my lap scratching its ears until it peed all over my leg. We kept on the freeway through the garish, subdivisioned outskirts of San Jose, and I stayed with him until he got to his home in Los Gatos. The sky had grown dark without benefit of sunset, a sort of slow and imperceptible graying into starless night.

I walked for a while, directionless, not even bothering to inquire my way back to the freeway. After a while I came into a small burg where the stores were dark and vacationing teen-agers were lined up in front of a movie theater to catch the eight o'clock show, the boys acneed and unsure, the girls small and lovely and soft and anonymous. At the other end of town I passed the railroad tracks and a big rambling wooden hotel and walked down a brief hill to a highway with a sign announcing California 17. I didn't know where this particular road went, but that was irrelevant anyway, as long as it went south.

Headlights burned out of the darkness and passed me without slowing. I walked about a quarter of a mile, then took off my jacket so my white shirt could be seen, and turned and stuck out my thumb. Almost immediately a car roared out of the darkness, passed me, honked its horn and skidded to a halt on the shoulder. I ran for it, putting my jacket back on as I moved. I didn't even notice that the car was familiar until I was inside with the door closed, gazing lethargically and not even astonished across the dark seat to the face of the driver.

"Small world," I said.

"Why, Chess," Merril exclaimed. "It is a small world, isn't it?"

"If it gets any smaller, it'll disappear. Where the hell are you going?"

"Got a client in jail in Santa Cruz," Merril said, pulling back on the road. "The indictment is early in the morning, so I thought I'd drive down tonight. But fancy meeting you here—of all people."

"Yeah, li'l ol' me. Just fancy that."

"This really is a surprise. I thought you would be having a drink with your old cronies in San Francisco tonight. Heh, heh."

"Heh, heh," I said. "Well, it was getting a bit hot."

"You found out something?"

"Yeah. I talked to my friendly family doctor and he said I had a disease. It's catching. Like anybody who comes within ten feet of me is liable to get sick, too. With maybe a bullet in the head. According to latest medical reports from the most reliable sources, that can be fatal."

Merril choked out what vaguely resembled a laugh. "You're exaggerating, of course. I mean these people would be stupid to harm anyone who might lead them to the microfilm."

"Yeah, that's what Custer said. Seems you've been thinking about it some."

"Just mild curiosity. You've got to admit your case has certain interesting aspects."

I slumped down in the seat and lit a cigarette and watched the pavement and trees rush away into darkness. "Oh, for chrissake, come off it, Merril. You must have been following me ever since this morning."

"Following you? Following you?" Merril stammered.

"That's right, following me. Look, Bob, you're a nice guy and you may be the greatest lawyer in the world, but you make a rotten detective. Damn it, if you're going to tail somebody, don't tip your hand by picking him up."

Merril laughed nervously. "I had to pick you up," he said. "I thought I was going to lose you. It's not too hard to follow a hitchhiker in the daytime—just remember what kind of car he got into—but at night all the taillights look the same."

"Okay. Now we're getting somewhere. Next question: Why?"

"Look," Merril said, pleading, "you've got to admit that what Marriane said this morning was worth some consideration—I mean about finding those laser plans first and selling them back to the United States."

"I'm not admitting anything."

"Well, at least I thought the idea had merit. I mean, it wouldn't be like stealing. The government throws away millions of dollars every year. And certainly the value of that microfilm—I mean, if we could keep it out of the hands of the Russians—I mean—well, damn it, Chess, just a million dollars isn't too much to ask."

"Yeah, and this year two and two equals five. You're talking larceny, Merril."

"We could work together—split it right down the middle. Don't tell me you couldn't use five hundred thousand dollars."

"Yeah, the doctor would take a whole lot of pins out of my eyeball for five hundred grand. Jesus Christ, Merril, wake up! Did it ever occur to you that if an amateur could follow me all over the countryside, there's probably two or three pros on your tail right now?"

"I thought about that. We just let them follow us until we find it, then we ditch them."

"Simple as that," I said. "You sure seem confident that I know where those plans are."

"I checked the bar—the one near the Llowell Hotel—after you left, and found your name on the bathroom door just like you did. It must have been a message left by Kreigger. And that picture around it, maybe that's the clue to the whole thing."

"Yeah, maybe it is and maybe it isn't. And maybe I'm not very interested in finding that microfilm. And as long as we're conjecturing, maybe the Ruskies don't especially want anybody else looking."

"That's a chance I'm willing to take."

I leaned my head back on the seat and closed my eyes against the oncoming glare of lights. Suddenly I felt intensely tired. It seemed that somehow in the preceding days I had almost welcomed the excitement, the excuse to vacate my self-imposed prison of gutters and dives. But now I was just tired. I just wanted to sleep.

"Is it really that bad?" I said.

"What?" Merril asked.

"Marriane."

Merril answered with an abrupt silence that must have lasted almost a minute. When his voice did emerge, it was shaking and choked in his throat. "I don't know what you mean."

"Try again."

"Well, damn it, Chess, what do you want me to do? Marriane's the best thing that ever happened to me. Look at me, Chess. I'm not handsome. I'm not the life of the party. How do I rate a wife like that? You don't know. You don't know what it's like just to be around her. I can't lose her."

"So what makes you think you're going to?"

Merril sounded like a brave little boy trying to hold back his tears after he's been spanked. "She was having an affair. I don't know who with. I don't care. I wouldn't believe it for a long time, but she kept getting more and more open about it—you know, coming home all messed up or staying out late—almost as if she wanted me to find out. Finally when I got up the nerve to ask her, she just laughed in my face. She said I wasn't enough of a man for her. She really did. She said she was worth better than me, and if I couldn't give her the things she deserved, she would find someone who could . . . and take our daughter."

"Why don't you just say it? She's up for sale to the highest bidder."

"Okay," Merril snapped. "If that's the way it is, then that's the way I'll take her. Damn it, Chess, my business is going down the drain. I can't keep my mind on a case. I've lost five in a row. It's gotten around. Why do you think I had so much time to put in on your case? And even if I was doing all right, it still wouldn't be enough. God, Chess, she's my whole life. What else can I do?"

That was a great question to ask Robert Chessick, who was successful at only one thing, ruining his own life and everything he touched. I thought about it. "I don't know," I said. "Christ, Merril, I don't know."

I caught a few minutes of near-sleep—a drifting, shapeless imagery like a drunken mosaic, a sort of mute floating horror with nothing to attach it to. Then I was awakened by lights piercing my eyes. We were inside a small town, well-lit and seething people, all going in the opposite direction from us. I could smell the sea. At the end of the road were the garish, multicolored lights of a carnival, twisting and arcing against the sky. I had never been here before, but I knew it was Santa Cruz, a beach resort that supplied the simulacrum of excitement for the dull subdivisions of San Jose and Salinas.

"Let me off here," I said.

Merril looked at me, startled to see me awake. "Let's talk a while," he pleaded. "I'll buy you a drink somewhere. Maybe we can make a deal."

"No talk. No deals," I said with more harshness than I intended. "Pull over."

Merril pulled to the curb and I got out and shut the door and leaned back into the open window on my elbows. Merril just sat there, his hands on the wheel, his head dropped forward on his chest. There was something intensely innocent and childlike about his posture. Maybe he had banked a lot of dreams on convincing me to join him in his search for the microfilm. He'd make a lousy corpse. He was too damned ugly.

"All right, Merril," I said, "let's get something straight.

I've had it. I'm fed up to my teeth. There's enough sonsa-bitches chasing me around without you joining the parade. If I see you behind me again, I'm going to slap you down so hard they'll have to take you to the hospital in a bucket." I felt dirty and ugly about playing the muscle routine with the one man who had come to my aid when I was down, but it was the only way. I had enough on my conscience without Merril's corpse.

"Ah, Chess . . ." he mumbled.

"Go on home," I said.

I waited until the car was out of sight, then started walking toward the beach, pushing against the tide of teen-agers and parents and squalling kids, all returning to their fat warm secure homes to catch a good night's sleep before the alarm clock woke poppa in the morning for work. It seemed strange that it was still Sunday. Too much had happened for it still to be Sunday.

Briefly I cursed Merril. If he hadn't picked me up, I might have gotten a good night's sleep myself, in the mistaken impression that I had eluded my followers. But now I could be fairly certain either the Commies or the F.B.I. or both were still on the track. But who? Aaron? Ladd? The dark-haired girl with the razor scars on her wrists whom I hadn't seen yet? I couldn't escape—I knew that. But perhaps I could force my tail to show himself.

I crossed through a narrow alleyway to the beach. It was typical of any beach carnival on any coast. A long cement "boardwalk" that dropped off into sand on one side, the other side a motley, uninterrupted string of tourist-fleecing shops, hot-dog stands and arcades. At the far end were the rides—Ferris wheel, roller-coaster and a dozen other cheap thrills. I bought a watery hot dog on a stale bun for fifty cents and stood watching the crowd for any suspicious characters. All America was there. Shiny-faced boys from Fort Ord, proud and cocky in their stripeless trainee uniforms. Teen-age girls, giggling and sexy in too-tight trousers, trailing an entourage of panting, diffident boys. Bespectacled old ladies gazing about them in rapt incomprehension of the horrifying loneliness of it all.

I ambled up the walk until I passed the Fun House, with its laughing dummies in the show windows, then turned and came back and bought a ticket. Inside were a series of slides, oversized barrels, moving steps, but I only glanced quickly around until I spotted what looked like an exit corridor. Once I was outside, anyone who was following me would have to come through one narrow little door. And I would be waiting.

I entered the corridor half running and suddenly found myself in a hall of mirrors. A few steps and I walked head-on into a sheet of polished steel. I turned back. All around me there were nothing but Robert Chessicks—thousands of them—diminishing away and disappearing in distance. I started up the corridor and slammed into another mirror. I put my hand on the steel wall and followed it slowly, looking at the floor. I seemed to be going in circles. Behind me I heard the first distinct footfall. I stopped and waited, trying to recall the fundamentals of my Army karate. All around me a thousand Chessicks raised their open hands into striking position behind their ears. The footsteps came closer. I could tell there were two of them now, but I could see nothing but the four-foot square in which I stood. They were bumping into the mirrors just as I had done. Someone cursed, close now. Suddenly the mirrors picked up a young man in a sailor suit and a fat girl. They both looked at me—some kook admiring himself. I grinned and scratched my ear with my poised hand. The girl giggled. The sailor walked into me and stumbled backward.

" 'Scuse, uh," he said. "Thought you was a mirror."

"Look at the floor," I suggested.

"That's cheating," he said and walked into me again. The girl giggled and grabbed his hand and pulled him out of my four-foot range of multivision. I could hear them laughing as they fought their way down the hall.

I sighed and closed my thousand eyes against the hideous

fly's view of Robert Chessick. There I was, running from shadows again. God, I was tired. I'd find me a nice quiet spot on the beach somewhere and sleep for twelve hours.

I opened my eyes and there was my follower, a thousand of them standing not a foot away and gazing with an abstract curiosity up at the grizzled face of a thousand Robert Chessicks, every one who had actually believed he was beyond surprise. Oh Lord, I thought, I'm too tired for this.

"Small world," I mumbled.

"Yes, isn't it though," Carla said.

ELEVEN

We drove in silence for several hours. Carla held the wheel, her face calm and void of expression as the Corvette lanced the darkness at eighty miles per hour. I slumped in the seat, watching absently the endless fenceposts beside the road whipping out of the night and into the headlight glow and then gone. We had cut away from El Camino toward the interior highway which would take us down through Bakersfield to Los Angeles. Now and then we passed a farmhouse, warm and beckoning with the soft yellow squares of lighted windows.

I turned my head against the back of the seat. Carla's face was that of a statue, an ancient eternal piece of cut marble on which some inspired chisel had trapped forever all of beautiful, hopeless, endless longing. Gone was the glistening façade of wealth, and in its place were the finely hewn features of a lovely, but ordinary, girl—somebody's daughter, somebody's sister. For all its beauty, it was an intensely human face. Hardly the face of a spy.

Even her story had a certain logic to it. After Deke had beaten me up, she had become depressed—guilt over first allowing me to stay in jail and then watching me get nearly ruptured by one of her friends—and she had deserted her party and driven around with vague hopes of locating me. After an hour or so of futile searching, she had suddenly found Frisco unbearably stifling and she impulsively headed south on the freeway, bound for nowhere in particular. She spotted me beside the road while I was being lectured by the cop. It took her a while to find an exit and circle back, and by that time I had already gotten a ride. She stayed on 101 for several miles south of San Jose, then believing she had lost me, she decided to go to Santa Cruz, a town she remembered with fond nostalgia from her high school and college excursions there. She arrived just as Merril was letting me out. Justifiably shy about approaching me, and not knowing exactly what she wanted to say, she hadn't called to me right away, but had followed me into the Fun House.

The story was so crude, so true to her personality—the aimless driving, the sudden shifts of mood—that it was almost believable. Almost. A week before, I would have accepted it without question, but somewhere along the line I had lost faith in simple coincidence. And yet it was nearly inconceivable that she could be an agent either of the Russians or the F.B.I. Nor could I escape the fact that our first meeting was the product of my initiative alone.

So I had to trust her, for the moment at least. She had a car, money, and she didn't care where she was going. She was my only chance of escape.

She pulled over to the side of the highway and turned the wheel over to me. I was sleepy and I opened the window to let the cool night air blow over my face. Carla put a small gelatin capsule in my hand. I looked at it curiously.

"Dexedrine," she said. "It will keep you awake. Dexamyl is better—a mixture of Dexedrine and sodium amytal. The two drugs sort of neutralize each other, so you just stay awake without getting high. But in San Francisco you can't always be too choosy."

"You seem to be an expert on drugs," I said.

Without answering, she curled up on the seat and closed her eyes. She was right about the effects of the Dexedrine. In about fifteen minutes I was wide awake, as though I had just gotten a good night's rest.

"Do you want to talk about it?" Carla said.

"Maybe I should ask you?"

She opened her eyes and looked at me with a slight smile curling her lips. "What's there to tell? Rich bitch. Spoiled rotten. On the make for anything in pants."

"You've been seeing too many movies. People aren't that simple."

"No," she said, "I don't suppose they are at first. But sooner or later everybody finds the right stereotype and fits himself into it. There's too much work involved in trying to figure out a novel pattern for your life."

"And my stereotype?"

"The educated lush."

"How did you know?"

"What? That you were educated? Some things show. But you'll never make it. You could hit the bottle for twenty years and never make it. You picked the wrong stereotype."

I knew she was right. I once thought it was simple to become a drunk. Just start pouring it down. Pour enough down and I wouldn't be Robert Chessick any more. But it was eight months, and I hadn't drowned the bastard yet.

"Your wife?" Carla asked.

"Maybe. No. It was a long time before that. I guess it started with a little kid playing Roy Rogers."

Carla smiled. "The Don Quixote complex. It's a sad thing in a world where there are far more windmills than dragons."

"You know too damned much about men," I said. "Anyway, I found my dragons. We called them a lot of things, but mainly Charlie."

Carla looked at me quizzically. "Viet Cong?"

"Yeah," I said. It still hurt. God, it hurt. But it was like a scab you had to pick at, had to bleed out and clean. "Yeah, I was a hero all right. When I was eighteen I was going to climb Mount Everest, capture the monster of Loch Ness, fight in an African revolution. But things came up. I didn't have enough money to hitchhike out of Indiana, let alone around the world, so I let my parents send me to college. It was easier. Four years studying the rotting corpse of philosophy. Then grad school to avoid the draft. Two more years and I've got a master's degree. Then I woke up one morning and discovered I was twenty-five years old and as dead as Thales."

"Who's Thales?"

I was surprised she was still listening. "Greek philosopher. Pre-Plato. Thought the world was made of water. Maybe it was, for all I knew. I had never seen any of it farther from Indiana than Chicago. So I quit school and volunteered for Army O.C.S. I was going to crawl in the mud and shoot people and be a hero. Right. After six months of ritualized insanity at Officer Candidate School, they gave me a little gold bar and sent me to Fort Dix as a flunky for the postal officer. Anyway, to keep up the illusion, I took karate lessons twice a week at night. Even got me a second-degree green belt, which meant I was highly proficient at kicking people in the knee—that is, if they didn't swing first and knock me flat on my ass."

"You shouldn't talk about yourself like that," Carla said, with more motherly compassion than I had believed was in her.

"Why not. Once you've lost your balls, it doesn't hurt to hack away at the roots."

Carla grinned mischievously. "You do very well for a castrated man, Mr. Chessick."

"Castration isn't always physical."

"How did it happen?"

"Forget it."

"I like to know who I'm sleeping with," Carla said.

I looked at that innocent, angelic face framed in white hair, and laughed. "That's blackmail," I said.

"Uh huh," she agreed.

"Okay. After the Army it was Indiana again. I got a job teaching English to a bunch of high school brats. Just two semesters and I would have a grand in the bank so I could go around the world. But I knocked up a girl. She wouldn't go the abortion route, so, like any hero, I faced up to my responsibilities."

"Did you love her?"

"No. Marriages for love went out with the Charleston. But I came to love her. I really did. It took a lot of hating first—hating for this final destruction of all my heroic dreams. We had a son—Ronnie. He's five now. But it wasn't enough. There was still the dream—and the home in the suburbs and a clean, soft job teaching didn't fill it. That was when the war in Viet Nam was escalating fast and you could see that the Green Berets weren't going to hold the whole show much longer. The regular line troops were going to be in it. This might be my last chance. I re-enlisted in the Army. Oh, it wasn't a very popular decision, but I think Lorrie—my wife—knew what was eating me up inside. She cried a lot, but she didn't try to stop me.

"I had stayed with the reserves, so they gave me my second-louie bar back. Nobody knew really who was going to Viet Nam, but there was a unit at Fort Benning called the Eleventh Air Assault that was training with helicopters—a new concept then—and I figured that was the best bet. It wasn't hard getting into the divison, since most everybody there was trying to get out. So there I was, a platoon leader—a damned good one, too. Ran my men until everybody from sergeant down hated my guts. But they respected me, too—and respect doesn't come out of a book."

"I remember reading about that division," Carla said. "Didn't they change the name to the First Cavalry?"

"Yeah. Proved itself to be a fine combat unit. Or so they tell me. I wasn't around long enough to find out."

I was speaking slowly now. Each word had to be deliberately and forcefully pushed up from my throat. I could hear myself talking, but I didn't know what I was saying—because my mind was remembering it, remembering the feel of the heat and the damp smell of the jungle. Behind me there was only the incessant shuffle of combat boots. I turned and looked back along the narrow path that was a canyon between two walls of cackling, impenetrable jungle. My men were spaced twenty meters apart. Up front, the point man—a baby-faced corporal from Cincinnati—was poking at the path in search of buried pungy sticks. Suddenly the corporal held up an open hand. I passed the silent halt signal back. The trodding died slowly and there was only the stridulant silence of the jungle. The men took up their ready position beside the path. We had been on several patrols before, but hadn't yet seen so much as a single sniper. This one was probably a false alarm, too. There was no place for Charlie to hide in the solid wall of jungle. The platoon sergeant moved up beside me, and ducking low, we waddled toward the point man. The jungle opened abruptly into a wide field of elephant grass.

I thought I heard something move out there, the corporal said.

It's a good spot for an ambush, Sargeant Reeves whispered. They've got us in a funnel.

I had known about this field from the map, and my response was automatic.

We'll move out one by one along the edge of the jungle, I said.

We were squatting in a tight group so we could whisper softly. The sergeant's and corporal's backs were to the field. I was about to return to my men when it happened.

All I remembered now was the explosion. It seemed to come from only a few feet away, and it erupted in one sharp ear-splitting burst. Hard objects pummeled my body. I could hear nothing but a high-pitched whine. My body was wet and sticky. I had been knocked to the ground on my back. Shaking with raging dizziness and nausea, I pushed myself to my knees. Even now I could remember vividly what I saw. My body was drenched from head to foot in blood and plastered with white particles of flesh and bone. And all around me, on the ground . . . And then the whine in my ears became a scream, and even then a small, rational part of my mind knew it was all over, all the dreams, everything.

"I cracked," I said. "Wide open. It was a claymore anti-personnel mine—a little box full of glass and wire on a tripod and backed by high explosive. We must have been standing directly in front of it. The corporal and sergeant were blocking me. Their bodies took the impact and shrapnel. It blew them apart. Both of them. Literally apart—plastered pieces of their bodies all over me. That's what I opened my eyes to see. Me, the Indiana boy who had never in his life even seen a corpse. And I cracked. I started screaming and kept on screaming all the time I was running. The battle lasted two hours, and when it was over they found me more than a mile up the path, shaking like a freezing man and trying to bury myself in the ground.

"I spent two months in a hospital in Saigon, then six more months in a booby hatch in California before they admitted I was a hopeless case and threw me out of the Army on a Section 8. Mentally unfit. Yeah, there's your hero."

Carla gazed at me questioningly, trying to understand. The loneliness, the defeat, the sense of failure, these were all within her realm of experience. But this part—the war—could be no more than words. She couldn't even hate me for being a coward, or feel the disgust my men must have felt. I could talk forever and she would never comprehend it.

"But surely a lot of men break . . ." she began.

"No. Not a lot. Just a few. But there's a helluva lot that go through worse than I did, who see horrors I never dreamed of, and still, somehow, manage to carry on."

Carla was quiet. There was a sadness in her silence and I knew that she felt ashamed that she couldn't share this with me. God, but she was a lovely girl.

"And your wife wouldn't accept you back?" she asked.

"On the contrary. Lorrie had never wanted a hero. I get a real kick out of these movies where women fall all over James Bond because he's so rugged and dangerous. If James Bond ever existed, women would run like hell. Heroes are myths created by men and for men. I've yet to meet the female who doesn't tremble in fear at the first threat to her comfortable dreams of security. No, Lorrie was quite elated. It was finally out of my system and we could settle down to a nice secure home—bridge on Tuesdays and P.T.A. Wednesday and a movie Saturday night, a good retirement insurance program. And she could mother me and pat my head as though I were a hurt dog."

"But you wanted punishment, not love?"

"I never thought it out that clearly. Yeah, something like that. But I don't suppose I ever really hated her. I loved them enough—my son, too—that I thought destroying the marriage would be punishment. I even hit her a couple of times, but even then she wouldn't grant a divorce. Finally I walked out. Got the divorce papers in the mail. She's married again, I hear. A full-fledged professor at Indiana U. She's moving up."

"You still love her?" Carla asked.

"Yeah."

For a moment Carla gazed at her folded hands in her lap. "I'm sorry," she said. "Truly I am."

"Thanks," I said. For the first time in over a year I wanted someone not to hate me. "Thanks," I said again.

Before dawn I pulled into a motel in the open country south of Bakersfield. Carla was asleep and I carried her in and laid her on the bed. I went in the bathroom and took a hot shower. When I came out, Carla was beneath the covers. Her clothes were draped carefully over a chair. I sat down on the bed beside her. She opened her eyes and smiled.

"It's not going to be like before," she said. "It's going to be lovely this time, isn't it?"

"Yeah," I grinned. "Lovely."

And it was. It really was.

I didn't sleep at all that night. The Dexedrine was still working. But I let Carla sleep in my arms until the sun was full and golden on the curtains. I took another shower and dressed before I woke her. She rubbed her eyes and looked up at me.

"You're beautiful," she said.

"It comes from clean living and reading the Bible every day. But you're so ugly, I don't understand how I ever let you seduce me. You sure that pill you gave me wasn't some sort of aphrodisiac?"

Carla laughed. "There were times last night when I wondered that myself."

"Enough of that talk," I said. "Up. Get up. We have to move."

"I don't know why. Honestly, Chess, you'd think somebody was still trying to throw you in jail or something."

I pulled her up, slapped her on the bottom and watched as she staggered sleepily into the bathroom. She peered in the mirror and let out a mock squeal of horror. "You're right. I am ugly! How do you stand me!"

"I like ugly girls," I said. "Now get a move on. You've got five minutes while I check out."

I stopped briefly in the doorway and looked back at Carla, who was making faces at herself in the mirror. Laughing out loud, I went outside and started toward the office. The red Corvette was parked in front of our door and I passed it without thinking. After a few steps I halted abruptly. Very slowly I turned back.

Both tires on the right side of the car were flat.

TWELVE

For maybe ten minutes I just stood there looking at the flat tires and feeling that old hopeless anger curdling my stomach as though I had swallowed a rotten fish whole. Carla came up beside me, grinning and rubbing the sleep from her eyes. No girl is ever more beautiful than the morning after a night of good, honest love-making. Whoever made up that cliché about beauty being only skin deep must have been talking about that. Carla's hair was hanging straight down, a few strands poking out in back, and her eyes were red and her lips slightly bruised, but for all that she was positively glowing, as if her bones were neon lights that had just been turned on. Sleepily she cuddled under my arm.

"Chess, you have the worst luck of anybody I know," she said, giggling.

"Luck hell!" I said, dropping down on my knees beside the car. No slits, no breaks, no nails. Somebody had just let the air out. "Damn, I bet there isn't a gas station for twenty miles."

"I guess we might as well go back to bed," Carla suggested.

"You lusty wench, you're insatiable." The prospect was intriguing, but I had a hunch that something was going to happen very soon, and I wanted to be possessed of all my faculties when it did occur. If someone had wanted to stop us completely, there were more efficient methods than letting the air out of the tires. I walked around to the rear of the car and opened the trunk to see if the spare was up.

There it was. A shiny little metal box clamped by magnetism to the inside of the trunk. Even a ten-year-old kid would have known what it was if he only went to the movies once a year. A homing device. No wonder I hadn't spotted any followers. This little box would be sending out radio signals which would be picked up on a receiving set in a car that was probably very careful to stay several miles behind me. There was no need to accuse Carla quite yet. Someone with a set of master keys could have put it on in Santa Cruz, or at any one of several cafés we had stopped at for coffee, or even right there at the motel. But whoever had flattened the tires must have known I would open the trunk, so they couldn't have been aware of the transmitter. Which meant I was still being followed by two separate groups and both were very nearby. I wished the F.B.I. and the Ruskies would at least coordinate their efforts.

I pulled the device loose—it was hardly larger than a pack of cigarettes—and looked around for another car to attach it to. The only other car in front of the motel was a big, fat white Buick, vintage about 1955. But before I could even move in that direction, the owner emerged from Room 3. He was a tall, thin man with the dry, sun-hardened face of a laborer, and he wore a multicolored flowered shirt especially made for tourists in the sweatshops of L.A. I watched him as he got in the car. He bent over briefly and shoved something in the glove compartment. The car started a little more smoothly and powerfully than a twelve-year-old should.

He stomped it in reverse and the car disappeared momentarily into a cloud of dust, then swung past us toward the highway. He looked at me as he drove by, as though he expected me to flag him down. I didn't. Let him make the first move.

He made it. The Buick halted at the highway, then bolted in reverse back to the Corvette. He leaned out the window and yelled, "Got troubles, mister?"

"Yeah," I said. "Little bit of vandalism. Nothing serious. You got a tire pump in there?"

" 'Fraid not. Vandalism you say. Dunno what the kids nowadays are coming to. Didn't notice they did anything to my car. Can I give you a lift? There's a gas station about five miles up the road."

"I'd appreciate it. Let me pull one of these tires off."

He sat in the car and watched me until I had it off, then he came around and opened his trunk and waited while I threw the tire in, offering me no chance to attach the transmitter.

"Can I come, too?" Carla asked.

"No. Go back to bed and lock the door. Don't let anyone in."

Carla's lips curled downward into a mock pout, and she slumped back to the motel. I watched her as we pulled out onto the road, feeling very warm and protective.

The Buick roared onto the highway, spewing dust and gravel from its rear tires like an angry dragon with its ends reversed. In about ten seconds we were pushing eighty.

"By the way, the name's Chessick," I said through clamped teeth.

"Yeah, Wilson here. Mike Wilson."

"You've got quite an engine in this thing."

"New Chrysler. Three hundred eighty horses. And take a

gander at that four-speed floor shift. A hot engine ain't no good without a good transmission, eh."

That was a lot of power for an old car, but it probably took a lot to tail some people. And the old body was a perfect front—the one car on the road you would never notice. I fingered the transmitter in my pocket. This baby would really give somebody a run for their money. My left hand searched under the seat for enough metal to hold the magnetic bottom of the device. No luck. The glove compartment.

"You don't happen to have a Kleenex?" I asked.

I didn't wait for an answer. I just reached out and snapped the glove compartment open. Wilson glanced away from the road and his hand reached halfway across the dash, but he stopped and settled back when he saw the deed was already accomplished. It was obvious that he would have appreciated more notice. Lying inside the compartment was a snub-nosed revolver.

"No Kleenex?" I said.

"I use a handkerchief." Wilson had begun to sweat a little around the hairline. His eyes held on the road.

"Gee, is that a real gun?" I asked innocently. I reached out and picked it up, at the same time fixing the transmitter to the roof of the compartment.

"Watch it," Wilson said. "That thing's loaded."

So it was. All six shells. I was no expert on civilian firearms, but I figured it for a .38. Nice size for a shoulder holster. "What do you use it for? You a cop or something?"

Wilson wiped the sweat from his eyes with the back of his hand, probably cursing himself that he hadn't locked the glove compartment. Maybe he couldn't afford to. Maybe he was in a profession where he might have to get to it fast. "No, no," he said. "I just keep it for self-defense. I'm a traveling salesman and, you know . . . well, you can't be too careful these days."

"Oh, a salesman," I said, examining the pistol. "I've met a

couple of other salesman in the last week—a shoe salesman and a real estate salesman. Owen and Aaron were their names. Maybe you know them?"

"No. I sell . . . uh . . . brushes."

"Really? I need a shaving brush. Do you happen to have one?"

"I don't sell no shaving brushes. Just toilet brushes, things like that."

"Well, now that you mention it, I could use a toilet brush."

"Sorry, I just gave away my last sample. Hey, would you be careful with that gun."

"What? Oh. Sure. By the way, could you slow this thing down a little."

"Sorry. I didn't know I was scaring you."

I leaned against the door with the pistol resting on my lap. The sweat was spreading under his arms now, soiling his flowered shirt. His eyes didn't move from the road. He slowed to fifty with short, chopping jabs at the brake pedal.

"Slower," I said. "Like about twenty-five. I never did get used to these fast cars."

"Yeah. Sure," Wilson said, braking down to twenty-five. " 'Cept I gotta keep an appointment."

"I'll try not to detain you too long. See that dirt road on the right? Pull into it."

"What is this?" Wilson mumbled, the words choked in his throat.

"I said pull in or I'll blow your damned brains out right here."

Wilson had a big Adam's apple and it started bouncing up and down the length of his throat like a ping-pong ball. Silently he swung right onto a dirt road. The road cut briefly through a patch of eucalyptus trees and then left again, running parallel with the highway but screened from it by foliage. On the other side was a barbed-wire fence and a vast plowed field.

"Stop here," I said.

He stopped. "Look, if this is a holdup . . ."

"Get out."

"You can have my money. I ain't got much."

"Out."

I slid out on the driver's side after Wilson.

"All right, walk over to that barbed-wire fence. And when you get there look at it real hard because I'm going to smear you all over it if you don't give the right answers."

I walked about six feet behind him. There's a karate method of taking away a gun held on you from behind, and I wasn't about to forget that Alpine Hat had received a couple of good kicks before he could use his sleeve knife. Wilson stopped about a foot away from the fence. The barbs were flecked with rust.

"Okay," I said. "Now who the hell are you?"

"I told you. Mike Wilson. I sell brushes."

"That's one. Try again."

"Look, I told you . . ." He started to turn, gesturing helplessly with his hands. I let him get almost all the way around, then I kicked him in the shin with the edge of my shoe and when he bent toward the pain I let him have the barrel of the pistol along the side of his head. He twisted with the blow and dove face-first at the fence. When the barbs caught his stomach he automatically tried to break away. I gently planted my foot on his spine and shoved. He fell back against the wire and hung there by his armpits, gasping for breath. I hoped he wasn't one of Ladd's flunkies. Well, that was the breaks of the game.

"All right. Who are you working for?"

He grunted something I couldn't understand, so I put my foot back on his spine and bounced him a couple times. With each push against the barbs he let out a tiny muffled scream.

"Awright," he groaned. "Awright."

"Who?"

"Markham."

I considered belting him again. But the world—especially

my world—was full of surprises. I might as well follow this lead. After all, the only real assurance I had that Carla wasn't involved was the accidental nature of our first meeting.

"Okay," I said, "we'll pretend you're working for Carla Markham. Next question . . ."

"Not Carla. Carl. Her old man."

That *did* make sense. I grabbed him by the collar and threw him on his back on the ground. Blood was spreading outward from a dozen little tears in his clothes and there was a bad slash over his eye.

"You're wide open for a kick in the balls," I suggested. "So keep talking."

"I'm a private eye. Work out of San Francisco. Old Man Markham hires me every now and then to retrieve his bitch daughter."

"Is Wilson your real name?"

"Yeah. Check my license. It's in my wallet."

"Hand it to me."

He groaned and reached for his back pocket. His face contorted with pain as he attempted to roll over on his side to tug the wallet free. Suddenly a spasm ran through his entire body, then he relaxed, spread-eagled on the ground. I didn't think I had roughed him up that badly, but there was a damn good possibility I had pushed his spine out of joint. Carefully I knelt beside him and struggled the wallet from beneath his inert body. That was a mistake. His knee slammed hard on my cheek and I went over on my side. He rolled up from the ground. His hand caught my wrist just below the butt of the pistol. My thumb had been poised on the hammer and I heard the sharp snap as I pulled it into full cock. His other hand pummeled at my face. But I wasn't worrying about that. He was fighting blind. The barrel of the pistol was shoved against his belly and the pressure on my wrist was pulling my finger back on the trigger. All I needed was a real murder on my hands.

"You damned fool," I tried to yell, but not much of it got

through the fist that was hammering at my mouth. I couldn't even fight back until I got that damned pistol out of his belly for fear it would go off. I tried to release the handle, but I was dug in too tight and the slightest motion would snap the trigger. I got my free hand up to his collar and shoved my thumb hard into the nerve center beneath his chin. He screamed and rose an inch. It was all I needed. I brought the empty hand across my face and hit him in the side of the neck. He rolled just as the pistol exploded. He clutched at his side and lurched over. I swung the pistol and caught him with the butt just below the ear. He fell off me and lay still.

Slowly I pushed myself to my knees and surveyed the damage. The bullet had put a black hole along the side of his shirt, but there was nothing but a slight burn on the flesh. Thank God. My old man had once told me never to point a gun at anything I didn't intend to shoot, and now I knew what he meant. I had come a fraction of a second away from killing Wilson, and this time I doubted if any phony witness would have gotten me off the hook.

I tried again for his wallet, this time with a little more care. But Wilson was out of it. Inside the wallet was exactly what I was afraid I would find. His name really was Wilson and he really was a private eye, and from the number of credit cards, I figured he did all right in the profession. It was at least pleasing to note that he had medical insurance coverage. It was also pleasing that he had over a hundred dollars in tens and twenties. I began to add up the charges. Ten years for assault with a deadly weapon. Five years for car theft. And, oh yes, life plus ninety-nine for kidnaping. I figured it wouldn't matter a great deal if I stole his money, too. Besides, as the ad said, you should never carry more money than you can afford to lose. And now that Carla and I were getting along so well, it just wouldn't do to have to put the pinch on her for spending money.

I returned to the car and examined my face in the rearview mirror. One eye was changing shades of black and blue even as I watched. Blood was smeared all over my mouth and nose so you couldn't even discern the swollen lip. I wiped it all away with my handkerchief except an artistic streak from the side of the lip down the chin. After all, in the movies whenever the hero got hit he never bled any place except from the side of the lip. And right now I was feeling quite joyously heroic. I had finally beaten up a bad guy. Well, maybe Wilson wasn't really a bad guy, but he wasn't a good guy either. Matter of fact, he had nothing to do with it at all.

The elation lasted all of the twenty seconds it took to drive back to the highway. Then I started seeing cops behind every tree. If they weren't there now, they would be as soon as Wilson recovered enough to stagger out to the road. No telling how long that might be. I was counting seconds now. Luckily the gas station was only a mile further on. I took it easy on the accelerator returning to the motel. No sense begging for the attention of the cops, especially when my face looked like last year's meatloaf and I had a .38 shoved into my belt.

When I got back, the first thing I did was transfer the homing device to the trunk of the Buick, concealed behind the spare tire. When the Corvette was ready to roll again, I woke Carla. Her reaction was what I had anticipated.

"Good God!" she said.

"Look, that guy who picked me up, he was the one who flattened our tires. He's one of your father's private eyes. I roughed him up a bit."

"You didn't kill him?"

"No. But as soon as he wakes up he's going to have cops all over us, so . . ."

"Not if he's working for my father. He wouldn't dare involve me in a scandal."

Carla was getting more lovable all the time. Well, there went my life-plus-ninety-nine years. But I still had good reason to move fast. Whoever was on the other end of that transmitter would discover soon enough that he was watching the wrong car.

When we were back on the road again, I said, "I thought your father's goons ran in pairs."

"They do," she said. "There was probably another one waiting up the road. Maybe they were going to beat you up."

"Maybe. Anyway, they're liable to pick up our trail again, so I suggest we disappear. What do you say to a vacation in Mexico?"

Carla grinned. "That would be fun. I know a place in Tijuana . . ."

"Tijuana! What was a nice girl like you doing in a rotten dump like T-J?"

"I used to dance the strip in a bar there," she said coyly. "But seriously, Chess, there really are parts of Tijuana that the soldiers don't see. And I know just the thing to cheer you up. Some of my friends from college rent a house there for the summer, and every night they have a party."

"A party!" I mumbled. "Oh, Christ, that's all I need."

"It'll do you good. You're too morbid. You should let yourself go."

I thought of Wilson lying half dead beneath the eucalyptus trees. Yeah, all I needed was to really let myself go.

A party yet.

THIRTEEN

The highway system in California was designed out of nothing more than pure, sneering sadism. Sooner or later all roads lead to Los Angeles. In those unguarded moments when abstract recollections of the City of Angels are able to force their way into my consciousness, I envision a vast confetti-flecked slime—akin to a wino's supper the morning after—which has somehow come alive and is spreading its pulsating tentacles out over the countryside, devouring everything it encounters. I have a built-in radar system that shoots a hot bolt of panic through my nerves as soon as I come within fifty miles of the insatiable monster.

The terror struck abruptly as soon as I saw that U.S. 99 had become California 5, and I swung abruptly to the shoulder and turned the wheel over to Carla. Being a native of the Great State, she could not understand my sudden metamorphosis into a blubbering idiot, but she was feeling good enough that she didn't argue the point except for a brief ad-monition that, "Really, Chess, it's all in your imagination."

She might have been right, because she moved on through the city at a good clip, staying on Route 5, and all I had to do was watch the inexhaustible houses, factories, apartments and stores of civilization gone nuts whir away beside the freeway. Los Angeles, like the Army, is pretty hard to insult, because everything nasty you can think to say about it has already become a cliché. After a while I gave up trying to think of anything new, and just lay back on the seat and closed my eyes and listened to Carla's stream of one-sided conversation. I wasn't sure what she was talking about—friends, daydreams, books, movies, things like that, I sup-pose—but if she showed her happiness in rambling, nearly incoherent jabbering, that was all right with me. At least she had a nice voice—except when she tried to sing. Now and then I would look at her blossoming, red-tinged cheeks and wonder whatever happened to the somber, tragic waif I had picked up in that Frisco bar.

It occurred to me that if Carla had been any less rich and beautiful, she might have been institutionalized. I had seen far less pronounced symptoms of the manic-depressive in the various hospitals where I had been an unwilling guest. But if Carla was crazy, that was all right, too.

The mood held all the way to the border and further, even though it seemed to me that her spring was wound too tight and must inevitably run down or break. Instead she kept soaring higher and higher, and with every foot she as-cended, her own fragile little foot descended a bit more on the gas pedal. When Route 5 swung into U.S. 101, I took over the wheel again, keeping a close eye on the rear-view mirror for any cars which might continually reappear in spite of my erratic slowing down and speeding up. I was no expert, but as far as I could judge, we were no longer being followed.

We stayed on El Camino Real—the world's only seven-hundred-mile junk sculpture—down through San Diego, and crossed the border into Mexico just before dusk. Tijuana isn't the bottom of the earth's garbage barrel as some people claim. It's the scum underneath the barrel. But one inch over the border and you've crossed outside the realm of values and thinking where something might conceivably be shocking or immoral, into a dirt and neon never-never land where you can gaze upon the wildest perversions with no more outrage than if you were casually perusing the wild, sick imaginings of a black humorist. Even on a Monday the main drag was surging with aimless marines and soldiers, bemused tourists, greasy con men, leering pimps and fat whores.

I drove on through the main part of the city without stopping and out past the jai-alai stadium and the bullring into a quiet area that I hadn't known existed. It was a motley conglomeration of ramshackle houses and pasteboard stores where honest, decent Mexicans were born and lived and married and bred and died in quiet oblivion to the oversized Gringo whorehouse a few blocks away. Carla pointed the way to a large colonial mansion that had been fashioned into a hotel. It was twenty minutes before we could break away from the friendly, garrulous politeness of the family that ran the place and get to our room.

I lay on the bed while Carla took a shower. The Dexedrine was wearing thin, and without much prodding I could have slept twelve hours straight. The party Carla had suggested didn't sound especially appealing, but she was flying too high to join her lethargic beau in anything as sensible as sleep. Besides, yet hovering about my thick skull was the vague suspicion that sweet, innocent little Carla was not all as innocent as she appeared. Nor could I dismiss the simple fact that ever since Santa Cruz, Carla had been calling the direction of travel. If my suspicions were correct, her party might be part of the overall design. If that was true, it wouldn't be all fun and games.

But I damned well had to find out.

It was a rambling adobe structure with thick walls and narrow windows and ancient wooden beams jutting from the corners. The front section looked as if it might once have been designed as a combination home and one-family fortress, but later more affluent and less endangered generations had added a second story and room after room out from the sides. I envisioned the place as the castle of a once-vast wine empire. Within the surrounding wire fence scattered and neglected grape vines had abandoned their neat rows and sallied forth to do battle against the stronger manzanita and scrub oak.

Beyond the fence, small wood and clay shanties had, like the ravenous wild brush, implanted themselves in asymmetrical lines among the lost vineyards, leaving the great adobe hacienda standing like an island monument to yesterday's dreams and yesterday's glory. It was almost night and a slight mist had fallen, leveling the shadowed shapes into dreary variations of gray and diffusing the lighted windows into yellow blobs against the walls.

Carla knocked at a massive carved wood door. We waited several seconds in the growing darkness, then she knocked again. I noticed this time there was an obvious pattern, a signal of some sort. After a while a woman opened the door. You wouldn't have recognized her unless you were in the habit of frequenting the Grade Z movies. I had seen her in a couple of low-budget horror films, maybe a western or two. She had a weirdo starlet name—Zelda Zorch or some damned-fool nonsense. I remembered in one movie the hero had looked longingly at her and said with a straight face, "Gosh, I never realized it before, but you're really beautiful." It was the funniest line in the movie.

"Whah, Carla honah," she gasped in an accent that might have induced Robert E. Lee to vote for Lincoln.

"Aimee, dear," Carla said with catty enthusiasm.

"Whah, Carla, Ah am suhprahsed. Ah sho didn't 'spect yoh ta sho up heah. Not in mah whole born days. Ah mean, aftah runnin' off lahk thet, an' raht in the middle of yoh verah own partah, too."

"Don't tell me the news has gotten down here already," Carla exclaimed.

"Whah, deah, aftah yoh disappeahed, Deke, he jus' up an' flew on down heah. Mah, but that man is hung up on yoh, deah, somethin' terrible, an' aftah all the dirt you done him."

"Deke's here?" I said.

"Sho is, honah. Carla, wheah did yoh fahnd this lovelah young man?"

"Good-by," I said.

Carla caught me halfway to the gate. "You coward," she giggled. "Deke won't hurt you. He's really a very nice guy."

"Look, baby," I said, "I'm not sure precisely when it happened, but somewhere between your party and tonight the law of averages totally fell apart. First I meet Merril, then I meet you—all quite by accident, of course—and then several hundred miles away I run into the same karate expert who practiced on me yesterday. Do you realize what is going to happen now that the law of averages has become inoperable? Everybody will decide to go for a Sunday drive in the same direction at the same time. Every car in the nation on the road all at once. A massive traffic jam. Just picture it! Twenty million babies born on April seventeenth and not a one on the eighteenth. The hospitals will be either overcrowded or deserted."

"You're being silly," Carla said, laughing.

"Baby, the law of averages rules the world. It says too many coincidences don't happen to one person within a single twenty-four-hour period. Think what's happening right now. The Las Vegas roulette wheels stop always on the same number. Everybody buys stock in General Electric—nobody in Westinghouse. Currency falls apart. Depression. Famine. War. Population explosion. Terror. Misery. It's the end of the world. I'm going to find me a new planet."

"Honestly, Chess, sometimes I think you're absolutely crazy. There's no coincidence to it. Deke has known me for a long time. I come here quite often in the summer when I want to get away from home, so there's hardly any mystery about how he knew where I was."

"Well, what the hell is he doing here?"

"Oh God, but you're exasperating sometimes, Chess. I mean really, isn't it obvious? Deke just happens to have a schoolboy crush on me. He follows me around like a puppy. I certainly don't encourage him, but really, what can I do?"

"Well, I don't want to encourage him either. So you just give him my apologies."

"Really, Chess, sometimes I just don't understand you. What are you so afraid of? I thought that police thing in San Francisco was all over."

"Yeah," I said. Her explanation of Deke's presence was reasonable. The only trouble was that when things stopped looking too coincidental, they began to look too logical. Life as I had always known it didn't fall into smooth little patterns. If you suddenly met an old friend on the street, you could grill him for hours and never get a fully reasonable explanation of how he happened to be there at that particular time. Now all of a sudden life had become simplified —the old row of dominoes falling one upon the other. All the causes were on view. That was just as hard to swallow as the total coincidence theory. But maybe Carla was right. Fear makes you look at the world in a new way, and if this— Carla, Merril, Deke, the private eye—had happened a month earlier I probably wouldn't have bothered to mark it up to either coincidence or logic.

I let Carla pull me by the sleeve back to the house. Aimee was still standing there, sipping her drink.

"Gosh," I said, "I never realized it before, but you're really beautiful." She gave me a vacant look as I passed.

"What was that all about?" Carla asked with a lovely tinge of jealousy.

"We're old friends from the back-alley Bijou," I said.

We were in a long corridor, with the trapped musk of old clay and rotted wood. A few candle holders had been left along the walls, but everything else of value had been removed, giving the bare corridor a somber, haunted-house quality. We passed several doors opening on candlelit, deserted rooms. At the end of the hall we came into a large room, lighted by a hundred or so candles in a massive chandelier. There were maybe thirty people here, yet there was a strange atmosphere of silence and unmovement. The air was heavy with the sweetish odor of exotic tobacco.

The guests were broken into a number of small groups of three or four, and each cluster seemed to have its own uniform. Middle-aged men in dark business suits with ladies a little too pretty to be their wives. The remnants of the Beat Generation had taken over one corner and were seated on the floor supplying the music—bongo drums and a folk guitar. Others were dressed in the latest in casual styles, the males resembling clothing models in *Playboy* ads, the girls in shapeless knit sweaters and bell-bottomed slacks. The crowd seemed to hold only one thing in common. To a man they reeked of money.

Deke was stationed behind a randomly placed bar counter—the only piece of furniture in the room. He hadn't changed his clothes since our last meeting, and the only alteration in his appearance was a few more wrinkles in his *Mad* sweatshirt and the nearly imperceptible acquisition of more dirt. I wasn't sure how he would take to seeing old buddy Chessick again, so I held my place in the doorway while Carla went to meet him. They talked briefly, then Deke looked past her to me with an expression of surprise and mild outrage. I prepared myself for a swift exit, but Carla said something that set Deke howling with laughter.

"Were yoh bein' insultin'?" Aimee said from behind me.

"What?"

"Thet what'cha said back theah. You din't soun' . . . well, sincere."

"Whah, honah," I said, "l'il ol' me was jus' referencin' ta one o' yoh movahs."

She gazed at me suspiciously, then her face beamed and her mouth widened to a grin. "Whah, yoh raht. Ah do remembah. Whah, wahn't thet the one wheah thet big beetle was mutated bah the mad scientist an' was gonna tahk ovah the whole wohld."

"I think it was a cockroach," I said.

"Whah, thet's absolutelah raht. Yoh did see it, din' yoh. Whah, yoh'd be suhprahsed how few folks Ah meet have seen mah movahs."

"Didn't you have a Brooklyn accent in that movie?"

"Whah, ain't that the mahk of a real actress—Ah mean, thet she kin reahly feel her paht—Ah mean deep down."

I was saved from an astute observation on Aimee's acting ability by a young man with carefully combed peroxide blond hair who sidled up beside me and asked in an obsequiously effeminate voice, "Pardon me, sir, but you don't happen to be . . . well, you know."

"Sorry, buddy, can't help you," I said.

"Get lost," Aimee said in a perfect Midwest accent.

He dismissed her with a flaccid wave of his hand. "Oh, shut up, Aimee. You just don't understand." He turned back to me. "Would you believe it, but the ones who are here are such absolutely unimaginable bitches."

"I believe," I said.

"Not my type at all. Really, you just can't imagine how it is—even for a person as talented and sensitive as myself."

Carla came back, grinning ear-to-ear at my company and dragging Deke by the arm. "I see you've already met the elite," she said.

"Carla, dearie," the young man said, "I find your sarcasm unwarranted and uncouth. It's the horrid society we must live in today. No one respects the courage to be different."

Deke looked at the floor, wiggled his foot and shoved a hairy hand out toward me. "Truly grieved about that,

Chess," he said. "I gird up my loins and repent in sackcloth and ashes."

"Really, I'm classical, you know," the young man said. "Ancient Greek."

I shook hands briefly with Deke. "Okay. No problems. Just remind me not to take a swing at you."

"Well, if there's any possible manner in which I might expiate my unpardonable offense . . ."

"I'll settle for a drink."

As we crossed to the bar, I turned and looked back. The Ancient Greek had cornered Aimee and was giving her a biased review of Plato's *Symposium*. Aimee was leaning against the wall, contemptuously waving her hand back and forth in front of her nose as though to rid herself of a stench. "Be gone, worm," she said with stage elocution.

Carla ducked behind the bar. "Scotch, bourbon, rum . . ."

"Beer," I said.

"Carla informs me you majored in philosophy in college," Deke said with forced friendliness.

"Only the B.A. Master's in English."

"Ah, philosophy," Deke exclaimed. "The true wisdom of the world. The bounteous harvest of man's intellect." He commenced a typically collegiate lecture on the beauties of ageless wisdom. It was the speech of a freshman who has accepted all the whitewashed garbage of an ivory-tower professor, the reduction of the blood-and-guts surge of the dirty earth to vague and pretty abstractions.

I let him ramble and turned to observe the guests. The party had visibly changed its shape and texture, taking on a solemn ritual atmosphere. The different uniforms had integrated and almost everyone was seated around the walls. There was little talking. I had the feeling that this was phase two—an interim between the introductions and polite conversation and whatever was supposed to happen at these parties. A Negro with a scraggly white beard was beating out a slow, almost inaudible rhythm on a pair of bongos. One of

his accomplices was tuning a guitar. A girl caught my attention. She was leaning against the wall on her forehead,
waving her whole body back and forth in a mildly sensual
rhythm. She turned slowly and I could see why I had picked
her out. Her face was familiar from the movies—but she was
no mere starlet like Aimee. This baby was big money. You
saw her in a lot of Otto Preminger films. She was pretty in a
vapid sort of way. Movie actresses invariably turned me off
cold. I felt insulted by what Hollywood thought I was supposed to like. To me sex is a subtle thing—a certain atmosphere a girl carries about her, an atmosphere of depth and
mystery. Without it a girl is about as sexy as a nude calendar. But Hollywood had no concept of subtlety. For one class
of idiots they gave you a pair of big tits. For the idealist they
had the sweet young virgin that snot-nosed kids were supposed to want to take home to mother. Between the bone-
headed professional virgin and the sex symbol, there is something loosely called a real woman. But Hollywood would
have none of the middle way.

This one was of the virginal school. She had recently made
the cover of a national magazine by spouting some rot about
free love. She was all for it. She was also for equality for
women and she thought that Winston Churchill was the
greatest of all living men. A real deep thinker, this one. I
wondered where she was when Churchill died.

"And speaking of science," Deke—who supposedly was
speaking of science because certainly nobody else was—said.
"Well, just take Freud. The theory of universally patterned
growth cycles—like, say, the stages of infantile sexuality—
would be unthinkable if the mind were still believed to be a
mere *tabula rasa*. Have you ever considered that Jung's col-
lective unconscious might be an extension of the Kantian *a
priori?*"

"Deke, deah, what ahh you talkin' about?" Aimee said,
approaching with the Ancient Greek on her heels.

"My dear friend Chess, here, has been a student of the
subtle profundities of philosophical speculation. We are in-

volved in esoteric discourse on the immense contribution of
Immanual Kant to modern science."

"Actually, philosophy died with Aristotle, you know,"
Ancient Greek said.

The virginal movie star moved away from the wall and
commenced a slow, sensual dance to the bongo. Her eyes
were glazed, staring. Her body lost the rhythm of the bongos
and merely swayed with a random motion. Her chin
dropped forward over her neck and her hair covered her
face.

Then suddenly she was standing straight and stiff as
though her body had become marble. Her eyes held on the
ceiling above my head. A tiny quiver rippled across her lips.
Then she screamed. It was a high, lancing scream that was
captured in the walls, hollow, muted, echoed, dying slowly.
No one moved. No one seemed to have even heard it. She
fell abruptly to her kneees, her hands clawing at her hair. For
several seconds she kneeled there, her throat making little
squeaking sounds. Oh. Oh. Oh. Oh. Oh. Then, still gripping
her head, she dropped forward. I heard her head make a
brief, dull thudding sound as it hit the floor.

I started to move toward the fallen girl. Aimee grabbed
my arm. "Whah, Mistah Chessick, yoh can't help her. Whah,
she's not even heah."

I swung back to Deke for an explanation.

"Bad trip," he said dryly.

"Ah say, what a lovelah, innocent young man you ahh,"
Aimee said.

"Lysergic acid diethylamide," Deke explained.

"Us poh un-intellectuals jus' call it LSD foh short."

I turned back to the counter. Carla had left an open beer
for me and I chug-a-lugged it halfway down. I felt like an
unsophisticated little kid. Except for maybe a vitamin pill or
two, and of course the Dexedrine that Carla had given me
on the way down, I had never had much to do with drugs. I
still retained that obsolete conviction that such esoteric
thrills were the exclusive domain of the slums. Deep down,
old Indiana boy Robert Chessick was still a prude. In the

last few weeks I had seen a man with a hat pin in his eye, had tortured an innocent private detective, and here I was surrounded by California's most beautiful people, and I was shocked. Cross over the border and you're in another world. Right, baby. You take your private world with you no matter how many borders you cross.

"Maybe you'd like to try it," Deke said, holding up a capsule he had removed from his shirt pocket. "Truly a surpassing experience in metaphysical contemplation."

I shook my head.

"A wise decision perhaps. Carla told me of your experiences with the mental health department."

I finished my beer and turned to look for Carla. The movie star was in the same position as when I had last seen her—on her knees with her face on the floor. Those along the wall had taken on a uniformly trancelike aspect. Their eyes seemed to be creating reality against blank walls and in empty air. Some appeared to be listening intently as though to great music, although even the bongo drum was still, and now there was only the hushed suck and gasp of heavy breathing. Someone hummed a few bars of a random tune and was silent.

Then I noticed Carla. She had been sitting against the wall, hidden by a vertical beam. She stood up and began to dance. It wasn't the softly sensual dance of the movie star. There was something primitive in it, a frantic compulsion to just move. The bongo picked up the rhythm of her body and the guitar joined in. She moved faster, challenging the music. The movie star rolled over on her side into the fetal position and began to sob. Carla's hair flashed like rippling flame in the candlelight.

"Her too?" I said.

"Not LSD," Deke said. "Too overwhelming for such an unstable personality. She tried it once and had to spend three weeks in a hospital. I'm not certain what she's on tonight. She enjoys variety."

I looked at the small group—Aimee, Deke and Ancient Greek—who still had their feet planted firmly on solid ground. "Aren't you going to join the party," I said sarcastically.

"Afraid we can't," Deke said. "Tonight we are the watchers. The watchers at the gate of heaven—or hell—whichever the case might be. It is our task to make sure one of our omnipotent and invulnerable guests does not wander out into a world which does not appreciate omnipotency and invulnerability. But if you would like to try something light—tea, perhaps—there's no need for you to bear with us squares."

"I'll skip it," I said. "Carla and I are going back to the hotel."

"Whah, Mistah Chessick, thet wouldn't be a good ideah ayat all. Ah mean, in the condition she is, an' with what the cops in T-Town are lahk."

Something clicked. I might not have noticed it at any other party, but suddenly things were becoming exceptionally clear.

"Okay, baby," I said, "let's you and me take a breather."

"Whah, Mistah Chessick, are yoh suggestin' . . ."

"No, but I might."

Aimee giggled. I grabbed her arm and pulled her back toward the doorway.

"Please, yoh don' hafta be so rough."

I ignored her. The whole thing had gone sour in my mouth. Sour and dirty and cheap. For a moment I believed I could run away from it, find myself a private little sanctuary where it would be just Carla and me. No Russians. No F.B.I. No corpses. No laser beams. The hallway was longer than I had remembered. I could see the little blue at the base of the candle flame. The pocked texture of the adobe. I felt vaguely dizzy. The aftereffects of the Dexedrine. There was something in my stomach. A growing razor edge of anger. Maybe terror. I couldn't capture it. It was cutting at my ribs.

We went outside. It was dark except for the lights of the windows and the hall shining yellowish rectangles on the twisted branches of manzanita.

"Whah, Mistah Chessick, please. Yoh hurhtin' mah arm," Aimee said.

I hit her in the face with the flat of my hand and knocked her back against the wall. She stood there staring at me. Her face was a neat pattern of overlapping shadows. She had green eyes. I could smell the color of her eyes. It was the odor of fear in a green meadow in bright sunlight. *Something is happening to me,* I thought.

"You bastard," she said. Her voice was like a thumbnail rasping down a blackboard.

"My name. Chessick. You've used it two-three times. Who told you?"

"Are you crazy? Carla . . ."

"No. I was with Carla every moment she was near you. Same with Deke. Both of them only called me 'Chess.' "

"That's insane. How should I remember . . ."

I grabbed her wrist and pulled it to the light of the window. "I thought so. Razor scars."

"So what's wrong with that? My agent told me to. It's standard procedure—just a way for a starlet to get publicity."

"The woman who was with Aaron in Frisco—looking for Kreigger—had razor scars."

"I don't know what you're talking about. Let me go."

I raised my hand to hit her again. But my arm wouldn't move, wouldn't touch the disgusting thing in front of me. I could see the pores in her flesh like giant craters. The face congealed around her eyes, leaving only two glistening pinpoints of black. Her mouth curved up on her cheeks into a garish half-moon grin. Ears grew out of her hair—sharp, pointed ears—like horns. Then suddenly I was staring not at flesh but at cold, hard, white ivory.

I shoved my fist in my mouth and bit down hard. My feet stumbled back into the dark, rasping bushes beside the walk.

Something is happening to me, I thought. *My God, something is happening to me.*

FOURTEEN

Then it was soft. I went down among the manzanita, where light perched upon glistening Negroid limbs like an ethereal bird of indescribable beauty, rippling effulgent wings outward into bright shadow. Then the bird melted by the heat of its own radiance, like a candle in a furnace, and flowed in liquid light upon the leaves and the earth. *I love all things that flow,* said Walt Whitman, and my eyes went out into the flow and felt the leaves and immersed them. I chose one leaf and watched it and touched it as it descended slowly into the ocean of my eyes. I could sense it breathing through chlorophyll pores and its breath was the gentle odor of childhood dreams in the afternoon when you would lie beneath an oak tree and conjure lovely phantasms out of drifting particles trapped and hovering in sun rays through the branches.

Another part of my mind—a rational part—was a round ball without dimension and it moved up through my skull and sat down on air about six inches to the right of my ear and above my shoulder. I looked down and saw Robert Chessick squatting among the bushes, gazing at his mind that was a puddle of light with a single leaf floating in it on the ground before him.

Aimee came up behind him. "Chessick," she said. "Chessick, close your eyes." Her voice was sparkling rain upon window-lighted puddles, falling in diamonds and rippling circles outward. Her voice was music and each letter of each word was a single raindrop note. The drops flowed into each other and became a pool and from out of the pool there was a stream and the stream was a sentence. "Close your eyes."

I sat down on the shoulder of Robert Chessick and told him to close his eyes as she said. The light on the earth flowed back into him like a waterfall in reverse. Now there was shimmering, incandescent blackness. The sweet odor of apples turning brown beneath a summer sky. Chessick reached out and touched the odor. It was hard and smooth like ivory.

"Can you talk?" Aimee asked. The words strummed like swift fingers over a harp. I looked at Chessick to see if he would answer, but I couldn't see him because his eyes were closed. After a while I heard him say, "Yes." His foot said it and the word had to wend its way through the web of blood vessels in his body before it could come out his mouth.

Then the blackness began to melt away like morning mist. Robert Chessick was standing in a Dali-esque landscape, vast beyond tangible dimension.

"What do you see?" Aimee asked.

"A road," I said through Chessick's mouth.

"Follow it."

Obediently Chessick moved off along the dark endless diminishing ribbon of road. There were no houses or people or trees or bushes or mountains on the landscape and he was very lonely. Now and then he would pass great boulders or little pebbles that were congealed sounds and odors and dreams beside the road and he would feel nostalgically happy or very sad when he looked at them. Summer passed and the earth became the color of autumn and the snow fell and the earth was white and shimmering. The disembodied head and arm of his platoon sergeant in Viet Nam lay frozen in the snow beside the road. He ran quickly past it and out of winter and into night.

"Where are you going?" Aimee asked.

"I have an appointment," Chessick said. "I have to meet the courier."

"Who is the courier?"

Chessick did not answer. The night began to rain. He looked at his watch. It was two days after eleven P.M. He was late.

"You've got to tell me. Who is the courier?"

"I don't know," Chessick said.

I sensed that Aimee was the enemy and Chessick must not lead her to the courier. I tried to yell to him to turn back, but I had no voice. He moved with a sense of urgency now, half running across the wet pavement. The moon came out and glimmered briefly upon the street. Suddenly he halted. Before him stood a man silhouetted against the shadows. Chessick waited. The man came forward slowly. He wore a green alpine hat with a red feather in the band. I called to Chessick to run, but my voice was silent. He took a hat pin from his pocket. The man in the alpine hat saw it. Suddenly the steel blade of a knife glinted in the moonlight, sparkling brief droplets of falling rain. Chessick waited, the hat pin slightly before him, gripped between his thumb and forefinger. Slowly the two men circled each other, gracefully as though in some ritual dance. The man in the alpine hat lunged. Chessick grabbed at the steel blade, clutched, felt it bite deep into his palm. Simultaneously he brought his leg up and kicked at the man's knee and before there was even time for reaction he kicked again to the groin. The man's body snapped forward into the rupture. Chessick tried to pull the hat pin back, but it was too late. He felt the brim of the hat touch his wrist. There was a sound like a man spitting between his front teeth. The man fell sideways onto the pavement.

For several years Chessick stood there above the corpse. Slowly he kneeled down on the pavement beside the body. He already knew what he would see, but he looked anyway. The corpse was a photograph in a soggy newspaper. There was a neat hole in his temple. Twenty-two caliber long, Chessick thought. The face was vaguely familiar. It was a thin, emaciated face with pronounced cheekbones. A bushy mustache. The face of an intellectual. Otto Kreigger's face.

There was a sound behind him. He turned, still kneeling. The stranger's hand was already poised above Chessick's neck for the blow. For one moment Chessick stared up into the face. It was different from anyone he could remember, yet there was something familiar, something . . . Then he knew. His body shuddered. His lips started to say the name.

Then he was liquid again, flowing down a long gutter in the rain, with cars going by in the street and people passing on the sidewalk. He washed over wine bottles and scraps of paper and brown cigarettes and swirled in circles over the metal grate of a drain and fell down into darkness. He fell for a long time, and while he was falling he thought of Alice plummeting into the rabbit hole of childhood dream, and he wondered if it would be better down there for him, too. He fell onto the floor of a great echoing cavern and he lay there exhausted. There was an odor of ageless primeval slime and the slow drip-drip of water. After a while he looked up—and screamed.

"What is it?" Aimee asked urgently. "What do you see?"

"The courier," Chessick said.

The courier rose a hundred feet above him, glistening white and smooth against the rough ochre of the cavern walls. Its flesh was solid ivory. It squatted there like a gigantic Buddha, its monstrous potbelly and black navel jutting out over carved toes. Yet for all its fearsome size, there was little that was terrifying or even unfriendly about its countenance. Its face was chubby, with fat cheeks and squinted oriental eyes that were mere black upward slashes against the ivory. The mouth, too, was no more than a single black line, a whimsical half-circle grin, the edges reaching almost to the long, pointed ears that jutted up—hornlike—on each side of the head.

"The courier," Aimee said. "What is it?"

"I don't know," Chessick said.

"Describe it to me."

"It's holding a pie," Chessick said.

And it was. In one massive hand it held up a fittingly large pumpkin pie, expertly sliced into a number of symmetrical pieces. The shapes of the pieces were continually changing as though in a kaleidoscope.

"The courier," Aimee persisted. "You've got to describe the courier."

Somehow I had to signal Chessick. He mustn't describe the courier. Aimee was the enemy. This is what she wanted. But Chessick didn't need my advice. He could smell her voice and there was the odor of death. He sniffed at the words as they echoed along the cavern into silence.

"You've got to tell me. Describe the courier."

Suddenly the ivory statue turned and lumbered along the floor of the cavern on legless feet, its body rocking back and forth like a hilarious imitation of the Frankenstein monster. Chessick understood. The courier had to deliver the pumpkin pie. But where? To whom? He struggled to his feet and ran along behind. Now he could hear a fierce growling and struggling from deep in the cavern. He was afraid, but he knew that the courier would protect him. He must not let the courier escape. Abruptly he became an eagle and flew up and perched on the great ivory head. The courier grinned and laughed. The laugh echoed away into the roar of the beast before him.

"Describe it! You must describe it!" Aimee was screaming now, her voice shrill and importunate. "Describe the courier!"

Chessick was a bird and he couldn't talk. He began to caw.

"Oh, for Christ sake," Aimee said.

Suddenly the tunnel opened into a great cave. A gigantic bear was chained to a stalagmite, struggling frantically against its bonds. Its savage claws fought the air, its dripping jowls champing at nothing. Its roars filled the cavern. Suddenly Chessick knew that it was to the bear that the pie must be delivered. He changed back into a man and began to scream at the lumbering statue.

"No! No! You mustn't!"

The courier, with its eternal fixed grin, moved on.

I drifted upward out of a light film of incoherent dream and opened my eyes. I was lying on the bed in the motel. Carla was sitting beside me stroking my forehead with her finger. I smiled and went back to sleep.

FIFTEEN

It was late morning when I woke. Carla was beside me, sleeping heavily. For several moments I just sat there on the bed watching her, not even with anger so much as a dull, churning sense of loss and emptiness in my stomach. I couldn't forget that I had only that one beer at the party, and Carla had opened it, which gave her the best opportunity to mickey it with maybe an eyedropper of LSD, maybe a fast-dissolving capsule. But the bottle had been sitting there for some time while I was watching the guests, and Deke, Aimee and the Ancient Greek were all standing nearby. Anyone of them would have had ample opportunity to drug the beer. Now that I thought about it, everything pointed to Aimee. She had been the one described with Aaron in the Frisco bar, she the one who had done the interrogation on me. Okay, I could accept that for the moment, but I would have to keep reminding myself never to trust Carla.

Besides, whoever had slipped me the LSD had done me a good turn. It might be my last good turn, so I had better take advantage of it. I knew what they were after now. Not only that, but I knew what it looked like and they didn't. How that damned grinning ivory statue got in my mind I could only surmise. Maybe it was something I had just seen somewhere in passing and wouldn't remember consciously. Maybe I had actually met Kreigger and was drugged when I saw the statue or maybe I had been drunk or perhaps somebody had bonked me on the head and given me temporary amnesia. If I recalled my college Freud correctly, had the statue been associated with some particularly horrifying incident, I might have repressed it—shoved it out of conscious memory. There were a dozen possibilities. But the whys and hows could come later. The important thing for the moment was to find out just what the courier was.

I dressed quickly, shoved Wilson's pistol in my belt beneath the jacket, and started for the door before I remembered I was still being watched. I turned back to the window and jumped into the alley behind the hotel, then walked several blocks and picked up a cab. I continued alternating long walks and cab rides until I was fairly sure I had lost any tail.

At a gas station phone booth in San Diego, I tore out the yellow page section on novelty stores, second-hand dealers and antique shops, and spent a couple more hours systematically checking each such establishment in a widening circle outward from the center of the city. It was a slow task. I couldn't even describe the statue to the shopkeepers and clerks for fear a possible tail would learn from them what I was looking for. That meant it was necessary to search the wares of each and every shop. After five luckless hours I bought up two dollars' worth of dimes and tried the phone. My first call was to Ma Fedlow's Antique and Curiosity Shoppe in La Mesa.

"A fat ivory statue with a grin and pointed ears," I said. "Probably pretty big. Maybe a couple of feet or more."

"No," Ma Fedlow said, "I don't believe we have anything like that."

"Okay. Thanks."

"I believe we have a little one though."

I almost fainted.

"You what? You have one? Don't sell it. I'll be right out."

"But, sir, this one is much smaller than the one you described."

That was an understatement. In fact, the thing was on a key chain and hardly an inch tall, not quite the imposing monster of my dreams.

"Do these things get any longer?" I asked.

Ma Fedlow was a short little lady with rimless bifocals and a red wig. "No, I don't think so," she squeaked. "After all, you're supposed to carry him in your pocket for good luck. See, you just rub his tummy and tickle his toes and you'll have good luck. That's why he's grinning, because he's always being tickled."

"Luck, uh?" I mumbled. "Where did you get this?"

"A local man who came from Alaska—a very nice man, I should say—passed away a few months ago and I bought up a lot of his possessions. I thought it was so cute, I just couldn't resist it. His wife—poor lady, she's so sweet—told me all about it."

"Alaska? It looks oriental."

"Oh no. Billikins are only hand-carved by the natives of Alaska, you know."

"Billikins?"

"Oh yes, didn't you know? I've been told they're even more popular up there than totem poles."

"But they don't come any larger?" I persisted. One of my pet theories was going down the drain—that the microfilm had been hidden underneath or inside a large statue.

"Oh no. Perhaps three inches is the largest."

"Well, would it be possible to cut some kind of hidden compartment in one of these?"

"Oh no. All the genuine billikins are carved from a single piece of solid ivory or sometimes moose horn. One couldn't cut it at all without being very obvious."

I scratched my head, perplexed. "Well, I guess I'll take it. Maybe it will bring me luck. I sure could use some. How much?"

"Is it for yourself?"

"Yeah. Of course."

"Then you can have it. You look like an honest man."

"Well, thank you, ma'am, but I wouldn't want to do that. It looks as if it must be worth at least five dollars."

"Oh, but it's part of the superstition, you see," Ma Fedlow said and smiled. "It wouldn't be any good if you bought him. He's only lucky if he's stolen, borrowed or given to you as a gift."

I stood in the doorway of Ma Fedlow's Antique and Curiosity Shoppe, studying the ivory carving in my hand. He wasn't a very forbidding character. In fact, he looked quite harmless, even friendly, gazing back at me with those black-slit eyes and that silly semicircle grin, his potbelly jutting out over a legless, footless collection of upturned toes. Rub his tummy and tickle his toes, Ma had said. I tried it. I didn't feel much luckier than before—but then I didn't feel any unluckier either.

Nor did I feel much closer or farther away from what I was after. Whatever that was. Clutched in my hot little hand was a billikin. But where the hell did it lead? To Alaska. And what's in Alaska? Glaciers, Eskimoes and igloos, that's what. Lovely. Then something clicked. Kreigger had spent several years at the Clear Radar Site in Alaska. Coincidence? Maybe. But there were too damned many coincidences. And there was something else, too. In my LSD fantasy, the billikin courier had been carrying a pie to feed a bear. And where were the biggest bears? Alaska. It wouldn't take a psychiatrist to figure out the symbolism. The courier was to make his delivery in Alaska.

It was too confusing to think about, and it suddenly occurred to me that there was a problem much more immediate. Somehow this billikin must remain absolutely secret, at least until I could establish its significance. If this was the clue they were looking for, someone might decide I was no longer relevant. I could already picture myself lying in a gutter with a pin in my eye. The decoration hadn't added much to the appearance of Alpine Hat, and I doubted seriously that it would improve my looks much. And if I had been followed, a quick chat with Ma Fedlow would reveal precisely where my interests lay. I fingered the pistol in my belt. It didn't give me much comfort. How could it when I didn't know the Commies from the F.B.I.—the good guys from the bad? I had damned near killed Wilson, and there was no guarantee that came with the gun that it wouldn't put a good-sized hole in the wrong person yet.

I shoved the billikin in my pocket and glanced up the street. There were a few people along the tree-shaded walk, but no one who looked suspicious. But then who did look suspicious? I tried to memorize the faces so if I met any one of them again within the next few minutes, I could at least start guessing. Abruptly I walked to the corner, then cut right up a side street. I wandered aimlessly for almost fifteen minutes. There were only a few scattered houses here and after a block the houses opened into a wide sandlot where a gang of boys were playing a noisy game of baseball. There was a sharp whack, and the ball flew high enough into the air to turn Mickey Mantle green. It disappeared momentarily against the sun, then dropped toward me, but I was too dumfounded to attempt to catch it. I could make a million selling this kid to the Yankees. The ball dropped on the sidewalk and bounced straight up about fifty feet. There went my quick million dollars. The kids were playing with a tennis ball. They were all yelling at me to throw it, and I chased it across the street into an alley that cut through a

closely wooded lot. A tennis ball has a nasty habit of bouncing in every direction except the one you anticipate, and it
took me a few moments of dancing a spastic's jig before I got
it safely in my hand. Panting, I stood up—and damned near
fell back down again.

There in front of me, almost concealed by foliage, was the
tail end of a white Buick. Wilson. So he wasn't a private eye
after all. He had had plenty of chance to retrieve Carla without following me from one cab to another all over San
Diego. But which side was he on? Maybe I should have
killed him when I had the chance. My hand automatically
dropped to the pistol.

"Mister?"

A little red-headed kid with a faceful of freckles was gazing up at me.

"Whaddaya want?" I said. "Get out of here."

The kid sniffed back a sob, turned and ran a few feet,
stopped, shoved both hands in his back pockets, contemplated
his foot, and mumbled almost inaudibly, "Kin we have our
ball, mister?"

I looked at the tennis ball in my hand. I had forgotten it.
"Yeah, sure, kid," I said, tossing him the ball. "Now get
lost."

As soon as the kid was back in the sandlot, I wrenched the
pistol from my belt and ran into the bushes beside the car.
My foot hit something. A pair of pliers, some wire and a
hunk of clay lay in the weeds below the bumper. Curiously,
I picked up the clay. Clay, hell! I had been in the Army
long enough to recognize plastic explosive when I saw it. It
looked as if I had better kill Wilson fast if I wanted to do
the job—or he would disappear in a cloud of smoke as soon
as he started his car. But whoever had set the bomb had
been careless leaving his tools around—too careless for the
professionals who were playing this game. He was either
close by or planning to return soon.

I dropped the plastic ball back in the grass and crept as
silently as I could into the trees. I hadn't stopped for more

than a second when I heard a dull thud, followed by a distinctly human groan from farther back in the woods. I crouched and moved, tree to tree, toward the sound. I had never been much of a stalker, even in the Army, and each cracking twig beneath my feet sounded like an explosion. But whoever I was stalking was making too much noise to listen. The voices were clearer now. I moved more slowly. Then, before me, appeared a small clearing, yellow with dandelions. Wilson was kneeling with his face against a tree. Behind him stood Aaron, holding a pistol with a six-inch silencer attached to the barrel.

Aaron smiled that winning, real-estate salesman grin of his. "I hate to be so nasty about all this," he apologized to his helpless victim. "But I really don't have much time. Please tell me who you are working for. Is it Chessick?"

"Get serious," Wilson muttered through his teeth, "I'm expensive. Chessick doesn't have a dime. I told you. Carl Markham."

I knew what was coming and I gritted my teeth against it. The steel silencer slammed against Wilson's cheek with a crunching sound and the silver steel turned red.

I rubbed the sweat from my eyes with the back of my gun hand. I wasn't exactly in love with Wilson, but I had gone to a lot of trouble to keep from killing him once. The idea of standing there watching him get beaten to death wasn't exactly my idea of good entertainment. But which was on what side? I couldn't very well put a hole in Aaron's head if he was really a good guy. Damn it, why didn't these people wear recognizable uniforms or armbands or something? One thing I did know. I wasn't about to stand there and witness a murder.

I moved very carefully now, circling around behind Aaron. His voice droned on in that same pleasant tone, as though he were trying to seduce Wilson into buying a haunted house. Suddenly there was an abrupt shushing sound, followed by a dull slap. I peered through the bushes. Wilson was gripping his thigh, blood seeping over his fingers.

That did it. I lunged. Aaron swung the barrel toward the sound. For a second I was staring into that deadly hole in the silencer. But he didn't fire. I didn't give him a second chance. I hit the silencer away with my left and slammed the pistol in my right into his solar plexus. Before Aaron even hit the ground, I had a grip on Wilson's sleeve and was dragging him, running, back toward the alley.

"For God's sake," Wilson screamed, "lemme get his gun. The bastard!"

"Screw his gun! Move, you sonofabitch."

Wilson cursed under his breath and staggered along after me, one hand gripping his wounded leg. Several times he fell and I grabbed him by the shirt collar and shoved him forward. When we reached his car, he fell against the door and hung there gasping.

"Get in," I said. "I've got to get a bomb out of that engine."

"There is no bomb. I caught him before he had the chance."

I looked back. Already I could hear Aaron stumbling through the bushes. "I'll take your word for it. Get in!"

"Damn it, I'm wounded. I can't drive."

"Well, you better learn fast, because your friend there is on his way to put a bullet in your head."

Wilson said something I didn't catch—probably unprintable anyway—and fell into the driver's seat. I got in on the other side and held my breath while he turned the key, still expecting to be blown into orbit. All three hundred eighty horses roared into action—but no explosion. I sighed my relief just as Aaron popped through the trees.

"Shoot 'im, Chessick!" Wilson yelled.

"Shut up and move."

I beaded my pistol on Aaron's face. Wilson hit the gas. Bushes and leaves exploded high into the air as the tires tore into the earth. I swung my aim to the rear window, ready to put a hole in Aaron the moment he leveled that silencer at the car, but he only stood there frantically waving his arms, his face contorted with yelling. Then he disappeared as we lurched around the corner. We ran a stop sign, dodged a kid, mowed down a row of hedges and took another corner onto the main drag and settled to a mere fifty.

I leaned back against the door and leveled the pistol on Wilson's side. "I'm almost beginning to like you," I said. "You're the only person I know who gets beat up more than I do."

"Go to hell," Wilson mumbled. "Where are we going?"

"Pick up the Cabrillo Freeway north. We've got some talking to do."

"Damn it, Chessick, I'm wounded. I'm dying."

"Yeah, that's what I thought once before and I almost lost half my teeth over it. You'll live. It's only a superficial flesh wound. It's not even bleeding any more. So drive. And talk."

"What about?"

"Let's start with what happened back there."

"All right. You've got the gun. I came back to my car to make a report. There's a radio under the back seat."

"What were you following me for?"

"Whaddaya think? To see where you were going."

"Oh boy, this is going to be fun," I said. "Go on."

"I found some wire and plastic explosive on the ground and figured somebody had planted a bomb. I opened the hood and checked. No bomb. As soon as I closed the hood, your fat friend sticks that silencer in my ear and takes me for a walk in the woods. Then we had a picnic."

"Yeah, it looked like fun. Who is he?"

"Name's Aaron. Same character who got you off the hook in San Francisco. That's all I know about him."

"How do I know you're not lying?"

"Damn it, Chessick, didn't you have the sense to look at my credentials when you stole my money?"

"Okay, so you're a private detective and Owen was a shoe salesman and Aaron's just a nice peaceable real estate salesman. Yeah, and the whole world's just peachy keen. We'll pretend you're telling the truth. Next question. Who are you working for. And don't give me any crap about Papa Markham."

Wilson was silent, staring at the road. We came out of the residential area and swung down the ramp to the freeway. I waited until we were on open road before I pressed the question.

"You've had a rough day," I said. "And I'm going to feel very guilty and sad about having to chop you up some more. But by God, if you don't . . ."

"Bob Merril," Wilson said.

I sucked in a hard breath and it stuck in my throat like a hunk of cactus. "Merril? How long . . ."

"Since Sunday morning. His wife must have talked him into it. He called me back less than an hour after you left."

"Called you back? Then you were the detective he phoned to check on Ladd."

"You're pretty slow sometimes, Chessick. Do you really think Merril could have followed you without being noticed after you left San Francisco? That took a real professional. I was following you—Merril was behind me. I had a small radio installed in his car as soon as I took the job, so he didn't even have to follow me. After you were dropped off in Los Gatos, I told him to give you a lift and try to make a deal. Then when he left you in Santa Cruz, I picked up the trail again."

"You said you were going to use the radio. Merril's here in Dago?"

"No, T-town. But you lemme at that radio and I'm gonna tell him I quit. This game is too big for us civilians. Chessick, you and everybody you touch is dead. These boys don't mess around. As soon as they find that microfilm, every Commie and F.B.I. gun in the country is going to be pointed right at your head."

"F.B.I.? What are you . . ."

"Wake up, Chessick. This isn't good guys and bad guys. It's just bad guys and bad guys. I don't know who Ladd is, but his department has a reputation. When you're fighting an enemy like the Commies, you've got to play just as dirty as they do. Did you ever wonder how Aaron survived even ten minutes after exposing himself by getting you out of jail? If he was a Commie, the F.B.I. would have gunned him down days ago."

"Are you trying to tell me Aaron's with the F.B.I.?"

"The Commies—the F.B.I., who knows? They both look just the same—just as ugly—when they're planting a bomb in your car or pumping bullets into you."

"Okay, what have you found out?"

"Not much. I talked to Ma Fedlow just after you left."

"Then you found out about the billikin. What about Aaron?"

"He doesn't know. He was too busy playing with plastic explosive to follow me after I left the car."

"Follow you? I thought he was following me."

"That's what I can't understand. Every time I ditch the bastard, I turn around and he's right on my tail again. He must be psychic or something. I lose him in Tijuana and right out of nowhere he picks me up again in Dago. I can't get rid of him."

I threw my head back and laughed. No wonder I hadn't noticed Aaron following me. This big hot-rod must have run him a merry chase. "Didn't you find that transmitter I put in your trunk?" I asked.

Wilson's face blanched white. "What transmitter? Is it still there?"

"It is unless . . ." I didn't finish the sentence. For a moment I just sat stark-still, then I whirled toward the rear window. "What kind of car is he driving?"

"A new Ford. Blue."

"Well, you better step on it," I said. "He's coming up fast."

He was way back, doing maybe ninety and weaving in and out of the rush-hour traffic like a drunken torpedo. The Buick shot ahead, pinning me momentarily back against the seat, and glancing sideways I saw the speedometer bolt suddenly then slow to a gradual climb. The blue Ford already had its speed up and that gave Aaron a good edge. Already I could make out his face through the windshield. He seemed terrified. Maybe hundred-mile-an-hour chases weren't in his contract. I lifted the pistol so he could see it over the top of the seat.

"Faster," I yelled.

But Wilson already had it floored and that wasn't enough. A red light was blinking far behind, but the roar of the engine drowned out any siren. Besides, I had other things to worry about. We whipped past two slower vehicles, and once we were clear Aaron moved up parallel on my side. I aimed the pistol through the window. One glint of steel in Aaron's hand and his face would have disappeared into hamburger. But his gun was out of sight. For a few seconds he was only inches away, his mouth open and yelling, his hand gesturing up and down.

"The brakes," he screamed. "The brakes!"

Wilson swung right. There was the sharp crash of metal as we hit glancing off the side. I grabbed at the arm rest as the Buick skidded, wagging her ass end like an excited dog, and slowly regained control. Aaron skidded away behind us, hit the shoulder, held momentarily, it seemed, in midair, then crawled slowly to a near-halt back on the road. It was all too fast for much thinking, but a rather terrifying idea was forming in my mind without benefit of words.

"Slow down," I screamed. "Slow down!"

But it was already too late. There was a small compressed explosion from underneath, hardly enough even to jolt the car, but no less frightening for that. My eye was already focused on Wilson's right foot. He hit the brake softly, but there was no resistance. The pedal just slid to the floor as easily as though Wilson had stepped into a plate of mush.

His reaction was automatic. His left hand shot out and wrenched at the emergency brake. Nothing. The car didn't even jolt.

"Oh my God Jesus Christ Almighty," Wilson said.

I didn't know whether he was cursing or praying, but God or devil, it didn't matter in the least who came to our rescue now. I glanced at the speedometer. We were up to a hundred thirty miles an hour, running smoothly in fourth gear. The two lanes in front of us were dotted sporadically with cars which seemed to be rushing in reverse straight at us. I looked again at Wilson. For a second his face was frozen with panic, his eyes glazed. Then quickly he reached out and turned off the key. We were coasting free now. The only sound was the rush of tires on pavement. I swung my eyes to the speedometer. Hundred twenty-five. Hundred twenty.

We were passing one car on the right. In front of us were two parallel cars covering both lanes. I closed my eyes tight. There was a bump as we hit the cement medial strip, three brief crashes as we clipped the railing, then another bump. I opened my eyes. Miraculously we were back on the road. I looked at Wilson with a sense of awe.

"I'm gonna try and slow her down," he yelled. He reached forward and turned the key back on. The engine caught and the car jerked slightly and surged on. His hand dropped back to the floor shift and shoved it into neutral. "Grab that doorknob, and when I yell 'Jump!'—you jump."

"What about you?"

"I'll kill a hundred people if I let this baby go." He revved the engine. His face was white, every vein on his forehead standing out. His right fist was clamped like a vise over the knob of the shift stick. "Pray for the transmission," he said.

The speedometer read ninety. I held my breath. He shoved his hand forward hard. The roar was deafening. The tires screamed. The speedometer dropped. Eighty— seventy—sixty. The roar merged to a high, piercing wail in my ears. I could smell something hot—burning.

I looked ahead. Only a few hundred yards in front the line of traffic had slowed in both lanes and was running bumper to bumper. We would reach it just about the time we hit an exit ramp and the solid concrete abridgement of the overpass. There was no shoulder to pass on and we were going too fast for the ramp. Beside us were a few feet of grass that dropped abruptly into a water-filled rain gutter.

I turned to Wilson helplessly. He was screaming again, but I could only make out isolated words. ". . . second gear . . . slow . . . jump . . ." His hand was again poised on the stickshift. I knew it couldn't hold. No transmission could hold. But he had to try. It was our only chance. He jerked back on the shift into neutral. The car shot ahead— freewheeling. Again he revved the engine.

We swerved right. For a second the tires touched the grass. Wilson's face was concentrated—listening to the engine. Then his hand moved. Back. Hard. The car seemed to explode. For one brief instant it seemed that we were standing still.

"*Now!*" Wilson yelled. His voice was lost in a loud metallic crash from beneath the car.

I jerked the handle and shoved. The earth went spinning out from under me and I was a little kid's tennis ball arcing up against the sun. Up. Up. Up. Right into the sun itself.

SIXTEEN

A hand gripped my hair and pulled my face from the water. I looked up. Aaron was standing above me.

"Come on, hurry," he said.

I groaned and tried to fall back. The water was cool and soft. Aaron stooped down, grappled one of my arms over his shoulder and stood up again.

"Come on, Mr. Chessick," he pleaded. "There's going to be cops all over in a few seconds. You don't want to talk to the cops, do you?"

"No," I mumbled, "I don' wanna talka da cops."

The embankment seemed like Mount Everest, and Aaron wasn't the best guide in the world. He did everything except use pulley and tackle to get me up. But we made it. Then I was sitting in the front seat of a blue Ford, gazing through the windshield at the crowd of cars and people gathered about a bonfire ahead of us.

That explosion I had heard just before I jumped had been the transmission. It had obviously blown apart. Wilson would have been freewheeling again. He had tried for the ramp but hadn't made it. The Buick had jumped the curb, crossed the triangle of bushy earth and slammed into the wall of the overpass. There was a black splotch running all the way up the cement where the flames had erupted from the first explosion.

Aaron pulled slowly into the right lane. A cop with a flashlight motioned us up the ramp. Aaron followed the ramp around on the overpass and down the other side and headed back south toward Dago.

"How'd you do it?" I asked, running my hands over my body to count the bruises. At least no bones were sticking out. And the billikin was still safely in my pocket.

"I was in vehicle maintenance for a while in the Navy," Aaron answered cordially enough. "And I learned all about brakes. You'd be surprised how little plastic explosive is required to blow a brakeline."

Which was, of course, why Wilson hadn't discovered any bomb. He was looking for it in the wrong place. Perhaps the explosive had been wired with a delayed detonator to the accelerator linkage to explode shortly after Wilson pressed the gas pedal to the floor. After tailing Wilson for a while, Aaron must have known something of his driving habits. The emergency brake wouldn't require any bomb. Just clip a few wires.

"You should thank me," Aaron suggested gaily. "After all, I did everything possible to warn you, even after you so rudely attacked me."

"I'd rather thank Wilson. He could have jumped himself, but he didn't want anybody else to get killed."

"Ah, isn't it a pity that all heroes end up too dead to boast of their exploits. It's a fact of life you might ponder, Mr. Chessick."

"Yeah," I said. I absently felt for a pistol, even though I knew I had lost it. Anyway, it was nice while it lasted. "Where to now? Some secret Commie hideout?"

"Quite the contrary, Mr. Chessick. If I had so desired, believe me I could have picked you up any of a dozen different occasions. Besides, you're assuming too much. How do you know I'm not with the F.B.I. and your friend was a Russian agent?"

"Oh, come off it. That nifty little trick you pulled on his car would have made a real mess if Wilson hadn't taken it off the highway. If the F.B.I. operates like that, I'll find me a new country."

"Well, the F.B.I. doesn't always have complete control over its operatives in the field. Now that you mention the possible consequences, I am deeply sorry about the whole affair."

"Oh, my God," I mumbled. "Well, before you go on a crying jag, how about telling me where you're taking me?"

Aaron smiled. "Why, back to your hotel, of course. We don't want to be any trouble to you, Mr. Chessick. We want you to just go on leading your calm, ordinary life."

Carla was sitting at the vanity in her panties and bra brushing her hair when I came in. She turned and her lips parted to say something, then formed a nearly perfect "O" and she uttered a squeak of astonishment from deep down in her throat.

"Chess," she exclaimed, "you've been fighting again."

"You oughta see the other guy," I said.

She started to run to me, but I moved away from her and sat down on the bed with my face in my hands. I could feel her standing above me, vaguely afraid, waiting. "It's two dead now. That's a pretty good score."

"You killed . . ."

"No. A man named Aaron. He may be a Communist assassin. He probably pulled the hat-pin job on Owen, too. What do you know about him?"

"Nothing. Nothing. Chess, tell me what's going on. I thought that thing in San Francisco was all over with."

I ignored her. "Aaron was seen with Aimee in a Frisco bar. That means they're on the same team. Last night somebody slipped LSD into my beer. Maybe Deke. Maybe Aimee." I looked up at her. Her eyes had formed quarter-sized circles to match the "O" of her lips. "Maybe you," I said.

"Chess, I don't know what you're talking about. Murders . . . Communist assassins . . . Aimee . . . Aimee's been a friend of mine for years. Everybody knows her. And I thought you took the LSD. Chess, I don't . . ."

I grabbed her wrist and jerked her down to her knees and held her there. Her face was as white as her hair. Her eyes began to wet with pain. "You're hurting me," she whispered, almost inaudibly.

"It's elementary logic, baby. Aaron's a Commie. Aimee is seen with Aaron. That kind of makes her a little pink in my book. Then you take me to a very convenient drug-feast where Aimee's waiting. *Waiting!* I wasn't followed. She was waiting. So just what does that make you?"

Carla began to cry. "I don't know. I don't know. It doesn't make any sense."

I let her go and lay back on the bed. She was right. It didn't make any sense. It was inconceivable that Carla Markham could be a Communist agent, inconceivable that I could meet an agent by such a convenient but improbable accident. But who the hell else knew where we were going? Deke? Okay, so I could play games with that surmise, too. Just by accident I meet a girl in a bar who just by accident happens to be the ex-lover of a man who just by accident happens to be a Communist agent who . . . No, the odds were still a billion to one against such fantastic coincidences. But if I ruled out the improbabilities, then just how the hell were the Commies following *ahead* of me.

At least one thing was finally clear. With or without Carla, I couldn't escape them. That left only one course of action. Find what they were looking for and try to get it to the F.B.I. before the Reds knew I had it. Until I had that microfilm clutched in my hand, I would lose nothing by believing in Carla's innocence. And after that . . .

"Chess," Carla whispered, still kneeling beside the bed, crying softly. "Chess, please don't hurt me again."

"Yeah," I said. "Come here."

She got up and lay down beside me with her tear-stained face burning against my neck. I stroked her hair gently. "All right," I said. "How's your checkbook holding up?"

She stopped crying and I felt her lips widen to a grin on my neck. "You gigolo," she murmured.

"I thought you might like to get away from all this. Take a little vacation somewhere."

Carla pushed herself up on her elbows and looked down at me, smiling, her face glistening with smeared tears. "Can we really, Chess? You promise. Someplace far away. The Riviera. Or Hawaii."

"Oh, those places went out with the twist," I said. "This year everybody who is anybody is going to Alaska."

Carla had slept fifteen hours straight after the party, and the aftereffects of the drug she had taken plus the overdose of sleep had effectively clipped the wings she had been flying around with the previous night. She had fallen into a mood which I had not yet encountered, a sort of quiet, sublime happiness, like a schoolgirl caught in the raptures of her first real crush. She spoke hardly a word all day, and that night when we made love her body responded almost without passion, but with a deeper, more honest intimacy than I had ever known. She didn't sleep at all, and when I woke gasping from billikin nightmare, she was there, smiling down at me through the darkness, her fingers moving softly over my brow.

The mood was still holding by the time we got to the airport the next afternoon, but the lack of sleep had mellowed her to the point where she could do nothing but hang onto my arm, her head resting on my shoulder, her eyes closed and an embarrassingly satisfied smile on her lips.

We got a prop plane out of San Diego to Los Angeles, where we were booked so tight we had about ten seconds—or so it seemed—to change to a jet that would take us to the Seattle–Tacoma airport, where we would change again to a jet through to Alaska. In the belief that not too many people would be following the same schedule I was, I had carefully observed the faces on the plane from Dago, so I could match them against the faces on the flight to Seattle. Only four passengers made the change—an old lady and a middle-aged woman, possibly mother and daughter, a marine lieutenant and a professorial type sporting a carefully barbered goatee. None of the faces was familiar, but I hadn't really had a good look at the professor since he somehow got to the head of the line on both flights and chose his seat far forward near the cockpit.

I had bought a new business suit before we left Tijuana, and I was feeling clean and respectable again. Some flesh-colored shaving talc had done wonders for the bruises on my face. Carla slept against my shoulder, breathing softly under the throaty hum of the turbines. When the FASTEN YOUR SEAT BELT light went out, I got a pillow for Carla from the stewardess and walked back to the toilet to survey the passengers behind me.

It was the usual collection of ladies, kids, servicemen and business executives. I checked out each face in turn, but could remember none of them. The man in the rear seat was reading a *U.S. News and World Report.* He was a ruggedly handsome man in his late forties, with receding, slightly grayish hair and wearing a gray business suit. I had checked him out in the waiting room and quickly dismissed him. Now my eyes came back to his face and held, not so much with recognition as a vague discomfort. He saw me looking at him and glanced up, smiled, nodded and returned to his magazine.

I entered the bathroom and for several seconds stood leaning over the sink. My palms and forehead had begun to perspire and there was a slight nausea in my stomach. I closed my eyes, searching the darkness for his face somewhere in the past few days. But it wasn't there. I felt with an absolute certainty that I had never seen the man before, yet the mere sight of him had filled me with a strange, indefinable horror.

It was several minutes before the nausea disappeared. I splashed cold water on my face and combed my hair in the mirror. Then I turned and opened the door.

The professor with the goatee was standing outside, waiting. For a moment we were face to face. The shock of recognition sent the nausea washing back through my entrails in cold waves. It was really an amateurish and absurd disguise —merely a dime-store beard glued on around the mouth and a hair tint. If I had gotten a good look at him from fifty feet away, I would have known that face.

"Merril," I whispered.

"Excuse me," he said and shoved past me and closed the door.

By the time I got back to my seat the nausea had settled to a dull dizziness. I couldn't understand it. I got on the plane knowing I would be tailed, so why get sick about it? It wasn't Merril. That was just a predictable shock at seeing him here. But even after I had recognized him, Merril had refused to recognize me, which meant that he knew we were being watched, perhaps even by who. His "Excuse me" had been spoken only loud enough to be carried a few chairs up the aisle, which brought it back to the man in the gray suit.

It wasn't hard to figure how Merril had found me. He knew what hotel I was staying at in Tijuana. As soon as he learned on the radio that his private eye was dead, he would have taken over the tail himself. Or he might have been watching the hotel anyway, tailing Carla.

My sickness was swiftly replaced by a burning anger. I already had enough problems without trying to keep Merril alive. Well, we would have to change planes in Seattle, and even if I had to knock him out and tie him up, that was as far as he was going.

I glanced back quickly along the aisle. The man in the

gray suit was still engrossed in his magazine. His eyes didn't even move toward me. If this man was on my tail, he was a damned thorough professional. Merril was just coming out of the men's room. I turned back and made a pretense of looking through the window past Carla's sleeping face. The stewardess stopped and asked me if I wanted a magazine. I shook my head and turned back to the window. I could hear Merril speaking with the stewardess. A moment of silence. Then there was a slight shuffle and something hit me on the arm. I whirled, my fist tight, my arm cocked for an upward thrust. I was staring into the bland, absurd, goateed face of Merril. There was a slight shine of spirit gum around the edges of his beard.

"You damn clown," I whispered through my teeth.

"Oh, excuse me," Merril said loudly. "I'm terribly sorry. It's these planes, you know. I get dizzy. One would think as much as I've flown, I would get used to it. It's the motion. Really, it's quite absurd. But you will pardon me, sir."

"Don't overdo it," I whispered, but Merril was already gone, weaving along the aisle, holding on to the backs of the seats and apologizing to each passenger in turn.

In my lap was a small folded piece of paper. I turned to Carla to make sure she was still sleeping. She opened her eyes, looked at me, yawned, smiled, closed her eyes and snuggled again into the pillow. As soon as I was certain she was asleep, I reached a safety brochure from the pouch in the seat in front, slid the note into it, opened it and read:

> I know how; I know who; I know why. And you
> know what. Together that information adds up to
> a million dollars. Meet me in the last toilet stall in
> the men's room at the Seattle–Tacoma airport.
> Don't allow yourself to be followed.

At the bottom of the note was a large underlined afterthought:

TRUST NO ONE!

SEVENTEEN

_____

We landed at the Seattle–Tacoma airport on schedule at slightly after eight. Carla was asleep under my arm. I didn't wake her until the aisles were clear, then I nudged her shoulder gently. She gave a slight moan in her throat and looked up at me with eyes that might once have belonged to a little girl. The stewardess came by and asked if my wife was feeling all right. That sounded good. Carla. Wife. I had been signing her as "Mrs." for a couple days now, but it was cheap then—like a traveling salesman's joke. But now it was innocent, like two kids playing house. No, my wife wasn't sick, just happy.

I helped her to her feet. She forced a grin and fell against me, so that I had to lead her down the aisle with my arm around her waist. Crazy newlyweds, the stewardess would be thinking. That sounded good, too. Chessick, the world's most practiced damned fool, was getting sentimental again. There would be plenty of time for that, I told myself, after the double cross. But there was too much warmth there. The complexion was too smooth, the hair too blond. Sweet young things don't double-cross. And leopards don't kill.

Inside the milling terminal I set her on an empty couch, where she could curl up and go back to sleep, and I headed for the PNA counter to verify my tickets through to Alaska. There was a forty-five-minute stopover, and I hadn't forgotten my latrine appointment with Merril, but I wanted to make sure I wasn't being watched. The man in the gray suit was like a cancer inside of me, a spreading virus of apprehension that was eating away at my guts. He was moving away from the ticket counter as I came up, swinging a leather attaché case at his side. The sense of familiarity was stronger in absence. From the back he looked like any other well-kept organization man. District manager for a loan company, probably. Home in Forest Park. Two kids. Active in the P.T.A. There was nothing terrifying about him. Chessick's imagination was working overtime again. Yet I was almost beginning to trust my imagination. That was about all there was left to trust.

I skipped the check-in counter—there would still be plenty of time for that—and followed the man in the gray suit, walking about fifty feet behind. He stopped a passing stewardess and asked her something. She pointed toward what I could see was the bar. He thanked her with a nod of his head and moved off toward it. The bar would be as good a place as any to get a better look at his face. I checked my watch. Still forty minutes. I started after him again.

Then I was standing still. For a minute I didn't even know why. The old feeling of nightmare horror was moving through my body, paralyzing me. My eyes were gazing across the lobby in cinemascope, taking in the whole area as though refusing of their own accord to focus on any one object. A man reading a newspaper. A fat woman shaking her finger at a kid. A group of tourists looking through the window at the darkening sky. Carla curled up and asleep on the couch. Several people milling about the paperback bookstall. Three nuns seated stiffly on a couch.

Then my eyes found him. Not the man in the gray suit, but another, even more familiar. He was walking with his back to me toward one of the ramps. A short, squat man, almost bald, wearing a plaid sports jacket. For a long time I just watched him, the blind terror wiping out rational thought. I shoved the fear down until there was at least enough room in my mind to form one word, one name.

Aaron.

I heard my throat bark out a sharp yell that rang with a metallic quality on the walls. He disappeared around the corner down one of the plane ramps without looking back. I ran after him. My footfalls rattled above a sudden hush. A baby began to cry. I yelled again. The long windowed ramp stretched away—deserted but for three or four people frozen in place and staring at me. Aaron was gone. I ran a few steps and halted. A door was open, leading down a metal stair to the field. I started toward it, but a voice called out sharply. I stopped and turned. A man came up wearing a blue pilot's uniform.

"Something wrong?" he asked coldly.

"No," I said, "I thought I saw a friend."

"Did you?"

"No. It was a mistake."

"Okay," he said without inflection. He moved by me and closed the offending door and locked it with a key. There was a sign on the door that said, FOR AUTHORIZED PERSONNEL ONLY.

I could feel people watching me as I walked back to the lobby and headed for the men's room. The terror was gone, replaced by the familiar sensation of fatigue and shame. I was floating in a void, isolated from all of humanity, from all that was good and decent and human. I pushed slowly into the men's room. A Negro offered me a towel and razor. I

passed him without speaking and walked into the aseptic
white corridor that was lined on one side with urinals and
on the other with toilet booths. I was outside of it now. It
was all far away. It tasted flat in my mouth like last week's
leftover beer.

When I got to the last stall, I didn't even bother to knock.
I shoved on the door. It was locked. I dropped a dime in the
slot and shoved again. Merril was sitting on the toilet, fully
clothed. He stared at me as I come in. His eyes bulged out
from their sockets, and you could see the tiny red veins
around the pupils. There was a slightly bluish quality to his
flesh. His face was wet, and long strips of damp brown hair
straggled over his forehead. The mouth was a gargoyle's
mouth, half open, contorted downward at the corners and
filled with a bloated tongue. The phony goatee hung down
from one corner of his chin. Half of his mustache was gone,
leaving a glistening smear of spirit gum on the left side of
his upper lip. I looked down between his open legs. The
other half of the mustache was floating in the pale, clear
water of the toilet bowl.

The technical aspects weren't hard to figure out. Merril
would have opened to Aaron's knock, thinking it was me.
Maybe Aaron had a pistol. Maybe just a sharp jab to the
throat or a chop to the neck. There would be a dozen ways a
professional could do it silently. I only hoped Merril was
unconscious when Aaron was holding his face under water.
No man should have to know he's dying that way.

I thought about Merril in college. I thought about his
bringing bum Chessick a modicum of hope in a Frisco jail. I
thought about the photograph of his daughter he had
showed me. I thought about the wife he had loved even to
death. I thought about a lot of things.

There aren't many certainties in this life. There's not
much you can plan and be sure of. But I knew one thing.
Aaron was going to die. He was going to die slow and ugly.

I shook myself from the trance, stepped inside and closed
the door. My motions were methodical now. At moments of

extreme horror, there are only two defenses. You either panic or your mind dulls over, obliterates all emotion. I was too far along for panic. That had all been expended long ago. There was nothing but a vague seething in my stomach, like air bubbles rising from the bottom of a pan of water just before it comes to a boil.

I pulled my handkerchief out and covered my right hand with it, then took Merril's handkerchief from his jacket and covered my left. His pants pockets revealed nothing out of the ordinary—the usual coins and keys. His wallet was in his inside jacket pocket. I skipped through it quickly. Credit cards, the pictures of his wife and daughter, social security card, selective service, driver's license, a long-expired note for an appointment, wallet calendar, three dollar bills, a ten and two twenties. Under the flap they used to call a secret compartment before it became so popular, I found a folded piece of slick paper. It was a page torn from a book, printed in small type in five or six columns. Something had been circled in red pencil. I shoved the paper into my shirt pocket and replaced the wallet intact. In the other inside jacket pocket was a checkbook and a folded green plastic case of travelers checks.

I took his jacket off and tied his hands behind him to the plumbing and then bound one leg to the toilet seat with his belt to make sure he didn't slip off or fall over on his face before I was at least a thousand miles away. If there was no rush on the bathroom which might cause some emergency case to knock on the door even after seeing the legs underneath, Merril might not be discovered for hours. I only needed about two and a half hours and I would be in Alaska. After checking over my work for anything forgotten, I flushed the toilet for the benefit of any passers-by, and while half of Merril's mustache swirled down the drain, I quickly wiped off the door with the handkerchief, ducked and looked underneath, then opened the door, rubbing the chrome coin slot free of fingerprints.

"Hey," someone yelled.

I spun. He was standing at the other end of the latrine, a thin man in a dark shirt with blue jeans. "Hey," he repeated again and started toward me at a skipping run."Hold that door open."

I slammed the door quickly and shoved the two handkerchiefs in my pants pockets. He slowed to a trot, then a walk, and stopped in front of me with a slight sneer curling his lips.

"Nice work, buddy," he said.

"What do you want?"

"I just wanted you to leave the damned door open. Is that so hard? I ain't got a dime. I only carry thousand-dollars bills."

"It's clogged anyway," I said.

"I heard you flush it. Didn't sound clogged to me, miser."

"It's clogged. Too much paper." I reached in my pocket and felt past the handkerchief and the billikin to the coins. "Here's a dime."

He looked at it curiously, then took it. "Okay. Better tell somebody about it being clogged."

"Yeah, I will."

I moved past him toward the door. After a few feet I looked back. He had moved to the last stall and was about to deposit the dime.

"Hey," I yelled, "I told you that one was clogged."

He turned to look at me with an ugly grin creasing his lips. "So I like 'em clogged," he said.

I walked back. "What the hell's the matter with you?"

"Look, fella, I don't take the screw from nobody. I seen you before. Big-shot organization man. All slicked up in your fancy pants and pretty tie. You see a guy on the short end of the stick, and just because maybe his shirt ain't clean, you wanna put the screw to him, uh. You heard me yell. You didn't hafta slam the door."

"Look," I said, "if I wasn't telling the truth, why would I have given you the dime?"

" 'Cause you're scared, mister. Scared. Well, I think you're lying, and I'm gonna find out."

He turned back toward the door, and I grabbed his collar and swung him around and hit him once in the solar plexus and brought my elbow up hard into his face. He stumbled backward, bounced off the wall and dropped forward on his chest.

There was a short, throaty "arf," like the barking of a seal, from behind me. The Negro attendant was staring at me with mouth and eyes wide open. He let go with the "arf" again and ran through the door. For the moment I was alone. The punk was out, but he wouldn't be out for long—and I needed maybe thirty minutes before the plane left. I reached down, adjusted his head to a better position, stood up and kicked him in the neck just below the ear. With luck he might not wake up for an hour or more and might not be coherent for days. I should have felt sorry for the poor bastard—just another slob who had been on the bottom for so long he thought anybody wearing a tie was the enemy. But I didn't have time for such luxurious emotions.

A man came in and went to one of the mirrors, glanced at it and turned to me with an expression of shock and incredulity. He started forward as though to say something, but it stuck in his throat. The door opened again and a man in a blue suit entered with the Negro attendant trailing behind.

"What's going on here?" Blue Suit yelled.

"Are you the manager?" I bellowed before he had even gotten the words out. "Well, I hope so, because I'm gonna make a big damned stink about this. What kind of place are you running here? The local pervert palace? I'm fed up to my teeth. When a man can't even walk into an airport without every gawddamned queer in the country making a pass at him, then you can bet it's about time something was done."

"Please, sir. Please," Blue Suit begged.

"Please, hell! I'm not without some influence in this town, and by God I plan to see that this sort of thing is cleaned up.

Do you realize that little children come in here! Just the thought of it makes me sick."

"Please, sir. This is very rare, and I assure you it will not happen again. We have an attendant here all the time in order to prevent such sordid people from . . ."

"I demand my rights. I want a cop. I plan to swear out a complaint."

"Please, sir, you can, of course, understand that any publicity would be detrimental to the terminal out of all proportion to the offense. And I'm sure a man of your standing must be very busy. You understand how time-consuming . . ."

"Well, I do have to catch a plane to Chicago," I admitted brusquely. "But I demand some guarantee that this man will be sufficiently punished."

"I promise you, sir, that I will take care of everything. I assure you, your outrage is no less than mine, but you understand, of course, the need for discretion in such sordid matters."

"Yes, I suppose I did lose my head for a moment. It was the thought of the children, you understand. You see, I have two boys myself and just the idea . . ."

"Yes, yes. I truly sympathize. I, too, have a boy. I assure you, I will personally reprimand this . . . this . . . pervert. Now, once I clean this thing up, perhaps I could buy you a drink."

"No, no," I said, heading for the door, "I'm running late now. You do what you must. And remember—it's for the children."

Once outside the door, I fell back against the wall and for a moment I thought I was going to be sick. But I made it.

Thirty minutes later I looked through the window past the sleeping face of Carla to the swiftly disappearing lights of the airport as we rose into the clouds. There was a good chance that Merril would not be found for some time. And I wasn't without experience concerning management's atti-

164

tude toward bums. No one would believe his story about clogged toilets. The pathetic bastard. If he thought he was being persecuted before, he would be lucky to end up somewhere this side of paranoia now.

For the moment I felt strangely safe. I had watched the people in the waiting room and neither Aaron nor the man in the gray suit had been among them. They knew where I was going, of course, and I was fairly sure to meet them again in Alaska, but for the hour-fifty minutes of the flight, it was just me and Carla. I felt exhausted and mildly elated. This was the short interim between horrors. But I could worry about the rest later.

When the NO SMOKING light went off, I reached in my pocket for a cigarette. Instead I found a crumpled piece of paper. I fingered it with absent curiosity. A nice little piece of paper with a guarantee signed by God to life, liberty and the pursuit of happiness forever after. It wasn't. It was the page torn from a book I'd taken off Merril's corpse. The same page out of the *Who's Who* that I had examined in the Frisco library two hundred years or so ago.

I thought with a smile that tearing that page out of a library book was probably the only crime Merril had ever committed. But that meant he must have thought it damned important. Among the list of Kreigger's published works— the multicavity magnetrons and the servomechanisms— Merril had circled a single title in red pencil: "A New Look at the Contribution of James Braid."

Was this Merril's big discovery—the discovery he had been killed for? It didn't make sense. The article was published in a German magazine in 1936, while Kreigger was still a student. And who the hell was James Braid? I vaguely recalled the name from my college science courses. A nineteenth-century scientist who had made a significant contribution to something or other. Since Kreigger at that time only wrote on optical physics, it must have been in the field of light. But I had never taken physics in college, so how would I have heard of some obscure scientist in that field. Unless it was in another field, one I had studied. Like biology. Or anthropology. Or psychology.

Psychology.

And then, very calmly, very slowly, without the sound of trumpets, like the steady drip drip of rain in a puddle, the whole incredible plot began to fall in place.

EIGHTEEN

Probably most tourists in Alaska see mountains, forests and totem poles. Not Robert Chessick. All I saw were billikins. They were everywhere. The airport gift shop had a year's supply of them glued onto everything from beer openers to silverware. Every travel brochure carried at least one picture of a billikin. The local newspaper advertised a Billikin Drive-In Theater, a Billikin Mobile Homes Sales and a Billik-Inn Liquor Store. Even the cabbie who drove us to a motel in Spenard, a suburb of Anchorage, had one of the grinning little ivory beasts dangling from his key chain.

That was bad news. If I figured right, Aaron and his friends weren't looking for microfilm at all. They might not know it yet, but they were looking for a billikin—any billikin. It wouldn't take even a low-order idiot long to draw a relationship between the ubiquitous ivory carvings and Kreigger's rough sketch in the bar in Frisco. Once they knew what they were looking for, my life would be about as valuable as the diary of Malcolm X at a Ku Klux Klan book-burning. That meant I had to work fast. I had to get it all together into a nice, neat package and tie it up with a prettty ribbon and hope that I could deliver it to the F.B.I. before the Commies picked me up.

The day was shot by the time we got settled in our motel room, so there was nothing to do but lock the door, say my prayers and go to sleep. I woke at ten A.M. Carla was gone. There was a note on the dresser informing me that she was out souvenir-hunting and would be back in two or three hours. That was fine with me. I had to move fast just to stay alive, and I didn't need Carla hanging on my shoulder.

Before I even dressed, I got on the phone to the Chamber of Commerce to find out what civilian organization had the contract for the Clear Radar Site. The sweet thing on the other end of the line thought it was Philco but wasn't sure and suggested I call Greater Anchorage, Incorporated. I tried that. She suggested that all radar installations were exclusively run by the Air Force, but I had better call the field office of the U.S. Department of Commerce. There I found out it was definitely the Radio Corporation of America.

At RCA I got hold of a secretary fourth-class who politely informed me that since Clear was not part of the White Alice Project, RCA had nothing to do with it.

"I know it's not White Alice," I said. "It's BMEWS."

"Thank you, sir," she said efficiently and switched me to another line.

Half an hour and a sore ear later I finally got hold of a man who had worked at the Clear Site in 1960.

"My name is Robert . . . uh . . . Luce," I said. "I'm a correspondent for *Time* magazine. We're doing a feature story on Otto Kreigger and I thought since you worked with him, you might be able to supply me with some information on the man."

There was a long silence. "I'm afraid, sir," the voice said stiffly, "that I could be of no help to you. I knew Dr. Kreigger only by sight."

"Well, perhaps you could refer me to someone who did know him."

Another silence. "Sir, I don't think you quite understand the position of RCA concerning Dr. Kreigger. We would, of course, like to pretend he never existed. Since that is impossible, our only other recourse is to avoid any further publicity concerning the matter. RCA has spent years establishing the high reputation it holds today, and you can understand the effect of such adverse publicity. We want only to make it quite clear that while Dr. Kreigger was working with us, his security record was unimpeachable. As you must know, Dr. Kreigger was working for the United States Government—not RCA—at the time of his defection."

"Yes, certainly," I said. "That's precisely the point we want to clarify in our story. All evidence points to the fact that Kreigger was an upright and honorable man who was stricken, at the end, with a fit of temporary insanity. You can see, certainly, that an angle of this nature would go a long way in erasing any misunderstandings concerning Kreigger's association with RCA which might have resulted from the early news reports."

Another silence. "Yes, I can see how such a story might be beneficial to this corporation. However, all employees have been instructed not to speak of the matter to anyone except authorized agents of the federal government, so I'm afraid I can't . . . No, wait a minute. One of Kreigger's best friends hasn't worked for RCA for over three years. He has a homestead near Chugiak. Dr. Sumner Cassidy."

Dr. Cassidy didn't have a phone, so I had to call a store in Chugiak that gave me the number of his nearest neighbor. The neighbor seemed apprehensive about how Cassidy would receive a *Time* reporter, but promised to pass the word on to expect me.

Fifteen minutes later I was driving a rented car east up Fourth Avenue, the main street of Anchorage. In arrogant disregard for its far north location, Anchorage was a sporadically skyscrapered city, quite similar to any of a hundred cities in the "Lower 48." There was no hint of the massive 1964 earthquake until you reached "D" Street, where for the next four blocks the entire north side of Fourth Avenue had dropped twenty feet into the earth, obliterating all the buildings. The last of the rubble had been long since cleared away, and the area was now churning with bulldozers and cranes and hard-hatted construction men attempting to reinforce the unstable ground.

But I didn't have time to play tourist. I stopped at the first hardware store I saw and purchased a small Colt .38 and a box of bullets. Luckily Alaska yet retained enough of its fading frontier quality to obviate gun registration laws.

Sumner Cassidy lived twenty miles north of Anchorage near a scattered collection of stores and junk shops called Chugiak. In this country it seemed that all it took was a bar and a privy to merit a dot on the map and the status of city. Cassidy was well known, and every gas station attendant along the highway gave me specific and exact instructions about how to get to his place, and each attendant was in direct contradiction to the last one I had asked. After almost two hours I found it—a track road jutting abruptly from the highway into the spruce and birch forest.

The road was little more than a jeep trail, and I could hear bushes making metallic rasping sounds along the gas tank. After nearly a mile the trail opened into a large cleared area. At least it was cleared of trees. The entire lot was sprinkled generously with rusting auto and tractor parts, tin cans, fallen tarpaper shanties, a collapsed privy, random piles of rotting branches, a stilted meat cache. The house itself was a small dilapidated log cabin that looked as if it might have been put together without nails. A flat-faced Eskimo child dressed in nothing but a filthy T-shirt and shorts stood looking at me with as vacuous an expression as

I've ever encountered as he absently scratched his enormous
potbelly. At the sound of my car, several other children of
varying ages, all bearing the same uncomprehending gaze,
appeared out of the woods. Feeling vaguely uncomfortable, I
got out of the car and started for the house.

Before I had gone two feet a man appeared in the doorway. He was a short squat man, bare above the waist. His
barrel chest was hidden beneath a carpet of golden hair. A
heavy beard covered the lower part of his face and hung almost to his solar plexus. Above the beard perched two intensely perceptive black eyes.

"Dr. Cassidy, I presume," I said.

For a moment his two black eyes seemed to bore into my
head. Then suddenly he burst into laughter that shook his
whole body and he clutched my hand in both of his and
pumped vigorously, almost crushing my hand.

"That's good! That's very good!" he bellowed. "Very a
propos. 'Dr. Cassidy, I presume.' Very good. That deserves a
drink." He turned back to the door and yelled, "Rosey,
baby. Get out the booze. We got company. Well, whaddaya
think of the place? Robert Chessick, is it? But they don't call
you that. Nobody calls anybody Robert Chessick. What is it?
Lemme guess. Bob. Robbie. Robert."

"Chess," I said.

"Chess. That's good. Good. Never woulda guessed it.
Well, come on in, Chess. Rosey, where the hell's that bourbon? You drink bourbon, Chess? What the hell. If it ain't
bourbon it ain't drinking. Rosey!"

The inside of the house was a compact approximation of
the yard, except it was so dark you couldn't tell what you
were bumping into. There was the enclosed must of tanned
hides, fish, old wood, books, burned frying pans, dogs, kids,
rotting fabrics, moss—each separate odor fighting to exclude
the last remaining morsel of oxygen. The place had origin-
ally been a single room and was now only subdivided by a
random collection of blankets and curtains. A plump woman
in a faded dress shuffled from behind a drape, carrying a

coffee mug of bourbon in each hand. "Jus' bring booze an' make baby," she muttered to no one in particular. "Jus' bring booze an' make baby. Someday I show him. I take pill. No more baby."

"Ah, Rosey honey, is that any way to talk about our charming family?" Cassidy guffawed, slapping her on the buttocks. She muttered something under her breath and shuffled back behind the curtain. I sipped at the bourbon while Cassidy struggled two chairs from the rubbish. "Have a seat, Chess. Don't let Rosey bother you. She's a damned fine hunk of woman, she is. She's just been getting these equality ideas in her head lately. God knows where she picks that crap up. But let me tell you, Chess, you want a real woman, you get yourself an Eskimo. Those gawddamned fancy-assed Caucasian broads—they don't want a husband. A man is just another status symbol, same as a pretty home in the suburbs, right? They crook their little fingers even when they're getting laid. Equality, hell! They won't be satisfied until every man is dressed like a faggot, smells like a pansy and reads *Ladies Home Journal.* Another ten years and the man will feel like some kind of pervert if he climbs on top. But what the hell. Whaddaya say, Chess? How do you like the layout?"

"Well," I stammered, "it's very . . . uh . . . interesting."

"In other words, you want to know what the hell a doctor of physics is doing living like a pig."

"I didn't mean that at all."

Cassidy laughed. "You mean you're too caught up in the social ritual to say it. Look, I'm from New York and California. Got my degree at Harvard. Forty years I played that game. Forty years. Then I came up here on the Clear radar job and I took a look around at these old sourdoughs and I discovered something that nobody had thought of for two centuries. You know what that idea was? Man was supposed to be happy. Sure, everybody says it. But I was the first man in two hundred years to believe it." Now that he was on a favorite subject, Cassidy's homesteader voice and manner suddenly changed into that of the lecturing professor. "You see, out there they believe in corporate happiness. Your boss or your neighbors or your life insurance company or the television commercials all tell you that security is happiness. Security is contentment and contentment isn't happiness. It's a disease that afflicts cows and pigs and allows them to be led easily to the slaughterhouse. Ah, but you didn't come for a lecture. You came from that paean to modern, mediocre man, *Life* magazine . . ."

"*Time*," I corrected.

"Same difference. In any case, you came to reinforce the high standard of American idiocy by pandering to the truly patriotic concept that because Otto Kreigger betrayed the country that nourished him, he must have been at once fascist, Communist, sadist, pacifist, and worst of all, thinker —all that is evil in our Great Society. Xilka, Xilka, besa, besa. A medieval incantation to demons, Mr. Chessick of *Time* magazine. But as you see, no demons appear. Demons, my friend, are products of the mind. And so the Otto Kreigger conjured by the press is merely a product of prevailing superstition. I fear you have come to the wrong place. I can offer you Kreigger only as a friend and a human being—not as a demon."

"Then perhaps I've come to the right place after all. If I believed that Kreigger was a demon, it would hardly require a trip to Alaska to verify that view. In my article I hope to portray Dr. Kreigger as an immensely human man—a man driven by simple misplaced idealism."

Cassidy looked me over curiously. "Aha, Mr. Chessick, you speak my language after all. We must hang a man for his acts, but we must judge him by his motives. You want a portrait of Otto Kreigger. I offer you Pontius Pilate and Neville Chamberlain. Kreigger, too, was a mediocre man of good intentions who was caught up in a surge of history too big for his comprehension. Like many a man before him, Kreigger was destroyed by a mentality that was insufficient to cope with the immensity of his idealism."

"Then you don't believe Kreigger was a genius?"

"A savant of science perhaps, but a genius, no. In theoretical physics he was an absolute wizard, but in the humanities he would never be more than a rank dilettante. He read sufficiently—actually, there was little else to do during the long nights at the Clear Site—but his mind had the typical sophomoric tendency to simplify complex problems into pretty abstractions. Pacifism, humanitarianism, utopianism —all lovely ideals which merely mask terrifyingly complex realities."

"You mentioned the long nights at Clear. Did Kreigger develop any hobbies or interests other than reading?"

"Hundreds of them. We all did. There was nothing else to relieve the boredom. Carpentry, model boats, painting, billiards, poker—even writing poetry—Kreigger tried his hand at all of them."

"Any others? Any persistent or compulsive hobbies? Something he might have become an expert at?"

Cassidy's two black pupils gazed at me from above the dark of his beard. "You have something in mind," he said.

"Hypnotism."

Cassidy laughed. "Ah, so you have done your homework, Chess. That little preoccupation was known only to his closest friends."

"He once wrote an article for a German magazine on the contribution of James Braid."

"Braid . . . James Braid . . ." Cassidy mused. "A nineteenth-century follower of Anton Mesmer, if I remember correctly. Wasn't he the one who gave the name 'hypnotism' to the art?"

"I think so."

Cassidy scratched his beard. "Well, it figures that he wrote that article in Germany. We're a bit more materialistic over here. Hypnotism still has the stigma of the occult. Like séances, it's too often considered a useless parlor game that always possesses an element of fraud. Kreigger was hardly the life-of-the-party type, and he was terribly shy about his interest in hypnotism. Seemed to think everybody would laugh at him. When he found out that I and a couple of others thought it was a serious avocation, he began coming up to my room every night for a little experimentation."

"What kind of experimentation?"

"Oh, the usual. Regression, physical insensitivity to pain, posthypnotic suggestion, that sort of thing."

"What about hypnotizing someone who didn't know he was being hypnotized?"

Cassidy sipped at his drink and thought for a while. "Seems to me we tried it once or twice, but it would only work on a good subject who had been put under several times before. No, wait a minute. I remember once we got in an argument over just that sort of thing. He claimed it could be done if a person were drunk or on drugs. I made a ten-dollar bet he couldn't do it, and I went down to the club and latched on to the first drunk I found—there was a large selection—and brought him back to the room. Kreigger gave him a bottle and got him talking about his home Outside. He was just a young fellow—homesick as hell—and he got pretty maudlin. After a while Kreigger convinced him if he stared long enough into a candle flame, he would see his wife and kid. Ten minutes and he was under. Deep, too."

"Then he could have done it again?"

"I don't know why not."

"What about hypnotizing a man who just plain didn't want to be hypnotized?"

"Well, there's a lot of debate on that particular subject. Kreigger never tried it that I know of, but personally I'm convinced it can be done. In fact, I would guess the Russians have been doing it for years. Have you ever wondered how Stalin got some of those purge trial confessions? You see, Pavlov proved that simply by physical deprivation an animal's will could be broken down almost completely. It would enter a highly suggestible state, very similar to a light hypnotic trance. This, when applied to humans, is brainwashing. But we're more sophisticated now. We can get the same—even more profound—effects with the use of drugs.

Take your so-called 'truth drugs'—pentathol, sodium amytal, scapalomine. All of them wear down the will to resist. The problem is that the barbiturates, which act on the central nervous system, also have a tendency to make a person sleepy and lethargic. Of course, depth hypnotism demands a subject who can concentrate, so none of these drugs would suffice alone. But there are other drugs that work directly on the brain. No pill could ever actually hypnotize a person by itself, but drugs can put a subject in a suggestive state that makes him highly amenable to the talents of a good hypnotist."

That explained a lot. Maybe too much. I couldn't forget that I had once commented on Carla's expert knowledge of drugs.

"Did Kreigger make any other significant experiments?" I asked. "Like, say, the use of a key?"

Cassidy had been slumped in his chair, and at the word "key" he suddenly sat bolt upright, spilling the drink over his pants. For several seconds he just sat there silently staring at me with those two inscrutable black eyes. "Jesus Christ," he muttered, then whirled back toward the draped blanket that hid the kitchen and yelled, " 'Nother shot, Rosey baby." Slowly he turned back to me. "You've *really* been digging, ain't you, Chess? I thought I was the only one who knew about that little experiment."

Rosey shuffled over with the drinks, mumbling almost incoherently, as though she had been sampling the bottle herself, "Bring booze, make baby. That all wife good for. Bring booze, make baby."

When she returned to the kitchen, Cassidy said, "It was a complicated experiment. The whole idea was to block off a portion of a person's mind that would be inaccessible even under further hypnotism, unless a certain object was shown. We did it on one of the engineers who had proven to be a good subject. Kreigger put him under and made him do various things—bark like a dog, stand on his head, the usual tricks. But then while the engineer was still under, Kreigger took a silver dollar out of his pocket, held it up before the engineer and sort of put him in a second trance. I don't understand the dynamics of it, but the silver dollar was a device for separating one compartment of the mind. Kreigger then opened the Bible at random to a page from Job and had the engineer read it, top to bottom. Kreigger told him he wouldn't remember any of what he had read, even under further hypnotism, until he was shown a silver dollar."

"And it worked?"

"Beautifully. To prove that the mind had actually been compartmentalized, Kreigger gave him another posthypnotic suggestion that he wouldn't remember anything that happened while he was in a trance. When he woke up, sure enough, he thought he had been asleep. A couple days later we brought him back up to the room and put him in a trance again. Once under he remembered everything he had done in the previous trance—barking like a dog and all—but absolutely nothing about the page from Job. In fact, he acted as if he had never heard of Job. Then Kreigger showed him a whole range of nickels, dimes, gold charms and what have you, but he still wouldn't remember. But as soon as Kreigger held up the silver dollar, the engineer quoted the page from Job verbatim. I'm not kidding. I was following along in the book and he didn't miss a word. Kreigger had simply closed a door on a certain portion of the engineer's memory, and the silver dollar was the only key that would open it. Not only amazing, but practical, too—especially since once the stored information has been reported, it can be locked up permanently merely by throwing away the key."

"I don't get it. How could you 'throw away the key'?"

"It's quite logical. Certainly if a posthypnotic suggestion can determine that only a coin will unlock the door, then it makes sense, doesn't it, that a further suggestion—that nothing, not even a coin, will do the trick—would close the door permanently, make that compartment of the mind totally inaccessible by any means?"

"I take it this little game could be played using some other object as a key."

"Sure, why not? Could be a real key, a beer can, a certain book—anything—even the Washington Monument if it was handy."

"One more question," I said. "Did Kreigger carry any sort of good-luck charm?"

Cassidy scratched his beard. "No, I don't think so. He wasn't very superstitious. No, wait a minute. Come to think of it, I gave him a billikin on a key chain for Christmas once. Yeah, he used to carry it with him all the time."

NINETEEN

So there it was, tied up in a neat package and ready for delivery. Sure, there were still a couple of details that didn't fit into the box, but I had a hunch the F.B.I. could answer a lot of questions that were outside my limited vision. Only there was one question the F.B.I. had better answer damned fast if the billikin courier was going to make its delivery to the right party. Where the hell were they? Ladd had said he would contact me, but so far he had shown no sign of doing so. Only one thing was sure. The Commies were still on my tail. There was something very un-American about the way Merril had been killed.

Coming out of Cassidy's homestead, I stopped the car only briefly at the highway, then swung north toward Palmer, away from Anchorage. I hadn't decided on running full bore yet, but I needed time to think. Once on the highway, I settled to a low thirty-five miles an hour that would force my tail to either pass me or show himself. A gang of high school kids swung around me in a new Chrysler, yelling at me to get a horse. I held my eyes on the rear-view mirror for five or six miles, then swung off on a dirt side road and drove into the bushes, where I could watch the highway without being seen. A green late-model Chevy passed, two campers and a station wagon full of kids.

One idea was slowly etching itself into my mind. What if the F.B.I. had lost interest in me in San Francisco or I had managed to ditch them along the line? That would mean I was stranded in Alaska with nobody for company but the Commies. I could always turn myself in to the police department or the Anchorage F.B.I. office, but even if the Reds were stupid enough to let me get that far, there was an excellent chance that I would be thrown out on my ear as a publicity nut or a drunk. The Commies had let me get this far because they wanted me to lead them to the key. Now whether they knew what it was or not, they couldn't help but be aware that I knew it. That meant the race was down to the line. They had no choice but to get me before I could contact the F.B.I.

Suddenly I saw it, screened through birch leaves and shaggy spruce. The green Chevy was coming back, moving slowly as though searching for something. I had been waiting too long for this moment for panic or even fear. My nerves settled into a calm anticipation. I reached under the seat and removed the blunt .38. The Chevy passed on out of sight down the highway. I got out of the car and crossed the dirt side road and waited in the bushes, watching the highway for any cars that might be following the Chevy's pattern. If there was going to be a shoot-out, I damned well didn't want to be trapped by thinking I was facing only one man when there might be a follow-up car. But there was none.

Several minutes passed. The Chevy would be searching every side road for perhaps a five-mile stretch. My palms and forehead began to sweat. I was slowly becoming aware of what cowboys meant when they talked about itchy trigger fingers. I had come several thousand miles to get to this little side road off the Glenn Highway, and right here, one way or another, it was going to end. A vague feeling of invulnerability encompassed my body like a glass shield. I had seen too much, come too far. Nothing could touch me now.

There was a slight rustling of bushes behind me. I turned. A gangly yearling moose, poised precariously on spindle legs, was gazing at me through the trees with a dull incoherence reminiscent of Cassidy's children. Presently the yearling was joined by its mother, and they stood side by side, staring at the absurd shadow of Robert Chessick, gun in hand, hiding like a kid in the bushes.

Suddenly both moose turned as one and waddled back into the bushes. Simultaneously the green Chevy swung off the highway and stopped, blocking the entrance to the side road.

A man got out. He was wearing blue jeans and a gray flannel shirt rolled up at the sleeves. A pipe was clenched in his teeth. He carried no gun, nor was there any place on his body where he might have concealed one. His face was vaguely familiar, and yet unfamiliar. He was perhaps forty-five years old, graying hair, deep-set eyes, clean shaven, wide mouth, narrow lips. The face was tough and smart, and you could feel its ingrained authority like static electricity in the air. He walked over to my rented car with long, easy strides and looked inside. Then he hooked his thumbs in his belt and turned and gazed at the bushes near where I was hidden. His face was turned fully toward me.

It took a while for the simple facts to fall together, but when they did there was no surprise. Perhaps in a way I had known it all along, somewhere outside of thinking. I had seen this same face only yesterday, in a jet out of Los Angeles smiling at me over the top of a *U.S. News and World Report*. And I had seen it before that in an LSD nightmare. And once before, out of memory, I had seen that face for one brief second as I kneeled beside the corpse of Alpine Hat, one instant before that practiced knife edge of his hand came down on my neck. And there were other times, too. A different face—a face with a beard.

"All right, don't move, Deke," I said. "Or is the name Ladd?"

I stepped out on the road, where he could see the gun. He watched me with an expression of exquisite boredom. It was Deke, all right—Deke, minus the phony beard, minus the wig, minus the pasted-on eyebrows, probably even minus the contact lenses that would change the color of his eyes, minus the deliberate slouching walk—Deke, the way he would look to his underlings in some monstrous F.B.I. office building in Washington.

"Haven't you had enough heroics yet?" he said. "Put that damned gun away."

"Well, let's just say my usual trusting nature has grown suspicious in the last few weeks. Let me see your credentials."

He removed a black leather case from his shirt pocket and tossed it to me. I noticed even the karate calluses on his knuckles had been powdered or painted over to a flesh color almost indistinguishable from the rest of his hand. The case opened in two halves, like a wallet. Set in the right side was a well-polished gold badge. On the other side was a laminated identification card with a lot of fussy scrolls, a photograph, fingerprints, the name "CN Ladd" and a physical description typed over the imprint of the Federal Bureau of Investigation. I closed the badge case and walked up to him and shoved both the case and the pistol into his hands. I felt sick to my stomach.

"That means Aaron is one of your boys, too," I said, spitting the words through my teeth. "Lovely crew that's protecting mom's apple pie."

"Aaron is a professional assassin," Ladd said dryly. "He's a madman and a killer. I'd like to put a bullet in him myself, especially over that brake stunt he pulled with Wilson. But this is a dirty business and we have to use the men who can do the job. There's a hell of a lot at stake."

"I'm crying," I said. "I'm really crying. I'm sure Merril's daughter will be happy to know her old man was murdered for the good of the country. Or did the Commies do that one?"

"You haven't been followed by the Communists since you left San Francisco. We made sure of that."

"Yeah, I should have known. But then you had an exceptionally stupid boy, didn't you? Here all the time I thought the Russians were the enemy. How dumb can you get! Okay, when do I get the bullet in the back of my head in the name of national security and peace and democracy?"

"That shouldn't be necessary. Once we have those laser plans, you can go your own way."

"Then why the hell kill Merril and Wilson?"

"Wilson was a mistake. Aaron found him following you and figured he was working with the Reds. Merril was killed by my orders. He was in the game for money. That's bad news. That meant if he got to those plans before we did, they might go up for sale to the highest bidder—either Russia or the United States. We couldn't take that chance."

I sat down on the bumper of the car and stared at the dirt. Somewhere it had gotten all screwed up. It wasn't at all like the movies where good and evil were kept in separate compartments. Good and evil were for comic books and John Wayne and for the people who manufactured fat children in warm houses with orange shutters. This was the middle realm, outside of simple morality, where the only ethic was power. Merril had been a friend of mine. He helped me when I needed help. Now he was dead, killed by a third-rate butcher named Aaron. And that was the way it had to be. No right or wrong. Simple expediency in the murderer's alley of international power. Merril had to die. I could see that now. But I didn't have to like it.

"All right," I said. "So now everything is peachy keen."

"Not quite," Ladd said. "We still don't know what the key is."

I laughed. "Then you've got your back to the wall, don't you? You can't reach those plans without the key. What if I don't tell you? Aaron would love to torture me, wouldn't he?"

"You're acting like a vindictive child, Chessick. If we had been aware you knew the key, we would have picked you up before you left California and we wouldn't have had to kill Merril. There's no reason why you shouldn't give it to us. It's for your own country. Besides, it would be a simple matter of hypnotizing you under drugs. The key is in your conscious mind now. And you are an exceptionally good subject."

He was right, of course. Everybody was always right, except Chessick. I just wanted to hurt them in any way I could, make them feel just a little bit of the pain Merril and Wilson had known. I reached in my pocket and threw the ivory billikin on the ground.

"I thought so," Ladd said. "As soon as I saw one in the airport gift shop, I thought that must be it. But we couldn't take any chances by picking you up prematurely."

I looked at the billikin in the dirt. The little charm would cost no more then three or four dollars in any gift shop in Alaska. And three men had been killed for it. The frozen grin on the ivory face seemed sardonic. What fools these mortals be.

"All right," I said. "You want to fill me in on the whole puzzle. There's still some pieces missing."

"I thought you had figured it all out."

"Not all. But let me try. When Kreigger defected, he burned all the records. There was no microfilm. All the formulas were in his head. So when he found a convenient drunk in the Frisco bar, there was no problem hiding the information. He simply got me up to his room, hypnotized me and fed the information into my mind and locked it up with the billikin as a key. Then he gave me a posthypnotic suggestion to forget I had ever seen him. The F.B.I. had picked up Kreigger's contact and had found out where the meeting was to take place and where a prearranged clue would be written if Kreigger had to leave. Aimee and Aaron took the contact's place but missed Kreigger. Aaron found the clue in the men's room and that put you on to me. Correct me if I'm wrong."

"You're doing fine."

"So you had my name and the vague outline of a grinning Buddha with horns, but you didn't have the slightest idea what it all meant. Or maybe you personally weren't involved yet. You were still sitting in an ivory tower in Washington while your flunkies did the field work. They didn't know enough about Kreigger to realize his interest in hypnotism, so the best they could do was put a tail on me and hope I would lead them to something. Alpine Hat was such an incompetent I doubt that you would have left him on a job that big. But finally you decided this was important enough for you to take personal charge, and you flew to Frisco from Washington, or wherever. And you *did* know about Kreigger's study of hypnotism. So you gave orders to have me picked up. You must have arrived the night I went with Carla to the hotel in Berkeley. Then maybe you came out to relieve Alpine Hat. Or was it a double tail, both of you watching me?"

"Owen—Alpine Hat, if you prefer—was supposed to make the pickup," Ladd said. "I was just there to make sure there were no slips. As you know, I have good reason for keeping out of sight."

"But Alpine Hat, in his usual bumbling, mock-heroic manner, screwed it up again. I suppose it was all smoothly planned. Alpine Hat would get me involved in a conversation and you would slip up behind and bonk me on the head. Too mundane for Alpine Hat. No, he decided to scare me with his pretty little sleeve knife. Only I didn't scare. In fact, I just about de-balled him with a kick, and then accidentally—or semi-accidentally—put four inches of hat pin in his eye. That part wasn't in the script. But you—cool to the end—weren't thrown off by my ad-libbing. You simply waited until I was down on my knees examining the corpse, then knocked me out. But I made one more mistake. I saw you. The rest I can pretty well figure out. A drug injection, a few soft words, a little interrogation."

"You're doing all right," Ladd said. "Except for one mistake. I had no idea that Kreigger had hypnotized you. We had a full dossier on him, of course, including his early interest in hypnotism, but it seemed a fairly minor hobby which had been left in Germany. We didn't know he had picked it up again. It was simply that you were the only clue we had, and from a background check on you, I couldn't see where you were leading us. To me it looked like a wild goose chase. We just don't have enough men for that sort of thing. I had you picked up simply to find out exactly what you did know, if anything. The killing of Owen wasn't in the plan, but it was no great loss, either. In any case, both of you were dumped in a car and taken to a house in Piedmont we use as a front. There you were heavily drugged, then revived and hypnotized while you were in a suggestive state. I could have questioned you without the trance, but there's a certain beauty in hypnotism in that you can wipe out memories, and if you were not important to us, it was essential that you have no recollection of the interrogation. That was my big mistake, because hypnotism got past Kreigger's posthypnotic suggestion that you remember nothing of your meeting with him. You told us everything—Kreigger's picking you up in the bar, taking you to his room, and so forth —everything, that is, except what we needed to know—that you had been hypnotized. That part—along with the laser plans—was blocked off with the billikin key. Since you mentioned nothing out of the ordinary occurring in Kreigger's room, I took it for granted that Kreigger had taken you to his room with the purpose of giving you the plans and then had changed his mind. It is quite conceivable that Kreigger—whose mind was working erratically at best—would make a last-minute change of mind."

"Yeah, that clarifies it a little," I said. "So there you were with a corpse on your hands and a bum who was of no use to you, but one worth watching. So you decided to solve both problems at once by framing me for murder. That way you could give a plausible explanation for Alpine Hat's sudden demise and at the same time have me thrown in jail, where I couldn't run out on you and I would always be available if something turned up that you needed me again. It was a simple matter to erase the memory of the interrogation and my brief glimpse of you. And just as an added precaution, you destroyed any chance of my pleading self-defense by erasing my fight with Owen."

"We would have preferred to dump your bodies back in the same alley in Berkeley, of course, to give your story some logic," Ladd put in. "But it was getting light then. There was too much chance of being seen. That's why we chose a deserted pier."

"Very pretty. And I was safely behind bars with nobody to try and get me out except a bored, court-appointed lawyer who was convinced of my guilt. But it didn't work out that way, did it. Merril came on the scene, one of the top criminal lawyers in Frisco. He could have really stirred up a mess if he investigated too far. That would make great headlines. 'F.B.I. Frames Man for Murder.' J. Edgar would love that kind of publicity. So it became urgent that you get me out of jail and get me out fast. By the way, thanks a lot. I keep wondering, though, if Merril hadn't come on the scene, whether or not you would have let me go all the way to the gas chamber."

"A moot question," Ladd said. "But as you can guess, it was a lucky accident for both of us that we were forced to free you from jail."

"Yeah, I can see that now. In our little conversation in the hotel, you seemed terribly surprised when I insisted that I had never met Kreigger. I remembered all that when you interrogated me under drugs, and then only a few days later I couldn't recall any of it."

"That, of course, was the beginning," Ladd said. "Before then it appeared that you were of no value to us. But your apparently sincere denial of having met Kreigger suggested that the memory had been blocked by posthypnotic suggestion, just as I had blocked the memory of your fight with Owen. Yet according to that theory, you should have remembered being hypnotized by Kreigger when I questioned you in Piedmont. But you didn't. That meant that a part of your mind was still inaccessible to us, even in deep trance. I assure you, I am no dilettante at hypnotism myself, but it took a considerable amount of research into the subject before I figured out what Kreigger had done. The idea of a key was the only answer. I naturally figured that the strange symbol Kreigger had drawn around your name in that bar's men's room was a rough outline of the key, but I didn't have the slightest idea what it was. Having never been to Alaska, I had never heard of a billikin any more than you had. The key might have been something Kreigger carved out of wood or it might have been a photograph of a hundred-foot statue in Tibet. One thing was certain, we had to know what the key was before we dared pick you up again."

"And since I was the only man alive who knew what the key was—even subconsciously—you decided to wait and let me search it out for you."

"It was a chance, of course, but it was the only one we had. We knew that you would not deliberately seek out the key, since you didn't even realize it existed, but your subconscious might. The subconscious can be a very powerful force, especially when it has all the resources of the F.B.I. to help it out."

"So that's why you latched onto Carla," I said. "To keep track of me and at the same time supply me with enough money to carry on the search I didn't even know I was involved in. Don't tell me she was a spy. She must have been recruited after I met her."

"That's true. We had pushed you to the point where you distrusted all strangers, so we needed somebody you already knew. Since you were being watched when you met Carla, we were aware of your relationship with her. A little digging revealed she was the type who would do just about anything for kicks. Even then I was a little astounded at the enthusiasm she displayed when I asked her to spy for us. The influence of the movies, I suppose."

"And when did you decide to get into the act?" I asked.

"Needless to say, I could hardly let Carla go it alone. She's a bit unstable at times, as you know, and I couldn't really trust her. I had to find an excuse to stay as near as possible, though of course I told her my presence was solely for her protection. By the way, you saved us a lot of trouble with your attempted blackmail—since otherwise I would have had to set up that meeting with Carla."

"And how did you just happen to be at that party—in disguise—when I did show?"

"For practical purposes, the disguise became semipermanent once I had used it to contact Carla. I had seen her just that morning, and as I was heading back to the city I called Aaron on the car radio. He was following you, and he gave me a description of your direction of travel. I guessed you were headed straight for Carla. When you arrived, I was right behind."

"So then you set up the meeting in Santa Cruz," I said. "That was pretty crude, but with me on the run, I suppose you didn't have much time. Must have been a real parade following me south from Frisco—you, Carla, Aaron, Merril, Wilson—God knows who else. How did you manage it without being spotted?"

"There were only two cars actually following you—both driven by highly experienced professionals—me and Wilson. I believe Wilson was in contact with Merril by radio. I didn't need any radio to keep Aaron on the trail, since I was driving Carla's Corvette and the electronic tracking device had been installed in the trunk before we left San Francisco.

Carla had already mentioned the party house in Tijuana, and when I turned the wheel over to her in Santa Cruz, I told her to get you there as fast as possible. Then after a quick phone call to Aimee, I hopped on a plane."

"Clever," I said. "But the real masterpiece was the LSD."

"Afraid I have to give Carla credit for that idea. Brilliant, if I do say so. LSD is the most powerful mind drug known, and if anything could break down the door that Kreigger had bolted, that would be it. I might mention that that was a very small dose—seventy-five micrograms—the amount used by psychiatrists in LSD therapy. If we had slipped you the standard acid-head dosage of two hundred fifty micrograms, you'd probably still be sitting in a corner somewhere singing 'Hare Krishna.' We brought in Aimee for two reasons—to get me into the party without too many questions and to keep myself and Carla out of it just in case the experiment failed. Aimee is one of our best agents in Hollywood. Knows everyone. It's very funny the way she tells it. Says you were cawing like a bird."

"An American bald eagle," I said. "I was trying to prevent the billikin courier from delivering a pumpkin pie to a Russian bear."

"A pumpkin pie," Ladd mused. "Pie would be the mathematical pi—the ratio of the circumference of a circle to its diameter. The number was probably used several times in the plans Kreigger fed into your mind. And didn't some screwball find some secrets in a pumpkin? Pumpkin pie—translation: secret formula. The subconscious can be a remarkable punster."

"But you still didn't know if I had discovered the key, or if I knew what it was when I had seen it in the LSD dream. But you knew that I knew where it was. That's why you allowed me to come to Alaska."

"And that's about it," Ladd said.

"All except for a couple of murders we skipped over. And maybe just two more questions."

"What questions?" Ladd asked.

I stood up and wandered away from the car. The sun was filtered in narrow rays through the branches, and I could hear the faint stirrings of small animals. It was calm, peaceful here. It was a good place for a nightmare to end. Except there was sadness, too. Carla. Carla who had loved me and betrayed me. But for all the terror, for all the running, there had been some good nights, some of the best nights of my life, when she was soft beside me. I suppose you can love harder in the midst of hell. Now she would go back to her world. I would go back to mine. Sometimes, sitting among her exotic plants and rare paintings, she might remember old bum Chessick with a sigh or a laugh. After all I had been through, I at least deserved that.

"What questions?" Ladd persisted.

"Probably nothing important," I said. "I was just wondering why you didn't simply search Kreigger's body for the key. Secondly, if you believed I was unimportant when you framed me for murder and got me free, why did you even bother to make contact with me in the hotel?"

Ladd chuckled softly. "On the contrary, those are very good questions. In the first place, I did not examine Kreigger's corpse because I had no access to it. Secondly, it was imperative that you be prevented from contacting the F.B.I. yourself. Therefore, I had to make you believe that the F.B.I. had contacted you."

I turned slowly. Ladd was standing near, smiling, my pistol hanging loosely at arm's length in his right hand. I'm too tired for this, I thought.

"You see, Chess," Ladd said, "what we have spoken of was the truth—with one minor exception. Just one last little lie. You're all alone. The F.B.I. never heard of you."

I looked at the pistol that was held at his side. He swung it quickly toward my temple. I watched it come. I'm too damned tired for this, I thought.

TWENTY

I've met people who can roll out of bed, be doing push-ups before they hit the floor and come up shadow boxing with one hand while they pull on their pants with the other. I've never been the type. Sleep is down—way down. It's deep and black and warm. Waking is like I'm at the bottom of the ocean and I just lost my weighted belt. I float up by buoyancy and all the time sheer will is trying to pull me back down. This time the ocean was mud and my mouth was full of rancid seaweed. There was no will left. A monster with a hundred forty-seven fishhook teeth had every one of them firmly imbedded in the back of my neck. There wasn't much sense fighting him, so I just let him tow me up toward a hideously rational surface, and I watched the horned Buddhas and the numbers and the pin-stuck dead eyeballs drift away and down into the sediment. When we got up to where the light could pierce my eyes, the monster swam away, leaving every one of his teeth clamped to my backbone.

Waking can be a pretty ugly thing when you've lost for the ninety-third time—this one for keeps. I pulled myself a few inches below the surface and stared at the mud and chewed the seaweed. A billikin swam by, grinning idiotically and begging to have its belly rubbed and toes tickled. Sorry, buddy, your luck I don't need. The grinning ivory blurred briefly out of focus and returned with white hair and a wide soft mouth and big innocent neurotic eyes. Carla baby, I trusted you. That's the worst part. Here all the time I thought you were just sewing on my long-lost balls. I needed you. Somebody to be a hero for. A face lovely enough to erase the image of ten seconds in the jungles of Viet Nam. Keep smiling, Carla. You make a damned fine spy. You don't just kill the enemy; you even destroy that last lonely vestige of remembered pride.

"All right, Chessick, come on."

Ladd's voice. Ladd or Deke or Korokov or whoever the hell he was. He grasped me by the shoulders and began to shake me. The teeth dug deeper into my neck.

"Get laid," I said.

"Come on. Wake up. You're missing some of the most beautiful scenery on the continent."

"I wouldn't want to miss the scenery," I mumbled.

I opened my eyes and the light washed over and through them like freezing water. My chin was down on my chest, and I was surprised to see there was a body attached to the pain. My wrists hung between my legs, tied together with a white nylon rope. I was sitting on some kind of bunk in a small, cluttered room that kept going up and down as though in a gentle earthquake. Wood steps leading up to a door. Green Coleman camp stove on the bolted-down table. Metallic box with dials and gauges—maybe a short-wave radio. Directly across from me was another bunk with Ladd sitting there grinning at me like a ruptured billikin.

"Beautiful scenery," I said.

He laughed. "The scenery's outside. Stand up. Take a look at it. Walk around. Get your blood moving."

"I'm glad you're so worried about my health."

"Believe me, Chess, I'm extremely worried about your health. You don't realize how valuable you are."

I struggled to my feet, bracing myself against the table. When the first dizziness had cleared into a steady throbbing, I looked through the narrow window at the top of the cabin. We were on some kind of a boat, and on either side a dark filigree of green trees and rock rose out of the sea to fade and disappear in the low-hanging clouds. There was a beauty to it, all right. It was the desolate beauty of naked forest and sea and sky. It was the beauty not of pastoral dreams, but of the stark, uncaring, relentless, eternal, heedless, headlong cycle of growth and decay. Against those savage mountains all your skyscrapers and automobiles and arty movies and dreary operas would be nothing but so much arrogant foppery. There was nothing petty here. Everything was reduced to the two simple essentials—life and death.

It was a helluva place to try to make an escape. Escape— yeah. I couldn't even hope for that last-minute cavalry charge by the F.B.I. There was no reason to doubt Ladd's contention that the F.B.I. had never heard of me. Even if they had seen my name on that bathroom wall in Frisco, it would have meant absolutely nothing among all the other scrawls. Probably the only reason that Ladd was able to decipher it was because Kreigger had informed the Commies precisely where he would leave a message if contact was broken. As Ladd said, I was all alone. And even if the incredibly clever Robert Chessick, who never did anything right in his entire life, was able to pull off a miracle this once, what good would it do? The Commies would never rest until they got me back. And if I did escape and turned myself over to some bona-fide F.B.I. men for protection, would they really allow me to go on living after they had extracted the information? No, they would do just what the

Commies would do—grab, question and kill. So where did that leave me? Total, absolute hopelessness must be a very rare experience. I suppose the only time a person really knows it is the exact instant when the firing squad pulls the trigger. Up to that point you can always hope for escape. But I was already beyond hope. Way beyond. I looked back through the window at the sea and the mountains, but there was no comfort there.

"Resurrection Bay," Ladd explained. "Rather sorry you had to miss the port of Seward. Fascinating town. It was almost wiped out by tidal waves during the earthquake. Has all the appearance of a ghost town that refuses to roll over and die."

"All right," I said. "You can forget the tourist speech. How about telling me where the hell I am and where the hell we're going?"

"Patience. We have several hours. This is a very slow fishing boat. Hardly the accommodations for an excursion of such importance, but it did cost us five hundred dollars to rent it for the day. I'm sure we could have gotten it for ten if this wasn't fishing season."

"I would have been happy to wait until fishing season was over."

"I'm quite sure you could wait—but we couldn't. Our timetable is rigid. There's a Russian trawler waiting for us about ten miles beyond the mouth of the bay."

"And I suppose no one will be suspicious of a Russian ship in these waters?"

"Oh God, no. The Russians fish the area all the time. The United States only has a three-mile limit, so the ship is well in international waters. However, as a precaution, you, Aaron and Carla will board after dark."

So Aaron and Carla were on the boat, too. Old Home Week for Commie spies. "And you?" I asked.

"Sorry to disappoint you," Ladd said. "But I'll have to leave the rest of you at the trawler. After all, somebody's got to return this boat to its owner."

3

"That's awful thoughtful of you," I said. "Parting will be such sweet sorrow. But I would think that you might enjoy escorting such an invaluable prisoner to Moscow yourself."

Ladd chuckled softly. "That might prove inconvenient. Besides, though I do plan to make some use of you, by the time we part ways you will hardly be invaluable to me or anyone else."

I gazed at him curiously. I had truly believed that at least everything was clear now—no more questions to be answered, no more mysteries. "I don't get it," I said.

Ladd looked me in the eye and laughed. "Don't you? Then let me explain. When you board that trawler—quite soundly asleep—you won't have any plans to give them. I assure you, your mind will be as innocent of lasers as it was before you met Kreigger."

I shook my head to clear the fog. I was still dizzy, maybe a little seasick. That must be it. I wasn't hearing right. "Throw away the key?" I asked incredulously.

"I beg your pardon?"

"Something Cassidy said—that the door could be closed permanently by a further posthypnotic suggestion that even the key—or billikin—wouldn't open the lock. But that means drugging me here—on this boat. Why? They must want to question me in Moscow under ideal conditions. I don't understand. I . . ." My voice trailed off into the rumble of the engine. Slowly I raised my eyes from the floor and looked at Ladd. A slight smile creased the corners of his lips —a smile as deadly cynical as I had ever seen. Then I began to laugh. It shot tiny pellets of pain through my head and down into my stomach. But I didn't care. It was too good a joke. "You bastard," I said. "You cold-blooded bastard."

"That's right, Chess," Ladd said. "What did Merril want? A few hundred grand? A million maybe? He was a fool. The Russians will pay me five times that without a second thought."

The laughter died, leaving a dry aftertaste in my throat. "So the Commies have their Kreiggers, too."

"Don't compare me with that miserable little utopian," Ladd said. "He thought he was saving humanity by selling his soul for some pathetic ideal. Oh, I know all about that kind of blind idealism. It took idealism to infiltrate the German Army for the Reds when I was eighteen years old. Later, as a trusted member of the Hungarian underground, it took idealism to betray some damned fine men to torture and death. Oh yes, I knew Communism was the answer. The faster we piled up corpses, the faster we'd get our lovely utopia. But twenty-five years in this sordid little spy business—twenty-five years peeping through keyholes at governments with their pants down—and you begin to question your pretty ideals. No, I've seen too much. Sorry, I can't buy it any more. Communism—democracy—what's the difference? It doesn't matter what flag they're waving. The line they feed the rabble is always the same whether the language is Russian or English or Chinese. 'We'll give you utopia to-morrow if we can use you as cannon fodder today.' No, I'm through playing their game. I've waited a lot of years for you to come along, Chess—so I could buy my way out with their money." He paused, his lips folded over his clenched teeth in a bitter grin. "All right, Chess, you've had your lecture on reality for today. Let's get some air."

I was getting dizzier. I staggered to the stairs and leaned my head against the door. Ladd came up beside me and I felt the hardness of his shoulder-holstered pistol against my arm. He opened the door. I stumbled through into the damp salt air. Aaron was at the wheel beside the door. When he saw me stagger out, his hand came up with a big, ugly Army .45, but he looked past me to Ladd and shoved the pistol back in his belt. I glanced at Aaron and tried to recall the drowned, dead face of Merril. But it wouldn't come. I was too tired to care.

Carla stood at the railing on the stern. The wind caught her hair and billowed it out across her shoulders. She was wearing black capris and she was huddled into an oversized leather fisherman's jacket.

My feet moved forward automatically, as though the pain of a lifetime had centered at the back of my neck and was driving me forward. She turned and for one moment I saw again those lovely, innocent, tear-stained eyes that had done their work so well. My hands came up, clasped together in a double fist against the rope. I heard it crack above the waves and the engine and felt the sweet pain like a ripple of flame on my knuckles. Carla fell back against the railing and then forward and down. Ladd grabbed my shoulders and pulled me back.

"You damned fool," he said.

She stayed down on her knees, her fists clasped between her legs, her hair down over her face and breasts. Then very slowly she looked up. Through the scattered strands of hair, her mouth was a shapeless mass of blood. A pale hand came up and brushed the hair away.

"I didn't know," she said. "Honest, Chess."

"Sure, baby," I said.

"I didn't. I didn't know," she cried. Real tears were streaming down her face, but I don't suppose it's hard for a woman to cry real tears when she's just been busted in the mouth. I couldn't understand why she felt it necessary to keep up the act—but she was giving a real Academy Award performance. She came up off her knees and buried her face in my chest, still sobbing that she didn't know. It might have been convincing if the role had been given to Sophia Loren, but after you live with a broad for a while you get to know the range of her emotions. Carla was capable of some pretty morbid depressions, but this heroine melodrama was phony as hell.

She was tight up against me, and I felt her hand press something small and cold into my palm. My first instinct was to toss it away, but there was something desperate, something frantic in her attempt to close my fist over what I now realized was two separate objects. All right, I had played her game this far.

"Come on," Ladd said.

He pulled me away. Carla slumped back to her knees on the deck, crying hysterically. With all that talent, she could have made it on Broadway. Ladd shoved me back in the direction of the cabin. Aaron was oblivious to everything. The wheel was set into the wall of the cabin to the left of the door, so he could steer by looking over the top. His eyes held with cold intensity on the empty expanse of ocean before the boat, and he didn't even turn as we moved around the side of the cabin.

"Keep moving," Ladd prodded. "You've got a lot of remembering to do and I want you fresh. And don't get any ideas about jumping overboard. We would just have to fish you out, and all you would get is pneumonia."

The sea was fairly calm, but there's only a few inches between the cabin wall and empty space on one of those boats, so you have to move carefully. The bow was empty but for a mechanized roller to pull in the nets and the lid of the fish hold.

"She was telling the truth," Ladd said. "What makes you think you're the only gullible bastard in the world?"

I didn't answer. There's a certain amount of relief when you suddenly discover that you no longer have any control of the situation. You don't have to think any more. Carla had changed that. Clutched in my hand were two tiny capsules of some kind. But what? Maybe this was Ladd's subtle way of making me hypnotize myself. Two capsules of pentathol or sodium amytal. More likely a drug a hell of a lot stronger than either one of them. I take them myself, thinking they're something that will help me, and all I do is save Ladd the trouble of shoving them down my throat. But what if Carla was telling the truth? What if she had actually believed Ladd was with the F.B.I.? But if that was true, then what were these pills? Cyanide? Commit suicide and save the world. Come off it, Chessick, where the hell would Carla get cyanide capsules? But what else?

Then all of a sudden it was there. We were pushing eighty south on 101. It was late and I had the window open to keep awake. Carla gave me a small pink capsule. Dexedrine, she said, It'll keep you awake. There's a drug called Dexamyl that's better. A mixture of Dexedrine and sodium amytal. The two drugs neutralize each other so you just stay awake without getting high.

If the two capsules in my hand were pure Dexedrine, there would be a slight chance they would counteract whatever hypnotic drug Ladd kept in his medicine cabinet. They would have searched Carla for weapons, of course, but it would have been impossible to detect objects of this size, even in a pocket.

But what good would it do even if I was able to keep from talking for a few moments? And even if through some miracle I was able to overcome Ladd and Aaron, I could never escape. If we didn't keep our appointment with the Russian trawler on time, every Commie agent in Alaska would be out gunning for me. No, the situation was absolutely hopeless.

Then it hit me. There might be a way out, after all. A way out of everything—Ladd, the Russians who would be searching for me if I escaped—everything. Okay, Carla, here's the last trust. Chessick's going to play hero again.

TWENTY-ONE

"All right," Ladd said, "back in the cab-
in." We moved around the side again. Ladd's voice droned
on behind me. "You don't really think we could have left
her behind, do you? And she's a little too important to kill
outright. I'm sure the propaganda minister in Moscow will
think up a plausible reason why the daughter of one of
America's more affluent capitalists should defect to Russia.
It's quite possible she may even write some letters home telling all her friends of the glorious life under Communism."

Carla's future was of no great interest to me at the
moment—unless I could figure a way to hitch that future to
mine. Don't talk, Chessick. Keep your head. Think. Memorize. You don't know how powerful that drug will be. This
is Kreigger speaking. Memorize. Memorize.

Ladd walked behind me, one hand on my shoulder, as we

passed around the edge of the cabin to the stern. The mountains at the mouth of the bay were fading into mist as the boat moved onto open sea. Carla watched me from the railing. Her eyes were expressionless. I felt the first drop of rain on my neck.

"Inside," Ladd said.

Aaron opened the door for me, leaning over from his position at the wheel and smiling his real-estate smile. I stumbled down the stairs into the cabin and sat down on the bunk. I had to get the pills into my mouth fast. If Ladd used a needle directly into my bloodstream, it might already be too late.

Ladd picked up a folded leather bag, like an oversized wallet, from the table. He didn't take his eyes off me as he unfolded the bag and removed a hypo and a small jar of liquid. The rain began to come down hard, rattling on the roof and the water.

The door opened. Carla stood silhouetted against the dimming light outside. Ladd turned to look at her. It was all I needed. I dropped my head forward and clapped my hand to my mouth. Ladd moved fast. The side of his right hand curled into a karate chop, and when it hit my wrist the pain shot all the way up into my shoulder. One of the capsules flew into the air and bounced off the wall with a tiny snap. The other capsule was sliding down my throat.

"Carla, sit down on the steps and stay there," Ladd ordered. Stooping, he reached and picked up the fallen capsule and held it up to the light. "Dexedrine?" he asked. "Benzedrine? I rather thought your histrionics were a bit overdone, Carla. It's an interesting idea, but quite stupid really. This pill might have some neutralizing effect on certain barbiturates, but I assure you, Chess, the hypodermic needle I have here contains nothing so mild as scapalomine or amytal. There are certain drugs one just doesn't mix. You should thank me, Chess, for saving you from a most agonizing experience."

That sounded ominous, but at least a little pain might

keep me awake. I had one pill down and Ladd didn't know it. That was my only edge—and not much even there. It might not have any effect at all. I could fight him—give myself a few more seconds for the Dexedrine to take effect. But I might break the needle and my only chance was to take the shot and trust to luck.

Ladd put the capsule in his pocket and filled the syringe from the rubber-topped vial. "If you plan to put up a fight," he said, "I would appreciate it if you started now, before I get this needle in your arm."

"No struggle."

"That's a wise decision." Ladd took his seat on the bunk across from me. I offered the vein at the crook of my arm, but he refused it and had me pull my shirt down over my shoulder. The needle went in just above my vaccination mark. Ladd was good at it. There was no pain at all until a few seconds after he removed the needle, then a dull ache began to work its way into the shoulder area.

I had to start talking. Anything to keep me awake for just a few extra seconds. "So Carla fell for it, too," I said. "Or were you telling the truth about being with the F.B.I.?"

"Me—a double agent?" Ladd replied. "No, I'm afraid that would require more cynicism than even I can handle. There is, of course, a code name Ladd who is department chief of counterespionage within the United States. I chose the name under the assumption that you might attempt to verify Ladd's existence. There was no chance of your actually contacting Ladd, since he is very well hidden away in the darker recesses of the F.B.I. Don't feel too badly about being fooled by my credentials. They were printed in Russia and would appear authentic even to an experienced F.B.I. agent. Of course, I used the same name when I asked Carla to tail you."

"And got a report on every move I made from a girl who thought she was working against the Russians. Very clever. But aren't you rather overdoing the clever bit now?"

Ladd chuckled softly under his breath. "You mean in betraying the Russians? That, I assure you, is planned down to the finest detail. I would have preferred to question you on land, of course, but there was a small matter of privacy. As you might have guessed, we were being watched even during our little conversation in the woods. Then Aaron passed on the news of your capture somewhat prematurely and I received orders from the top to deliver you to the trawler myself. Inconvenient—but I have long experience in turning such minor irritations to my advantage. You see, several agents from Moscow headquarters are waiting on that trawler to interrogate you. They know all about the billikin. I told them myself. When you arrive, however, you will be fast asleep. Carla, too. I carry a very complete pharmaceutical supply. You will both remain asleep for at least thirty-six hours. Since I was not ordered to accompany you any further than the trawler and since no one there has the rank to delay me, I will return immediately to Seward and quietly disappear. When you awake they will interrogate you with the billikin, of course, but what you will offer them will not be a message from Kreigger, but rather a message from me—stating that I alone hold those laser plans. You will also do me the favor of giving them my detailed stipulations for the transfer of five million American dollars for the information."

I glanced at Carla. She was silently staring in open-mouthed incredulity at this new double-cross. She blurred momentarily out of focus. A slight, almost imperceptible buzzing began in my ears. Keep talking, I thought. "Pardon a stupid question, but is it really that easy to permanently destroy information that is firmly imbedded in the mind?"

"One of the problems of hypnotism," Ladd explained, "is the difficulty in predicting with any degree of accuracy. Even the most scientific of experimenters are continually contradicting each other as to what is and what is not possible. However, we do know that even under the most intensive hypnoanalysis, certain repressed memories are nearly impossible to root out. As Freud discovered, the subconscious constructs amazingly strong defenses against intrusion. This was what Kreigger utilized in concealing that information in your mind in the first place. There is no agreement on the basic nature of hypnotism, but there is one theory—put forth by a Dr. Estabrooks—that posthypnotic suggestion operates in much the same manner as the emotional trauma—repressed memory—which well explains the total amnesia aspect. It's quite complex, but in simple terms one might say that my suggestion that you permanently forget the information will be one trauma placed on top of another trauma—Kreigger's suggestion. Whether the effect will actually be permanent depends considerably on you as a subject—but I can guarantee that it will last long enough to serve my purposes. The laser race is so close that the Russians simply can't afford to spend six months or a year digging through your mind for that information. And, of course, I will be sure to let them know that any unnecessary delay will result in my seeking another buyer."

The buzzing in my ears ceased. My skull felt strangely hollow, like an enormous cavern, heavy with fetid air. "What about Aaron?" I said. "What if he tells them before you get back to Seward?"

"Aaron can't tell them. He doesn't know. I'm sure headquarters will be quite peeved at him for not being more aware of what's going on around him. I suppose they might even consider him expendable. Too bad."

"Tragic," I said. "Okay, so you get the plans from me, close them off permanently by posthypnotic suggestion and at the same time make me your messenger boy. I suppose I'm also very useful in disposing of any doubts your Commie friends might have that you don't really possess the plans. Real pretty. And of course everybody in this game is so lily-cheeked with charm and trust that there's no chance the Russians will pull another double-cross and grab you when you come in your rented truck to pick up the money."

Ladd laughed again. The old boy was having a grand time. "You underestimate me, Chess. Of course they'll try to grab me. And if they miss the first time, they'll spend their lives trying to grab me. That's the fun of it, isn't it? But there isn't a trick in the book that I don't know. Too bad we don't have more time, or I could give you a detailed report on the various methods of collecting and depositing large sums of money without ever going within a thousand miles of the pay-off man. I even have some techniques stored away that my peers in Moscow never heard of. And after that it's simple. That bloody idiot Merril couldn't have run a mile after selling those plans without being gunned down, but they'll have a harder time catching up with me. I can anticipate their every move. Besides, I know which of our agents are for sale, and you can bet that half the men that are chasing me will be on my payroll. No, Chess, they won't get me. I haven't been head of the entire spy apparatus in the United States for the last eight years for nothing."

The only gasp of awe or surprise was Carla's. I didn't give a damn any more. The drug was taking effect. It was like watching the lights go out in a large building. The janitor was moving from floor to floor in my mind, blacking out each room in turn with a gentle flick of a switch. I saw Ladd reach beneath the table and emerge with a small transistor tape recorder. He set it on the bunk beside him. Hold on, Chessick. The Dexedrine will have to take effect sooner or later. Just hold on. Keep awake. Keep talking.

"And I suppose after you've sold the plans to the Russians, maybe you'll figure the United States might want to get rid of a few million, too?" My voice was far away, echoing back to me down a long corridor.

"That would be foolish," Ladd said. "Even with my knowledge, transferring information for money is always a dangerous business. Why should I take the chance twice when I can get all I could possibly use from Russia alone? They would pay ten million if I asked. Really, they have no choice. But I would hate to be greedy."

"One should always be considerate of former employers," I mumbled.

The drug was pulling me down—down into the black mud again. It looked warm and gentle down there. Let yourself go, Chessick. It's just sleep. Beautiful, comfortable sleep. No memories. No worries. No one will blame you. No one will care. Except . . . Carla!

A bolt of pain shot up my arms as I twisted my wrists hard against the binding rope. A few lights went on. Ladd set his hand on my bloody wrists.

"Don't fight it," he said.

Yeah, don't fight it. Let go. Down, down into sleep. The Dexedrine won't take effect anyway. Ladd said it wasn't enough. He should know. You weren't cut out to be a hero. Let someone else save the world.

My head slumped forward on my chest.

"That's it," Ladd's voice said, muted with distance. "Let go. Sleep. Sleep."

Images drifted across my mind. Carla, her white hair scintillating on the pillow beside me in the darkness. Lorrie. Little Ronnie. Growing up in a lousy world of fear and sudden death. My son knowing all the hopeless desperation I had known. My platoon in Viet Nam. The men who had believed in me. And I let them down. I ran. Just like I was running now. Running down into sleep. Grab something. Hold on.

I can't, damn it. I can't.

Hold. Hold.

Down.

Sleep. Soft, encompassing sleep.

I heard the click of the tape recorder. Ladd's voice droned on outside of my closed eyes. "You will hear no voice but mine . . . sleep . . . count . . . backward from ten . . . nine . . . sleep . . . six . . . five . . ."

With each diminishing number a few more lights went out. Soon there would be none. A thin voice from far away cried, *Hold on.* But there was no will any more. Nothing. Nothing but sleep and blackness.

"Three . . . two . . . one . . ."

Blackness.

"Chess, can you hear me?"

"Yes."

"Listen closely. When you open your eyes you will see a billikin. You will tell me everything that it brings to your mind—everything Kreigger told you. Do you understand?"

"Yes."

"And once you have told it—when you have told everything—you will forget. You will forget everything that you have told. Nothing will ever make you remember again—not even the billikin. Do you understand? Not even the billikin will make you remember."

"Yes," my voice said.

"Open your eyes and look at me."

The eyes opened. The mind was blank—disattached. Something rumbled in my stomach.

Ladd held a small ivory carving before me. It hung from a gold chain and swung back and forth with the motion of the boat.

"Look at the billikin. Concentrate on it. I want you to tell me everything that comes to mind."

I could almost tangibly feel a door swinging open in my brain, hear its weight moan upon rusty hinges. Inside there was light. A room full of floating, drifting numbers. One by one, in orderly procession, they began to pass through the door and disappear. I could hear my voice—far, far away—picking them out of the air and repeating them in a lethargic drone. The rumble in my stomach was growing.

Something began to happen in front of my eyes. The movement was slow, amorphous. The glint of white hair. Carla leaning across Ladd's knees, struggling her hand toward the ivory statue. The billikin disappeared. A dull thud. A scream, halted abruptly. Silence. A void in front of me.

Then, suddenly, as though the disappearance of the billikin had been a signal, the rumble in my stomach burgeoned into a raging storm. My entire body exploded as though struck by lightning. And then the shattered flesh congealed again. It was in my head now—two irresistible forces having a tug-of-war with my brain, pulling it apart.

A single tiny light went on.

The Dexedrine was taking effect.

A cramp clutched at my groin and I bit my teeth against it. But it was pain. Beautiful pain. Feeling. I was alive again. I could feel it seeping back through my limbs. Another light went on in my brain. I focused on it. The cramp moved up to my chest and settled as a throbbing ache in my heart and began pumping through the veins and arteries into my head. I put all my weight against the billikin door and shoved. Numbers floated past and in the distance I could still hear my voice saying them in dull monody.

Outside of it, the other struggle had ceased. My eyes began to pick up separate objects. The bunk. A magazine. Carla. She lay on her face beside the table. Ladd knelt beside her. He felt her wrist, then, seemingly satisfied, returned to the bunk and picked up the fallen billikin.

The ivory charm didn't work any more. I shoved all the pain in my racked body against the door. It slammed shut. A few more lights went on. But the hypnotic drug wasn't about to go away. I had to fight for every second of consciousness. It wouldn't be long before the Dexedrine was overcome by the stronger drug. A minute. Five minutes at the most. Hold on, Chessick. Don't let him see you're being torn apart. Straight face. Talk in the same monotone. Don't show him any pain.

Silence.

"Come on, Chess," Ladd said. "Look at the billikin. Concentrate."

The door began to open again. All I had to do was close my eyes or move my head away, but that would let him know. Talk fast, Chessick. You can't last much longer. Think. Calm now. Forget the pain. You memorized the speech. Don't force it. Let the drug pull it out.

"This is Kreigger speaking," my voice said. "I have made a terrible mistake."

Ladd gazed at me curiously and reached out with one hand and turned up the tape recorder. "The plans. Go on with the plans."

"I do not know who will be hearing this," I continued, "whether American or Russian. This is my suicide note. My final expiation. For the first time in many years my mind is clear. Though I still believe in Communism, I cannot forget my greater allegiance to humanity. The plans that I have discovered and stolen are too destructive to be released to any government. I must die with them."

"What the hell are you talking about?" Ladd said, his voice rising toward hysteria. "The plans. Get on with the plans."

I continued softly, concentrating on each separate word. "It is in me to be a traitor to the United States, but I cannot betray humanity. I beg forgiveness of whoever hears this for the sins, including murder, I have committed for these plans. My only justification is that now they belong to no one, which is an absolute necessity until man achieves a spiritual wisdom consummate with his scientific knowledge. As for my sins, I pay the full price. Death."

Perhaps for the first time in many years, Ladd was shaken. Not merely shaken—terrified. His open hand whipped twice across my face. "The plans, damn it! The plans!"

"This is my suicide note, my final reprieve. For the first time in many months my mind is clear . . ." I knew I wasn't repeating it verbatim, and if Ladd realized it or played the monologue back on the tape recorder, he would know what happened. But Ladd was broken. He seemed to shrivel into a fraction of a man, to sink down into his clothes—beaten, destroyed. No rational thought, no careful logic would enter his mind for at least several minutes. And that was all the time I had anyway. "I still believe in Communism, but I cannot forget my obligation to humanity . . ."

"All right. Shut up!"

I shut up. Gladly.

Ladd slumped back against the wall, his eyes gazing into nothing. He had swallowed it. Every tasty morsel. But hadn't he been the one who had set it up? Had he himself not told me that the new traitor—Fuchs, May, Ponticorvo, Kreigger—was an idealist who sold his soul to the devil, thinking it was God? And hadn't Ladd admitted to being an idealist himself in his youth—a romantic of the first order? Of course he believed it. He had to believe it. Because at one time, if he was Kreigger, this is exactly what he would have done.

Slowly he rose and crossed to the radio. His body was tired, drained. At his feet Carla stirred and lifted her head from the floor, rubbing her temple with delicate fingers. Ladd turned on the radio and adjusted the frequency band. I wondered how many dreams I had just destroyed. Five million dollars. Five million dollars' worth of dreams. How many years had those dreams rested latent in his mind as his idealism faded to cynicism and cynicism to hatred? How long had he waited for this opportunity—despising his job, his employees, the government that paid him—despising even himself and surviving each day only with the prayer that his chance would come? And it had come and he had lost it. Gone. Obliterated.

A crackling voice emerged from the radio, speaking Russian.

Ladd turned the knob to another frequency. It was obvious that they had it set up so each would give a coded message—probably outwardly about fishing—on their own marine frequency. That way anyone monitoring the message would believe an American boat was speaking to another of his kind. Right now, in a Russian trawler somewhere out there on the open sea, a group of special agents would be crowded around a short-wave set, tuning to the American fishing frequency and listening with drooling anticipation.

Ladd didn't even bother to use code. "This is Cressida L. Nine zero zero three. C drugged and shown billikin. Nothing. No plans. Repeat. No plans. After a few formulas, K changed his mind. Left nothing but an apologetic suicide note. Over."

Ladd turned the knob again. Angry Russian voices poured through the set. I wondered if they were giving him hell for not coding his message, or perhaps for drugging me prematurely. Or maybe they didn't give a damn either. Ladd listened in patience. When they ceased speaking, he turned the knob again and spoke with restrained anger and renewed authority. "I'd like to remind you who you're talking to. The next sonofabitch who gives me that crap will be shoveling manure in. . ." He caught himself. Perhaps he was going to say, "Siberia." He continued with slow restraint. "I'm just as sick about this as you are. But it's over. Done. Pass it up the line." He paused a moment, then added, "There's no use boarding with only rotten fish. I'll have to dump them here. Over and out."

Even through the pain I could feel the slight thrill of electricity along the hairs on the back of my neck. It hadn't occurred to me, but of course Ladd had to kill us himself. He could neither let us go nor deliver us to the Russians— not after what he had told us of his planned double-cross. Think, Chessick, think.

Ladd turned off the crackling radio, put the mike back in its cradle and stood as though in a trance of his own. Okay, it was set. The Russians would have no use for me any more. The information had come from one of the big boys, so it would be accepted without question. If I could escape, I could go my own way without fear of being tailed. And if Ladd simply disappeared, they might even surmise suicide. But the problem of making an armed karate expert disappear wasn't so easy to solve, especially when my guts were being torn apart by two antithetical drugs, and Ladd's stronger concoction was gaining fast on the Dexedrine. I was already slipping under. Sleep. Oh, baby—sleep. No minutes any more. Just seconds.

I had one advantage over Ladd. He thought I was well lost in my dream of pi-eyed billikins. I had to use that. Fast. No elaborate schemes. My mind wasn't up to it. But with my wrists bound, I couldn't even throw a decent punch. The only thing I could do was go for his throat, attempt to strangle him. But Ladd had already shown me how easily he could defend himself against such an attack. That afternoon at Carla's mansion when I had grabbed his throat. What did we call it back in Army karate class? The windmill. Bring your right arm beside your head and come down hard on the attacker's wrists with your armpit. Simultaneous knee to the groin and elbow to the nose. In class we practiced on thin air, and every time I tried it I damned near fell on my face. When you didn't actually connect with that knee, you were about as off balance as you could get.

Come off it, Chessick. You're meandering. Concentrate. Think.

But of course. That was it. Ladd's defense was pure reflex. My only chance was to anticipate his move—use his own skill against him.

There was no longer time to think it out clearly—not with my body about to erupt in flame. Ladd was still standing quietly beside the radio. Then his right hand moved up, disappeared inside his jacket, then down again—the dark blue barrel of the pistol resting thoughtfully at his hip.

I lunged. Straight up, pushing with everything in my legs. I caught Ladd with both hands at the throat and drove him back against the wall. The look in his eyes was one of total surprise, but his body reacted without any help from his mind. The hand with the pistol shot straight up over his head. His whole strength was centered momentarily at his armpit as he thrust down over my wrists. Or rather where my wrists should have been. He came down on air. At the same instant his knee rose, his elbow drove at my face. That was exactly what I had been waiting for. I swung my entire body to the side. For one brief second he was poised on one foot, the focus of all the energy he possessed in his elbow and upraised knee, propelling him forward into thin air. I brought my clasped fists around until I felt them touch my left shoulder, then I swung with everything I had. The knuckles caught him hard on the back of the neck and he fell straight forward on his face across the barely conscious body of Carla. Maybe he was already out, but I wasn't taking chances. I brought my foot up and stabbed hard at his spine with the point of the heel. His body contracted into the break and then erupted into a single gigantic spasm. My heel came down again and again, until it wasn't hitting bone any more, only mush.

The two drugs inside of me weren't neutralizing each other. What had for a while been a minor skirmish had broken into open war. Tanks, flame-throwers, machine guns, claymore mines, H-bombs. The cramp caught me in the balls as though someone had hit me with a sledge hammer. I doubled up and went over on my face.

Aaron! The bastard must have heard the noise.

I struggled around in a circle like a ruptured centipede and looked through tears at the door. It was still shut. Of course, it was raining like hell outside. Aaron wouldn't be able to hear a thing.

Carla had pushed Ladd's body off her chest and was sitting against the table leg, still in a daze. She would be no help. With my elbows dug into my flaming stomach, I wriggled back to the fallen pistol and clutched it in both hands. I had to get Aaron before I passed out. And that wasn't going to be long. If only I could attract his attention. My mouth tried to scream. Only a gasp of pain emerged. I crawled toward the stairs. A cramp seized my balls again. I doubled under—paralyzed. My legs wouldn't move. Blackness was closing in.

Slowly I struggled my head from the fetal position like a shy turtle peeping from its shell. There it was, just below the stairway, about three feet in front of my eyes, where it had rolled when it fell from Ladd's hand or pocket. It lay there on its side, its ivory face grinning at me in slant-eyed mockery. The floor seemed to assume a Dali-esque perspective, stretching away and away to where the billikin gazed at me from the end of infinity. I couldn't remove my stare. The lights began to go out again. The door opened.

The gun, Chessick. Hold on! The gun!

I could hear my voice flowing through the door in an endless parade of meaningless numbers. The billikin grinned.

My stomach exploded, erupting up through my chest and
bursting from my throat in a muffled scream. I clutched at
the pain before it could escape and held on to it. Two immense arms pushed out in front of me across the vast desert
of the floor. The pistol was clasped in a double fist. The
billikin grinned at me from above the front sight. My lips
were still moving, the numbers droned on. I tried to pull my
eyes away from the billikin. Which side of the door was the
pilot wheel on? Left side entering. Right side going out. Or
was it right side entering? Which side is right? Hold fork
with right hand? Which hand?

The pistol was a lead weight. My body shuddered as I
strained the barrel up from the floor. Every muscle I owned
was exerted into the act of lifting. For a split second the tip
of the barrel blotted out the billikin. The door slammed
shut. My mind screamed. *Right side!* The pistol weaved to
the right. The billikin reappeared. The door opened. My
voice gasped the numbers again. My hands were slowly
deadening. Novacaine seemed to be seeping along my arms.
My mind sought the correct finger, trying each in turn. Pull.
Pull. Pull.

The numbers droned on—down, down into darkness.

Pull. Pull.

The explosion shot a white-hot lance of pain along my
arm and through my guts and out the soles of my feet. The
wood burst away from a tiny hole beside the door. A splinter
fell beside the billikin. He grinned. I pulled again. The roar
echoed like a superball rebounding back and forth within
my skull. A vortex of blackness swirled around me. Pull
again. My voice droned on. The billikin grinned. Blackness
swirled. Pull again. Again.

And then a pinpoint of radiant ivory was grinning at me
in a universe of total blackness. And my voice droned on.

TWENTY-TWO

I came out of it slowly—a growing awareness of sunlight and the sweet fragrance of spruce needles and wild flowers. I lay there with my arm over my eyes, taking inventory of the remains of Robert Chessick. There was a dull pain somewhere in the vicinity of the base of my neck, but I was surprised to discover that I felt strangely refreshed, as though the sickness had been spent in the delirium of the preceding days or years or whatever that I recalled only as the amorphous meanderings of a lost dream. I opened my eyes and sat up. I was in a sleeping bag in a meadow beside a cove. The tide was out and the boat was tilted half over in the dark silt, only a few inches of propeller and rudder in the water.

"Lie down," Carla ordered. "You're sick and I insist on my female prerogative of nursing you."

She was behind me, kneeling beside a random pile of twigs which she was abortively trying to light with wet matches.

Vaguely I realized that I might finally have won a game, and I searched my mind for some immortal words to honor the occasion. "Where the hell's Aaron?" I said.

Carla gave up on the fire and came over and shoved me gently back down onto a dirty pillow. "Dead,'" she said, with more emotion than I thought the statement justified.

"Then my aim must have been good."

"Not quite," Carla said. "You didn't hit him any higher than the knee. He must have hung on to the wheel all the time you were shooting, because the bullets just about took both his legs off. It was horrible. I managed to put tourniquets on, but he was crazy—crying and screaming—and he wouldn't let me get him in the cabin out of the rain. He just kept crawling around in circles all night until he died."

That evened a couple of scores—Merril, Wilson. But somehow there was no pleasure in it. "And Ladd?" I asked.

"Dead, too. When I woke up he was lying across my legs. It was all quite nightmarish. You were on your stomach, staring at the billikin on the floor in front of you and babbling all kinds of numbers and things. That went on for almost fifteen minutes, then you stopped talking and started laughing. I thought you had gone crazy. Then, as if to prove it, you got up on your hands and knees and crawled over to the billikin and put the barrel of the gun on its belly and pulled the trigger. I'm glad the bottom of the boat is thicker than the cabin wall or you would have sunk us for sure. Anyway, there are little pieces of ivory all over the cabin."

"Serves the little bastard right," I said and grinned. "But I'm shocked that such an upright gentleman as myself should behave in such an unseemly fashion."

Carla laughed. "Well, if you don't believe me, you can just listen to the tape. I played it back to find out what happened, and it's all there."

"The tape recorder was still running?" I said. "Can you make it out?"

"Not all of it after you fell on the floor. The rain and the engine drowns some of it. But after you were done with all that shooting, you really got wound up and started bellowing it out as loud as you could yell. It's really quite comical."

"It's more comical than you think," I said. "That tape is going to make a nice anonymous birthday gift to the F.B.I. We might have to do a little erasing—names and such—and wipe off a few fingerprints . . ."

"I don't suppose it would be a very good idea to visit them in person," Carla said.

"No, thanks. I put in a full day's work trying to stay alive, and I'd hate to see so much effort go to waste. The F.B.I. never heard of Robert Chessick, and I'd kind of like to retain that association intact."

"Then why give it to them at all?"

"Patriotism, my dear. Lasers for mom and democracy. Besides, once they have that information back in their bloody little paws, they will probably stop looking for it. I'll leave enough on that tape to give them at least a vague hint of what happened, and if Ladd's call to the trawler comes in loud and clear, they'll know the Russians aren't interested in me any more. That little suggestion that the information be closed off permanently should convince them that no sideshow hypnotist is going to latch onto it by accident. No, I doubt that even the F.B.I. has the resources or patience to spend ten years searching the world for a man they never heard of when they have every reason to believe that man can be neither a help nor much of a danger to them."

"Well, I don't suppose it's going to make much of a difference anyway, unless we can find some way to get back," Carla said. "After you went to sleep, the engine stopped and we drifted in here. Luckily you woke up, but you were still out of your head, so I just pushed you over the side and in the direction of shore. Anyway, we're quite stranded, I'm afraid."

"A dire situation indeed," I said with a smile.

"You never take anything seriously enough." Carla pouted. "We might be here forever."

"Not if the radio still works. And if the tide beached us, I suppose it might just as well unbeach us. But then, what's the hurry? I think we both deserve a vacation."

"Oh, can we? Can we really? There's enough food on the boat for a week or more and sleeping bags and rifles to protect us from bears and moose and things and . . . and I've never been in the woods before, and, gee, I'm learning how to light a fire . . . and . . . but, really, it is lovely, isn't it? Say we can stay, Chess. Promise."

"Well, I'm in such lousy shape," I groaned, "that it might take at least a week before I'm strong enough to move."

Carla bent down quickly and kissed me on the mouth. "You're lovely," she said. She jumped up and ran back to her pile of twigs. "You stay right there, and as soon as I get this fire going, I'll make you a can of soup."

I rolled over on my stomach and watched her fiddle with the twigs with an excitement that seemed to have been resurrected out of the dreams of a lost childhood.

"Carla," I said, "marry me."

For almost a minute her body was motionless, not stiff, but merely suspended. Then she turned to me with an expression of profound sadness. "I'm very flattered," she said softly. "And I really have fallen in love with you. I thought about it, you know. I thought about it a whole lot. But remember what you said once, I mean about how women are afraid of heroes because what they really want is a nice, quiet, secure life with a home in the suburbs and the P.T.A. and the bridge club on Thursday."

"Yeah," I said.

"Well, in the last few days I've very much developed a desire for that kind of life. I'm sorry, Chess, but you're a hero. You're just too damned dangerous to live with."

ABOUT THE AUTHOR

T. C. LEWELLEN was born in Reading, California, and has spent his years, not yet thirty of them, roaming the world. He's worked at all sorts of jobs, including being a fire fighter. He actually reached Havana in the hope of joining the revolution and spent a month in Alaska sleeping in his car while job hunting. Despite all this, he managed a college degree and a hitch of Army training. He is now a promotion copywriter, but is beginning to get the itch to take off again. Random House hopes to keep him here until he finishes the book he is now working on.

obert Chessick was just a bum. Ex-
schoolteacher. Ex-lieutenant. Ex-
husband. Ex-everything. Just a
bum. No money. No secrets. No dreams. No
nothing. Just a bum wandering the cement
canyon back alleys of San Francisco in
search of a bottle or a dime.

Just a bum—followed, framed, drugged,
beaten…

Just an ordinary bum caught in the center
of the deadliest game of all, a game played
outside the law by the professional killers of
the two most powerful governments on earth,
a game where the losers might end up like
Louis Owen—a four-inch hat pin in the eye.
They said Robert Chessick had done that,
but he couldn't have. No, he was not a murderer. He was just a bum—running blind,